HIS UPTOWN GUY

A Landmarks Series Novel

by
FELICE STEVENS

His Uptown Guy (Landmarks #2)
January 2019

When Jesse Grace-Martin loses his father on 9/11, his charmed life is gone forever. People look menacing, and the streets no longer seem safe. After experiencing a brutal mugging, Jesse retreats to his apartment in the landmark Dakota building. Five years later, his first attempt to walk outside those famous gates again is a disaster—except for meeting the gorgeous maintenance worker who helps him through his crushing panic attack. Jesse can't stop thinking about the guy but hesitates to reach out, knowing he has little to offer.

Dashamir Sadiko has big dreams. Money in the bank tops his list, and his glimpse into the life of the uber-wealthy at his job at the Dakota is all the incentive he needs. Struggling to work full-time and go to college, Dash desperately wants to break the cycle of poverty his parents had hoped to leave behind in Albania. When the two men become friends, Dash isn't sure what to expect but can't help his growing attraction to sweet and sexy Jesse. It's nice to see how the other side lives, but his affections can't be bought; Dash wants to be his own man.

Defying the Dakota's co-op rules, the two share lunches, their hopes and dreams, and ultimately their hearts. Jesse slowly regains his courage, but he's worried he'll never be the person he once was and that he's not good enough for Dash. And Dash isn't convinced the son of poor immigrants has a place at the table with a blue-blood, trust-fund man. Jesse needs to realize that money can't buy happiness and love, while Dash must learn to trust that what they have is real, that he's more than Jesse's walk on the wild side with an uptown guy.

Follow me along in my readers group, FELICE'S FUN HOUSE a fun and slightly crazy place to talk books, share kisses and talk about life, love and margaritas. facebook.com/groups/FelicesFunHouse

Want exclusive content, notices of sales and specials? Join my NEWSLETTER No spam ever!! landing.mailerlite.com/webforms/landing/c3h8p3

Dedication

To my friends who keep me sane.
You know who you are.

Acknowledgments

To my editor Keren Reed, who still puts up with me, despite my timeline issues and the fact that I can never spell T-shirt correctly. To Hope and Jess from Flat Earth Editing, you are superstars. Thank you for always putting everything and beyond into my books. And to Dianne from Lyrical Lines, thank you for that keen, keen eye. I'll train you into New York-isms soon enough.

To my wonderful readers, especially my group in the Fun House, thank you for buying my books and supporting me. I know there are a ton of books to choose from, so thank you for reading my stories. I treasure you all.

Author's Note

The Dakota is one of the most photographed buildings in the world. However, you cannot find one interior photograph of the hallways or the elevators (the scene in *Rosemary's Baby* where she is shown fleeing through the hallways was filmed in a different building). Nor can you find an up-close photograph of the interior courtyard. For these reasons, I've taken a bit of poetic license with descriptions and hope you'll understand.

Chapter One

THE BIG APPLE baked in the oppressive heat, the sun a shimmering disc sitting high in an endless blue August sky. Jesse Grace-Martin sipped his coffee. From his window seat, he had a sweeping vista of Central Park and the people swarming the streets in tank tops, shorts, and flip-flops. He spread his palm flat against the window; it was the only way to allow the heat of the sun to touch his skin. He imagined standing outside, lifting his face to the sky to soak in its warmth, and the gentle, welcome stirring of a cool breeze.

Another year had passed, and soon September would be upon them.

His mother never made it to the memorial ceremonies, but he couldn't fault her—neither did he. She hardly ever came back to the city now that she'd remarried—once a year for his birthday. They'd make uncomfortable small talk, and she and his stepfather would rarely stay more than a few hours. And as for Jesse?

His fingertips trailed down the windowpane to rest in his lap. The summer was at its hot and hazy zenith, yet he shivered from a chill not of his air-conditioned apartment. It was another year that he'd broken the promise to himself to try. To force himself, if he had to, but to somehow walk outside his apartment door.

He could lie to himself and say he tried, but he hadn't. Bad things happened out there. Bad people waited who wanted to hurt him. Jesse knew this, and so he stayed in his cocoon. He took another sip of coffee.

"Jess?"

At the sound of his name, he turned to greet Miranda, his personal assistant, who stood in the archway separating the living room from the hall.

"Come on in."

When his mother left New York City with her new husband to move to Connecticut, he'd hired Miranda to be his assistant-slash-life-coper, as he called her, but their relationship had morphed into friendship, and she'd become more like a cherished family member.

"You want something to eat? I made a run to the bank, then picked up your medicine and went shopping to get you some new jeans and T-shirts." Her hands were laden with shopping bags from several department stores.

"Thanks, but you didn't have to do that. I already ordered some new sneakers and other stuff online. I could've added to the order."

Miranda set the bags on the wide, chintz-patterned sofa. The room was huge—around thirty feet long, and like almost every apartment in the Dakota, it boasted fourteen-feet-high ceilings, intricately laid wooden floors, and large leaded-glass windows. All the main living areas faced Central Park, while the kitchen, bathrooms, and smaller rooms faced the interior courtyard. The Dakota was built between 1880 and 1884 and was designated a National Historic Landmark in 1976. Jesse's family had lived there since 1961, when the building went cooperative.

Jesse possessed a coveted corner unit boasting a view of both Central Park and 72nd Street. A white-brick fireplace took up one wall of the room. Family pictures once graced the mantle, but except for two—one of him and his father, and one of their family—Jesse had put them all away, and in their place he'd set glittering rock formations of quartz and other stones he'd purchased for his collection. The colors matched the modern art pieces gracing the walls. Darkness might rest inside him, but Jesse tried to counteract it with bright, happy paintings and prints.

"It's okay. I wanted to take a walk on Columbus Avenue and get some stuff for lunch. I hope you're okay with sushi."

"Of course. What's the hot new sushi restaurant now in the city?" Jesse recalled visiting Nobu for one of his last meals out, before the noise, the crowds, and the pressing in of everything and everyone around him after his father's death in the terror attacks made it impossible for him to leave his apartment. If he looked out the front windows, he could see the tourists standing in front of the Dakota—this beautiful building where numerous celebrities and public figures lived, but which for Jesse had become his prison. Self-made, he knew, but the walls in his mind preventing him from stepping outside were as high and deadly as those of a correctional facility with barbed wire running around its perimeter.

"Oh, there's lots. SUGARFISH is a big fave. But only if you like waiting on line for a few hours. I do takeout. Hold on—I'll get you a fresh cup." Her heels tapped on the shining wooden floors as she left for a moment, then returned with two large iced coffees. Jesse took the one she offered.

"I wouldn't wait hours for anything, especially three slices of salmon on a piece of rice. Is it as crowded outside today as it looks, or are people just heading into the park?" His gaze returned to the window. Aching. Wanting. Wishing he could join the throngs but knowing he couldn't when the very thought made him ill. He drank his coffee, barely tasting it.

Every day when Miranda came back from her errands, he'd quiz her about the goings-on in the city. He'd tried to explain to his mother and his therapist. It wasn't that he didn't want to go outside, walk around, and breathe the fresh air. He couldn't. Not yet.

Miranda flopped on the sofa, kicked off her shoes, and sighed. "I've been waiting all morning for this. I can brew it at home, but I swear there's something in this coffee that makes me crave it." She sucked noisily at her straw. "Mmm. Yeah, it's pretty crowded. End of season sales and lots of tourists."

"I used to love being in the city during the summer. It was so nice and quiet. Most of my friends were in the Hamptons or Fire Island. I could go to the park and sketch, walk to Lincoln Center and hang out in Barnes and Noble." He studied his straw. "It's closed now, right?"

"The store on Columbus is, yeah, but the one on Broadway is still open. We could go sometime. You and me."

"Miranda…" He shook his head. "You know what I'm gonna say."

"But you've been making progress. This is the first year I can remember that you have an interest in what's going on outside. And I heard you talking with Hector the porter, so you're becoming comfortable with other people, aren't you?"

Her wide, pleading eyes sent a pang of longing through Jesse. "Don't you think if I could, I'd be out there? Do you know how badly I want to?" He swept his hand toward the window. "Every day I wake up and think, maybe today. Maybe…but I can't. I choke and can't breathe at the thought of all the people out there." Jesse hung his head. "What if someone hurts you when we're outside? I wouldn't be able to help you, and I'd never forgive myself."

"Oh, Jess. Nothing's guaranteed."

"It is if I stay here. I'm okay, then. Nothing can hurt me."

"But—"

"No." He knew it was irrational, but he couldn't help it. "We've had this conversation in one form or another over how many years now? I'm fine."

The small shake of her head and sorrowful downcast expression in her brown eyes were enough of an indication that she didn't agree. And because he hated seeing her unhappy and upset, and because he was also a people pleaser—another personality fault he couldn't get under control—Jesse blurted out before he had a chance to think, "Maybe if you come with me, I could go to the lobby today?"

The beaming smile on her face did little to alleviate the sheer terror those words sent spiking through him, and though Jesse regretted speaking them even as they left his lips, he vowed to try. It was all his mother, Miranda, and his therapist wanted. "Try it, Jesse" had become the weekly mantra he heard at the end of every session with Dr. Mingione. And, "Please try, sweetheart" ended the infrequent conversations with his mother.

Right now, all he wanted was to throw up.

"It'll be okay, Jess. We'll take it slow. Out the door to the hallway first, and then we'll see how it goes from there."

It all became too much, and he strode away from the window to throw himself into the club chair. "Why? Why am I like this? I want to be normal. I want to go and do and see everything, but every time I think about doing it, I choke and can't move." Jesse set the coffee on the table with a bang. "I don't want to be like this." His words echoed against the walls.

The fragrance of Miranda's light perfume enveloped him as she hugged him close. "I know. I know. It'll be okay. I promise. One step at a time. You're such a beautiful, sensitive soul, everything gets to you and goes straight to your heart."

"My beautiful, sensitive soul wasn't enough to keep Sean, though."

"Don't mention that idiot." Miranda held him by his shoulders, her eyes flashing fire. "That man had no feelings whatsoever. You're better off without him."

Easier said than done when you'd been with someone for three years and they dumped you. "He had a right to have a boyfriend who wanted to leave the house. To be with a man who could go out and have fun and do everything couples do."

"There's more to a relationship than going out clubbing and having a good time." The steeliness of her voice surprised him.

"I know, but it was my fault we couldn't do those things."

"You had a problem, and he should've tried to help you work through it instead of running away like he did."

"Have. I still have the problem." He grabbed his plastic cup and sucked down the coffee.

"My point is that when you care about someone, you stay with them and try to help them get through their tough times." A bit softer now, she gave his arm a squeeze and returned to the sofa. "Sean didn't love you enough, and you deserve to have someone who does. Simple as that."

If only. Ready to end the conversation, Jesse held up his hand. "Enough, please. I'm going to take a shower, get dressed, and meet you in the foyer in ten minutes. Okay?"

"Of course." Sympathy creased her smooth brow. "I'm sorry, Jess. I didn't mean to upset you."

"Or nag?" He said it with a smile, so she'd know he

wasn't angry.

"Isn't that part of my job description?" Her expression shifted from morose to merry. "And don't forget your medicine." She dug through the plastic bag to hand him the bottle.

"I'd love to wean myself off this stuff. It makes me feel so dopey and weird sometimes. Like I'm inside a glass jar."

"I know. Maybe you can, if you take that first step."

Jesse's heart gave a thump, and he forced out a smile. The mere thought of taking that elevator ride down to the lobby shot his pulse into warp speed.

"Maybe."

Trying to maintain some semblance of normalcy, Jesse walked out with his head high and his body straight, but as soon as he crossed the threshold of the living room to the hallway, he collapsed against the wall and closed his eyes, hoping the steady, deep breathing his therapist recommended would calm his jangled nerves.

"I can do this," he whispered to himself. "I have to." During his last session, Dr. Mingione had encouraged him to step out of his comfort zone and challenge himself. He might not be ready to take the step of walking outside on the sidewalk, but getting out of the apartment and going down to the courtyard would be huge for him. More than he'd been able to accomplish in years.

In the shower, Jesse ran his hands over his body. In college and throughout his early twenties, he'd been an avid runner and cyclist, and weekends would find him and his friends in the park, outdoors, worshiping the sun while playing Frisbee on the Great Lawn. Now, though his body was still muscular from his workout regimen in the apartment, his skin was sadly pale. Jesse even longed for the freckles that used to sprinkle across his shoulders and the bridge of his nose that made him look annoyingly younger than his years.

He exited the shower stall and towel-dried his hair, then dressed quickly in a light-blue T-shirt and gym shorts. A quick check of his watch showed he was right on time. Ten minutes and he walked into the foyer, which for some apartments in New York could be the entire apartment, but for the Dakota was average at around a twenty-by-twenty space. He'd never liked the black-and-white, diamond-checked pattern of the marble tiles and once again considered replacing them.

"Ready?" Miranda had on her determined, perky face, and he nodded, the sweat already dampening under his arms and down his back.

" 'K." Although Jesse's stomach roiled, he squeezed his eyes shut for a second and expelled a whoosh of breath. "Let's do this."

Like the previous month when he'd made the attempt to leave, Miranda went first and held out her hand to him. That time he'd made it to the threshold of the front door before the floor tilted below his feet and vertigo robbed him of his ability to see straight and stand. Funny how the mind worked. When Jesse knew he was only opening the door for deliveries, he was fine. But when it came to him walking over that threshold to go outside, he could barely breathe.

And once again he only made it to the front door before nausea threatened. This time, determined not to fail, Jesse took several deep, cleansing breaths and focused on the opposite wall down the hallway.

"I can do this. I can do this," Jesse repeated to himself, lips moving like he was reciting the refrain to a prayer.

He pushed one foot over the threshold and then the other, and for the first time in five years, he stood in the hallway. Gulping down air and swaying as if a giant hand pushed him side to side, he put out his hand to get his balance and touched the wall.

"Jess. I'm so proud of you." With tears in her eyes, Miranda hugged him, and he clung to her, although he wasn't certain if it was for the praise or simply to hold him upright.

Sweat trickled down his back from exertion, and he hadn't even taken a step down the hallway. "I can't," he whispered.

"Take all the time you need. I'm not going anywhere." She held him close, and Jesse began to breathe more normally. To his surprise, the nauseating feeling passed.

"Okay. I think I'm gonna be all right." He let go of her and set his jaw. "Let's see what I can do." The walls closed in, and his feet moved as though weighed down by lead, but he persisted. On one side he held Miranda's hand, but with the other he trailed his fingers along the wall. The thought of all that wide-open space terrified him—someone could come up to him and touch him…hurt him again. All irrational thoughts, but ones he couldn't help.

Miranda stopped. "Jess," she whispered. "You did it. Look."

He'd been so trapped inside his head, he hadn't realized they'd reached the elevator.

Joy and terror warred within him, and he braced both hands on the dark wood-paneled wall. "I-I never thought…" His voice dwindled away as tears threatened and his body trembled.

"But you did. I'm so happy." He glanced up to catch her brushing tears off her cheeks. "Do you want to go back to the apartment or try to get on the elevator and go down to the lobby? No matter what, I'm so proud of you, and you should be too."

As much as for himself, Jesse wanted to do this for Miranda and the dedication she'd shown him over the years.

"The lobby." Even as he spoke, bile rose in his throat, but as always, Miranda knew what Jesse needed before he did.

"Remember the way your therapist told you to calm yourself?"

Jesse did. *Take deep, calming breaths. Inhale. Exhale. Clear the mind.*

"Push the button."

I can do this. I will do this. I have *to do this.*

No longer would he sit at the window like some dreamy Juliet overlooking the park waiting for Romeo. His therapist was right. One step would lead to another. Maybe not outside the gates, because the thought of all that open *space* terrified him, but what could happen in the courtyard?

Miranda held on to him as they waited for the elevator, and he rested his forehead against the cool expanse of wall, his heart tripping and his breathing growing steadily more difficult with each passing second.

The doors opened, and he jolted out of his trance.

"Jess?" Miranda stood in the elevator's entrance. "Are you ready? Are you sure? You can go back right now, and it'll still be an amazing accomplishment."

Oh, sure. An amazing accomplishment to walk down a hallway for the first time in five years. "I want to try."

Her lips trembled. "Okay," she whispered. "Let's do it."

Trying to look braver than he felt, Jesse stepped into the elevator, and like a person suffering from seasickness, kept his eyes focused on a point in the distance—in this case, the high corner of the elevator—so he didn't have to think about descending. Lucky for him, the building wasn't one of the new monstrous skyscrapers he'd read about popping up all over the city. The Dakota was only a ten-story building, and the elevators were on the four corners of the courtyard. No big lobby teeming with people walking in and out all day. He could go outside, maybe find a place to sit in the secure courtyard and get some sun.

With a bump and a shudder, the elevator ground to a halt, and its wood-and-metal door creaked open. Clutching Miranda's hand tightly, he stepped out of the cage and into the lobby.

The Dakota didn't have one large main lobby like most apartment buildings in the city. Then again, the Dakota was like no other building in the world. Once you made it past the security at the famous front gate on West 72nd Street and walked through the huge stone archways, you entered an oval-shaped interior courtyard with beautiful stone fountains and cement benches. The sidewalks surrounding the building were paved in bluestone, while granite stone pavers filled in the interior of the courtyard. The fountain and planters were all hand carved.

Jesse stood next to Miranda and peered out through the wood-framed glass front door. There was, of course, a concierge standing at the ready, waiting to assist the visitors who came through, as well as delivery people and residents of the apartments.

"Ready? Or do you want to stay inside?"

His shirt, now drenched in sweat, stuck to his back, and the queasiness he'd been avoiding hit him. He swayed, needing to hold on to the wall for balance.

"Jess," Miranda called out. He closed his eyes and felt himself slipping. A strong pair of arms wrapped around him and held him firmly so he didn't fall. The man smelled warm, like long-forgotten summer days spent lying in the grass in the park.

"Are you okay? Can you walk?" Low-timbre and gentle, his voice sent a shiver through Jesse despite the heat.

He opened his eyes, his cheek pressed against a well-muscled chest. The man seemed to be around thirty, with a sweep of thick, dark hair and fathomless eyes the color of jet or perhaps onyx. Jesse cursed himself. Here he was, being held by a man for the first time in years, and all he could think about were rocks.

"Yeah, I'm all right." His voice cracked, sounding unused and dusty, as if he were badly in need of water. When he tried to stand, a wave of dizziness hit him hard, and he clutched at the man's broad shoulders. "Uh, maybe not."

"It's okay. I'll help you. Eddie, a chair?" the man called out to the concierge, who stood with Miranda. He hurried over with one he brought from behind the small wooden desk.

"Can you sit?"

Jesse nodded, and the backs of his legs hit the chair as the man slid it under him. With a grunt he dropped down, still breathing heavily but missing the strength the man's arms around him provided.

"Better now?"

At his nod, a wave of relief passed over the man's face, and he broke out into a beautiful smile that took Jesse's breath away. He was gorgeous, and Jesse couldn't help but stare. The man caught Jesse's frank admiration, and an awareness passed between them, unspoken but recognized; a spark of interest burned until Jesse, unused to such close scrutiny from strangers, dropped his gaze to the floor.

"I haven't been well."

"Jesse, it's good to see you down here." Eddie handed Jesse a bottle of water, and with a grateful smile, Jesse accepted it and took a sip.

"Thanks." Jesse glanced up at his rescuer, noticing

for the first time that he wore a porter's uniform. "I don't know your name, but thank you for helping me." Hoping the man wouldn't see, Jesse wiped his hand on his shirt before extending it, hating how it trembled. The man took his pale, nerveless fingers in his hardened palm for a moment, and his warmth and strength radiated through Jesse's body like an electric shock.

"I'm Dashamir, Dash to my friends. I hope you're okay now." He bent to pick up the broom lying on the tiled floor at their feet.

Jesse said nothing, unwilling to trust his voice. He watched Dash sweep the area near the doorway until Miranda came over and touched his shoulder.

"Maybe that's enough for today? We can go back up."

Jesse hated himself and everything he'd become. It shouldn't be a big deal to sit outside on a beautiful summer day or to have a conversation with an attractive guy, but safety awaited him upstairs in his quiet apartment with his collection of rocks.

But inanimate objects could only satisfy for so long, and desire, something Jesse hadn't felt the stirrings of in years, now waited on the other side of fear. The urge to live again, to belong, rose thick and fierce in his blood.

"Let's do it." He took her hand, and they walked to the front door.

Chapter Two

DASHAMIR SADIKO WAS no fool. His mother raised him with strict values: get a good education, obey the laws, and be kind to people. Education and getting a good job were key to breaking free of the poverty that afflicted their family. Dash desperately wanted to give his mother more. She and his sister meant everything to him.

His father? That was a different story. Growing up, Dash barely saw the man. His mother's excuses that he was busy with two jobs might've worked when Dash was young, but he knew better now. He'd seen his father hanging out with men who made up some of the more dangerous Albanian gangs in their Bronx neighborhood. To the public, they appeared respectable in their expensive suits, gold watches, and slick smiles. But Dash wasn't fooled and watched his father become dazzled and drawn in, leaving his mother alone and unaware.

It had taken Dash almost six years, but he was two semesters away from graduating with an accounting degree, and he'd spent most of his time this past summer brushing up his résumé. The job at the

Dakota, even as a porter, was too good to pass up. His salary was okay, but tips from the tenants when he delivered their dry-cleaning and packages, plus the extra favors like walking their dogs and feeding their pets when they went away, helped pay for his tuition and the small studio apartment he rented near his parents. He was canny with his money because he'd seen how the rich lived and he liked it.

"Eddie, who was that? I've never seen him before. New owner or what?" With the lobby swept, Dash leaned against the desk to chat with the doorman. Through the glass door, he saw the man sitting with the woman in the courtyard.

"Jesse Grace-Martin? Nah, he's lived here since he was born. Parents and his grandparents have had their apartment since the building went co-op. Original owners. Real old money."

"Huh." Pondering that information, Dash recalled the man's fearful green eyes and the cool touch of his hand. "I've never seen him."

"Well," Eddie said, leaning forward on the desk and preparing, Dash could tell, for a nice, gossipy chat. "He's a funny one. Regular kid growing up, no troubles. Always said hi to everyone. Then September eleventh happened. His father worked in the towers and didn't make it out."

"Shit. That's horrible. Any brothers or sisters?"

"Nah, just Jesse."

Dash peered over his shoulder to see the woman put her arm around Jesse and give him a hug. "Seems like he has a nice girlfriend, at least. A bit older than him, but anything goes these days, I guess."

"Oh, Miranda ain't his girlfriend." Eddie's voice dropped to a conspiratorial whisper. "The kid's gay. Not flaming, obviously, but he used to bring a boyfriend here. They were together a few years. He hired Miranda around five years ago. She helps him."

So he hadn't been mistaken. There'd been an undercurrent...a feeling when they'd shaken hands. Again Dash glanced over at Jesse, but this time he allowed his gaze to linger on the sleek lines of the man's back and the long, pale throat peeking out from beneath the waves of dark-blond hair. Dash forced himself to look away and ignore the tingling in his groin. This was his job. Sure, he'd heard stories of residents sleeping with the hired help. He'd been propositioned more than once by the pretty young widow who lived in apartment 37, whose elderly husband had passed away earlier in the year. The seventy-five-year-old Oscar-nominated actor in 52 liked to brush against him whenever he passed Dash cleaning the floors, but he never failed to give Dash less than a fifty-dollar tip for delivering his packages, so Dash didn't bother to complain.

But a man like Jesse Martin—*Jesse Grace-Martin*, for God's sake—could be dangerous to him. He'd never known a guy with two last names before. They were close in age, and there was something about him....*No.* Dash set his shoulders and deliberately turned his back to the door. No way was he tasting that forbidden fruit. Dash had a plan for his future set in place: finish college, get a good job in an accounting firm, become partner, and one day afford an apartment like the ones here in the Dakota. Right now he needed this job more than he needed a fun time in the sack, no matter how hot the guy was. But something Eddie said stuck in his mind.

"Helps him? Like his personal assistant? What does he do? I can't believe I've never seen him before. I know I've only been working here a few weeks, but I thought I knew everyone in the building." A thought sprang to his mind. "Oh, wait, is he the guy everyone says never comes out of his apartment? The one who lives in 70?" There'd been talk among the workers that he was a Satanist, that he never got out of bed, or that he was simply crazy. Being the new guy, Dash had said nothing, but now, having met Jesse and looked into his deep-set eyes, Dash didn't believe any of the chatter. Sadness radiated from Jesse, coupled with loneliness and pain. Besides, they were obviously wrong, as he was outside in the courtyard. He should know better than to listen to gossip.

"Oh, he writes about rocks."

"Rocks?" He scratched his head. "What do you mean?"

"He's got all these stones in his apartment, Pete used to say. Like crystals and turquoise. He gets stuff delivered all the time from all over the place. I think he studies them before they're made into jewelry. Anyway, he writes about them for some magazines. What do I know?" With a shrug, Eddie picked up the buzzing phone. "Good afternoon. May I help you?"

Dash picked up the broom he'd left propped up

against the desk and darted one last look at Jesse. Unaware he was being spied upon, Jesse sat with his eyes closed, his face held up to the sun while the slight breeze ruffled his hair. An expression of dreamy contentment rested on his half-smiling lips.

Damn, he's good-looking.

Dash thrust the image of Jesse out of his mind and hurried down the hallway to put the broom away. Next on his morning work agenda was sweeping the interior courtyard. The broom went inside the utility closet, and Dash removed the special outdoor broom. One thing this building had was a lot of rules, and Dash was still learning them.

The sun beat warm on his back when he stepped outside, so he unbuttoned the top part of his work shirt. He wished he could take it off completely and work only in his sleeveless T-shirt, but that wasn't allowed. Another rule. He started at the arched entranceway, at the opposite end of where Jesse and Miranda sat, and worked his way around the semicircle. People came and went, cars pulled in and out, and yet Jesse spoke to no one and seemed to become more withdrawn and agitated as time passed.

"I can't." Jesse jumped off the bench and sprinted toward the door, but his steps slowed, and he sank to his knees. Dash dropped the broom, and without a thought, grabbed Jesse around his waist, preventing him from collapsing on the ground. His shirt was wet with sweat, and he smelled of fear and shook violently in Dash's arms. He wondered if the man was having a seizure. Miranda rushed to his side.

"I'm sorry. Let me try and talk to him. Jesse." She kneeled at his side, and Dash, still holding Jesse's stiff, unyielding body, remained silent and watchful. "Are you okay? Do you want to go back upstairs?" She rested her palm against Jesse's flushed, sweating face. Dash felt helpless, not knowing what to do. Jesse's breathing came in short erratic puffs, and his eyes were shut, the dark lashes fluttering against his cheeks.

At his quick nod, Dash tightened his arm around Jesse, and Miranda glanced at him for the first time. "Thank you so much for staying here with us. Would it be all right if you helped him up to his apartment? I don't think I can lift him."

"Of course." Dash bent to speak directly to Jesse. "Can you stand?"

"I don't know."

The sentence was delivered in a monotone so chilling, Dash shivered. It was as if Jesse had changed from the sweet-faced, slightly shy man he'd first met into someone broken.

"Come. Let's try. I'm here. I'll help you."

Jesse opened his eyes, and Dash winced at the despair in their depths. If, as his mother always said, the eyes were the gateway to the soul, Jesse's was fractured and in pieces.

When he tried to stand, Jesse's arms grasped him around the neck so tight and forcefully, every inch of him molded to Dash. "No, don't. Don't let go." Startled, Dash held on to his trembling body.

He wasn't soft and pliant as Dash thought he would be, but rather unexpectedly hard-muscled, and

Dash let Jesse cling to his shoulders until his eyes fluttered open again, and with an almost guilty start, he attempted to let go.

"I'm sorry. I didn't mean—"

"It's okay. Let me help. You can hold on to me." Not wanting to frighten Jesse further, Dash kept his voice quiet and soothing. Several moments passed before Jesse loosened his stranglehold on Dash's neck, and with his arm supporting Jesse, Dash rose to standing.

"Better now?"

An infinitesimal nod. Jesse's head hung low, his face obscured by the curtain of wavy hair. "I'm...I'm sorry."

"No need to apologize. Do you need me to help you upstairs?"

"I think that would be perfect," Miranda said. "Thank you so much. Come on, Jess."

"I can make it. I don't need help." Sounding a bit stronger, Jesse pushed the hair off his face. "I don't need to be coddled."

"Jess, come on. It'll be fine. He can help."

After glaring at Miranda, Jesse shifted his gaze to him, and Dash gave what he hoped was a reassuring smile, since he had no damn clue what the hell was happening. "It's my job. Service with a smile."

Jesse wiped the sweat from his brow. His face remained a sickly pale shade of white, and he kept gnawing at his bottom lip. "Well...okay. You don't really have to, but thanks."

With Jesse tucked into his side, Dash followed

Miranda to the elevator. They didn't speak, and in the silence of the hallway, Dash became acutely aware of Jesse's uneven breathing and how stiff he held himself.

What was the deal with this guy?

The door creaked open, and they entered the elevator cab. At this point, Jesse released his grip on Dash's waist, leaned up against the wall, and shut his eyes. Miranda pursed her lips and shook her head, staring at Jesse with her brow puckered. Dash knew he had no right to question, but he had so much running through his mind.

The door slid open, and uncertain now of his place, Dash held back. Jesse opened his eyes and blinked.

"Jess? Okay?" Miranda held out her hand, and Jesse took it obediently, like Dash's sister did when she was young, and stood by her side, his gaze firmly rooted to the floor. "Thank you," Miranda said to Dash. "We appreciate your help, but I think I can take it from here." She hugged Jesse's arm close to her, and with their heads together, they slowly walked away. They turned the corner, and the sound of keys jingled, a lock turned, and a door opened and closed. And that was that.

A little annoyed he'd been dismissed so quickly, Dash nevertheless couldn't spend his day staring down an empty hallway. He needed to power-wash the interior courtyard, then see about delivering the dry-cleaning and packages to the apartments, plus take care of other side duties he did for the residents. Yet during those errands and throughout the rest of the day, Dash wondered about Jesse Grace-Martin and why he behaved as he did.

At six o'clock, with his shift finished, Dash changed from his uniform into his regular clothes, and with his knapsack hefted over his shoulder, walked through the service entrance doors out onto 71st Street and Central Park West. The uptown train was right on the corner, and while he waited on the platform, he spied Miranda tapping away at her phone. Deciding he wanted some answers to the questions rattling around in his head, Dash hesitated only a moment before walking over to her.

"Hi, it's Miranda, right?"

In typical New York fashion, she gave him that side-eyed glare. The one that said, *Nice try, buddy, but I don't know who the hell you are, so stay away.* When recognition dawned, her smile was apologetic.

"Oh, hi. Sorry. I was so engrossed, and then when you spoke, I figured you were one of those annoying subway creeps." She slipped her phone in her purse. "It's Dash?"

Surprised she remembered, Dash took the knapsack off his shoulder to rest between his feet. From the illuminated signage, it appeared the train would be another eight minutes, so he might as well get comfortable.

"Yeah. Sometimes people don't recognize the staff when we're off duty and in our regular clothes. But I wanted to make sure your friend Jesse was all right. He looked kind of upset."

At the mention of Jesse's name, Miranda's smile faded, and her posture stiffened. "He's fine. Thanks for asking."

Sensing her withdrawal, Dash realized he'd made a mistake. "I, uh, I wasn't prying or anything. I was concerned. I've only been working there a month, so I don't know everyone yet."

"I know Jesse appreciated your help, and so did I."

For Dash, that was a non-answer, so he tried to come up with a way to word it differently. Why had Jesse looked as if the devil was chasing him?

"If you ever need me for anything in the apartment, let me know."

"Thanks, I will."

When it became apparent she'd share nothing more, they stood in awkward silence. The train pulled in, and they waited for the passengers to exit.

"Look," she said. "I've been with Jesse for five years now. I know the staff gossips. So I'm not about to get into a chat with you about him, no matter how helpful you were to us today. I have to make a phone call, so I'm going to wait for the next train."

She stepped backward, leaving Dash stunned and a bit pissed off. The bells rang, indicating the doors were about to close, and instinctively he moved inside the train car. The doors slid shut, and Miranda watched him with the phone pressed to her ear, but Dash would bet a week's salary there was no one on the other end. She needn't worry. She and her pal Jesse could keep their secrets. They didn't interest him in the least.

As the train pulled away and rocketed into the tunnel, Dash couldn't help but remember the real pain and fear in Jesse's eyes and how he shook in his arms. Saying it was one thing. Forgetting Jesse Grace-Martin might prove harder than he thought.

Chapter Three

JESSE CLOSED THE laptop. With his deadline made, he could take a break and do some fun reading of his own. He picked up *Smithsonian Handbooks: Rocks and Minerals* and happily settled in on his couch. It had been a while since he added to his collection, and he was now caught up in the beauty of the amethyst. He loved the varying shades of purple, from the faintest lavender to the darkest violet.

He avidly read their updates, noting the impressive finds of the semiprecious stone in the Southwest of the US and the largest concentration in Ontario, Canada. Jesse trailed his fingers over the pictures of caves and gorgeous collections of stone.

One day I'll get there. Maybe.

He opened his laptop again—this time to pull up the dealers he bought from, and after an hour or so of clicking and looking, purchased four different crystals. One store was only two blocks away, and after some online chatting, they agreed to deliver to him that afternoon. It was Saturday, and as Miranda had the weekends off, Jesse had the apartment to himself.

"What to do now?" he said, his voice echoing as he

wandered about. As always, he found himself a bit lost on the weekends without Miranda around to keep him on track and be his support. None of the friends he'd had in high school and college stuck around once he'd become unable to leave the apartment. His stomach rumbled. "I guess I'll eat lunch."

Before heading into the kitchen, he flipped on the television for some background noise. He peeked into the refrigerator and saw Miranda had left him rotisserie chicken, so he decided to heat that up while he prepared a salad.

With the chicken in the oven and smelling mouth-wateringly delicious, Jesse cut up cucumber, tomatoes, and peppers and added them to the lettuce, then drizzled on balsamic dressing he made and took the bowl and a beer into the living room. He propped his feet up on the coffee table and watched the Yankee game while he ate. No matter how well or badly they played, he watched as a tribute to his father, who'd been a tremendous fan. When he was a kid, his father had season tickets, and every spring the two of them had gone to opening day, eaten disgusting, greasy ballpark food, and had the best time. Jesse had a box in the closet with every ticket and program from the games they attended, tucked away with all his other memories.

Today the Yankees were tied with the Red Sox, and Jesse finished his beer and stood to get another, when the buzzer sounded. His heart kicked up, but he shook his head at his stupidity.

"You're in your apartment. Nothing can happen,

you idiot."

He hit the button. "Yes?"

"Delivery, Jesse. From Gems on Columbus."

That was quick. "Thanks, Eddie."

"I'll have Dash bring it up."

Jesse thought about telling Eddie to leave it downstairs, but instead blurted out, "Okay, sure."

What the hell am I thinking?

He ran to the bathroom to check himself out and winced at the reflection staring back. Gray-green eyes in a too-pale face. Though Hayden, the first guy he kissed, always commented on his full red lips and how he could spend hours kissing them.

This was stupid. Dash was coming to drop off a package and probably wouldn't even set foot inside the apartment. He definitely wouldn't remember who Jesse was. He ran a hand through his wavy hair and smiled to make sure none of the lettuce was lodged in his teeth.

The doorbell rang. "Coming." He hurried across the living room and opened the door to see Dash standing there with a large box.

"H-hi."

"Hi."

They stood, staring at each other for a moment, and Jesse realized Dash was waiting. "Oh, um, I'll take it." He extended his arms.

"I can bring it in and then take out the box after you open it. If you want me to, of course. I always ask 'cause some people don't want us coming inside their apartments unless it's to fix things."

"Oh no, come on inside." Stepping back, Jesse opened the door wider. "I'm not formal like some of the others."

I'm the guy who can't leave his apartment without having a panic attack. That's all.

Dash remained on the threshold, a wary expression etched on his face. "You're sure?"

"C'mon in. You can put it on the coffee table in here." He walked farther into the apartment, and with Dash following him, entered the living room. He muted the game and pushed his salad bowl to the side to make room for the box. Dash set it down and stood back.

"Like I said, if you want to open it, I'll take out the box for you."

Wondering if Dash said that because the other building workers had gossiped that he never left his apartment, Jesse set his jaw, determined not to live up to everyone's low expectations.

"Thanks, I can do it, but I'm going to open it anyway. Want to see what's inside?"

A bit taken aback, Dash shifted on his feet. "Sure. If you want."

"Have a seat." Jesse pointed to the sofa, then picked at the tape holding the box together. "I ordered it this morning, and they know me, so they sent it same day." The tape pulled off, and he opened the box and lifted out the carefully wrapped package surrounded by packing peanuts. A couple of the white pieces fell on the floor, but he ignored them and set the package on the table.

"I've got a few more coming in the next day or two, but this is the one I wanted most." He glanced over at Dash, who gave him a polite smile.

"What is it?"

Jesse tore off the wrapping and picked up the chunk of amethyst, holding it to the light. "Amethyst. Isn't it beautiful?" The sun streamed in through the leaded-glass windows, hitting the crystal, then bouncing off, creating a rainbow of colors. The amethyst glittered in his hand like it was alive.

"Oh, wow," Dash breathed out and stood. "That's gorgeous. I've never seen anything like it."

He took a few steps closer, and Jesse's heart tripped. He was so big, his muscles shifting under the smooth olive skin of his biceps. A bit dizzy with the unexpected wave of desire rolling through him, Jesse wanted to be held in those arms again. Dash's warm scent brought a rush of blood to Jesse's cock, and he swallowed hard.

"Yeah. This piece is from Siberia, where one of the biggest amethyst caves in the world is located." He held it out to Dash. "Do you want to hold it?"

Dash's dark eyes widened. "Really? But isn't it expensive? I wouldn't want to ruin it."

Jesse could see he wanted to, and smiled. "Unless you plan on throwing it at me or out the window, I think we're safe. Here." He placed it in Dash's hand, and at the touch of his hot, rough skin, prickles of goose bumps shot up Jesse's arms.

"It's heavier than I thought." Dash cradled the giant crystal formation and held it this way and that, admiring it. Jesse happily watched him as he studied it from every angle. "Oooh, look how it catches the light when I hold it up. It's so cool."

"Do you want to see my collection?" Jesse spoke without thinking. This guy, this gorgeous guy, had better things to do. He must get hit on all the time.

"Is that your hobby?"

"More than that, I guess you could say. I write about it for magazines and some books. I've always been interested in gems and rocks."

"That's cool. Yeah. You have more stuff like this?" He handed the amethyst back to Jesse. "I've never seen it in its natural state. Only in stores like for earrings and necklaces. My mom has one she wears on special occasions. Purple is her favorite color."

"I sure do. I have uncut emeralds, rubies, and lots of others. They look like nothing in the rock, but when you know what to look for, it's fascinating to find. Come. It's this way." He walked down the hallway and into the smaller bedroom he'd set up as a place for his collection, once his mother had moved out. Dash stood beside him in the doorway.

"This is awesome."

Warmth flushed through him at Dash's admiration. It had taken him months to set up the room the way he wanted, and there was still more to do. Clear shelves lined the walls, each holding a collection of stones or a crystal. A plaque with the name, date, and identifying information sat next to each stone. In the center of the room were small tables with his more valuable finds on display under glass. There was a large uncut emerald, one with a ruby, and then several small uncut diamonds.

"I've been collecting since I was ten years old. My parents and I would go on trips all around the world, and my father introduced me to his passion of collecting. A few of his pieces are in museums. I lent them out after his death."

"I'm sorry to hear about what happened. Eddie mentioned it to me."

So they had been talking about him. Jesse stiffened. "What else did he say?" His throat tightened. "That I was the crazy guy who never came out of his apartment?"

"No, wait."

Humiliated, Jesse turned away from Dash and walked blindly back into the living room. The only reason Dash came up to the apartment must've been to stare at him like he was a freak show. He *was* a freak. It had taken him all day to recover from venturing out into the courtyard for those ten minutes when he'd first met Dash.

"Hey, Jesse. I'm sorry we were talking about you, but it wasn't like the way you thought." The warmth of Dash's hand on his arm froze Jesse in his tracks. The pace of his breathing quickened.

"N-no? How was it, then?" The dark pools of Dash's eyes caught him in their depths.

"Uh, Jesse? Are you cooking something?" Dash sniffed the air. "I think something's burning."

"Shit. The chicken." He took off at a sprint to the kitchen, where black smoke puffed out from the stove. Remembering to grab an oven mitt first, Jesse opened the stove door and was greeted by a dark, smelly cloud. Coughing and his eyes tearing, Jesse reached inside and pulled out the charred remains of his chicken. He took the pan and dumped it into the sink, then poured cold water on it, which sent up another cloud of steam. The smoke alarm blared, and he waved a towel ineffectively under it.

Dash dragged a chair over, hopped on it, and pushed the button to stop the alarm. Jesse stared at the mess in the sink.

"Dammit. That was my lunch."

"You had it on four hundred degrees. How long was it in there?"

"It was already cooked. I was just reheating it." He checked the clock on the oven, startled to see it had been there for over an hour. "Shit. Yeah. It was over an hour."

Despite the steaming mess, Dash chuckled. "Um, yeah, that's a really long time. News flash, Jesse? It probably needs no more than fifteen minutes."

"Now you tell me." He made a disgusted sound. "Guess I'll be ordering in." He poked at the watery chicken carcass. "Yuck."

"Well, um." Dash rubbed the back of his neck. "If you want to wait a little bit, I get my lunch break in like half an hour or so. I have leftovers from my mom's dinner last night. It's chicken too. An Albanian recipe. There's plenty to share. If you're interested, of course."

"Lunch? Me?"

"Well, no. Lunch would be the chicken."

His face burning, Jesse bit his lip. "Very funny. I

mean, you want to have lunch here with me?"

Looking adorably shy, Dash ducked his head. "Yeah. Only if you want. But my mother makes a mean *pule me oriz*. That's chicken and rice, in case you don't speak Albanian."

"I don't, but I do love chicken and rice." If he sounded breathless, Jesse didn't care. The prospect of spending time with this gorgeous man was an unexpected yet wonderful surprise.

"So, um, is that a yes? Maybe I'm breaking a bunch of rules by hanging out with a resident. When I interviewed I was told we should be seen and not heard."

Annoyance spiked through Jesse, and he huffed. "That's bullshit. You're entitled to do what you want on your lunch. They don't own you. And if anyone gives you shit, it's on me. Tell them I asked you. I'd like to see them try and tell me what to do. My family has lived in the Dakota since it went co-op in the sixties." Those people on the board were so uptight about everything. It had cost the building plenty over the years in monetary settlements when the building's board of directors was sued for discrimination by shareholders. Jesse could only imagine their petty prejudices against the working staff, and it made him angry for Dash.

A small smile teased Dash's lips. "Okay, then. How about I give you a chance to clean this up"—he gestured to the soaking-wet chicken and pan in the sink—"and by that time, I'll be ready for my lunch and I'll be back." He consulted his watch. "Say, two thirty?"

"Sounds good. But I'll let you heat it up."

The sound of Dash's laughter echoed through the airy rooms of the apartment. "You got a deal." He turned solemn. "Look, man. I really wasn't gossiping about you. I've only been working here a little while, and I wanted a chance to get to know the people in the building. Most of all you. I've thought about you since that day in the courtyard. A lot." Dash's gaze met his, and Jesse sensed his honesty.

Warmth fluttered in his chest, and Jesse gnawed at his bottom lip. It had been so long since he'd talked to a guy his own age. And though he suspected Dash might be gay, Jesse wasn't about to bring it up or even make a pathetic attempt to flirt. Five years of sitting in his apartment with Miranda as his sole contact with the outside world meant he knew little about men and what people were looking for these days. In Dash, he sensed a person who was real and honest, but what if he wasn't? At this point, Jesse wasn't yet ready to take that risk.

"Thanks. I...I don't have much contact with the outside."

"No worries. I got you."

Chapter Four

I T HAD BEEN a risk to suggest having lunch together, but Dash honestly liked Jesse and found him interesting to talk to. It didn't hurt that he was cute with those big eyes and shy smile, and what could be better than spending an hour flirting? Plus, Dash wanted to learn more about Jesse and why he didn't go outside. He couldn't mean he stayed in the apartment all the time. That was crazy. Maybe that he didn't date? But recalling how he'd had what looked like a panic attack that day in the courtyard, Dash wasn't so certain.

All those questions ran through his mind as Dash swept out the lobby and delivered packages to other apartments in the building. It was a little more than forty minutes after leaving Jesse when he returned the broom and checked in with the doorman.

"Gonna take my lunch, Eddie. See you in an hour."

"Okay, kid. Catch you later." Eddie waved at him as Dash took the service stairs down to the community room where the workers congregated to eat their lunches or have quick coffee breaks. Dash took out his lunch bag with the chicken and rice he'd brought from home.

"Whatcha got there?"

Paul, one of the other porters, stuck his face in Dash's, and at the blast of his cigarette breath, Dash took a step back.

"Just some stuff I brought from home. Gonna go eat in the park." Not that he didn't trust Paul, who'd never been anything but nice to him, but Dash didn't think he should be spreading his personal business around the Dakota. His and Jesse's.

"Enjoy, see ya later." Paul sat back down at the long metal table and picked up the newspaper to check the racing forms.

Careful to be discreet, Dash used the service elevator that went to Jesse's floor. The Dakota was built with different stairwells leading to separate floors, and Dash had tried to memorize them all, as he and the other porters were responsible for knowing every part of the building.

He reached Jesse's floor, and after knocking on the door, had to wait only a moment before Jesse pulled it open.

"Hi." He lifted the bag with the container of food. "Your lunch awaits."

"Oh, hi, uh, great. C-come on in."

A bit surprised at Jesse's nervousness, Dash wondered if he'd made a mistake about their earlier agreement. "We did say about half an hour, right? I know I'm a little late. Is that okay?"

"Yeah, it's good. Come in." Jesse stepped aside to let him pass, and Dash caught a whiff of freshly washed skin and a light, citrusy cologne. A sweet warmth spread through him at the thought of Jesse changing and getting ready for him. "I made a little cheese platter to have while the food heats up."

"Sounds good."

"I'm going to let you take the lead on the hot food," Jesse said, humor curving his lips in a smile. "One disaster per day is enough."

Dash followed Jesse, admiring the shape of his firm butt. It had been a while since he'd been with a guy, but he didn't have the time. Aside from an occasional hookup, nights were spent studying and doing homework, and now this job would take up most of his other free time. But damn, Jesse's butt looked fine.

"Dash?" Jesse stood by the oven. "What temperature?"

"Oh, sorry." A bit embarrassed at being caught daydreaming, he ran a hand over his hair. "I need a pot with a lid. It should be heated on the stovetop."

"Okay, let me see what I have." He bent, and Dash forced himself to look away. "Here you go." Jesse straightened up, a large pot in his hands. "Will this do?"

"Yeah. Perfect." He took out the container from the bag and popped the lid. Immediately the aroma of paprika, onions, and garlic hit his nose, and his mouth watered. "You like a little spice?"

"I guess. I've never had Albanian food before, but this looks and smells really good."

"It is. Wait until you taste it."

Dash turned the flame between low and medium. "Do you have a spoon I can use to stir?"

Jesse fished a large wooden spoon out of the drawer. "Finally all the stuff my mother left when she moved is going to get used."

"Oh? Where did she go?" Dash stirred the rice into the pot and placed the pieces of chicken on top. He set the lid on with a little opening to allow the steam to escape. Like his mother taught him.

"She remarried and moved to Connecticut with her new husband. Harry's retired now, and they both wanted to move out of the city. Harry had a big house in Greenwich. It's nice if you like being in the country."

Dash laughed. "I think the most country I've seen is Central Park." Tight lines stretched across Jesse's smooth forehead and bracketed his mouth, and he could've kicked himself for joking. "Do you like her new husband?"

"Yeah, he's a good guy. He makes her happy, so that makes me happy. Losing my dad…it nearly killed her. Both of us, really."

Hearing the gossip from Eddie was one thing. Dash had heard enough stories of the disaster of September 11, but he'd never met anyone who'd lost a family member. Time didn't heal that wound. The grief and pain painted in his eyes would be with Jesse forever.

"I know it sounds really ineffective, but I'm sorry." He put his hand on Jesse's shoulder and gave a squeeze. "I couldn't imagine how horrible it was for you."

A shrug and Jesse walked out of the kitchen and down the hall. A bit disconcerted, Dash didn't know whether to follow him, but he decided the man shouldn't be alone with his thoughts. He first looked in the living room but then found Jesse back in the room with his collection.

"Hey, if you want me to leave, I understand. But maybe you could use a friend?"

Jesse ran a finger over one of the rocks. "My dad started me collecting. After he died, I took his stuff and added to it. Sort of my way of keeping in touch with him, you know?"

"I get it."

There was an almost tragic beauty in Jesse's finely etched features. Dash was drawn to him but kept his distance, not wanting to intrude, wondering if he should leave. Jesse glanced up at him.

"I'm sorry. I didn't mean to drag you into the sad story of my life. Let's go back out to the kitchen before that dish goes up in smoke too."

Relieved, Dash attempted to lighten the mood. "That would totally be your fault, my man. You've got a black thumb in the kitchen. Black for smoke."

"Ha-ha."

The spark of laughter in Jesse's eyes made Dash happy, and he vowed to keep it there for the rest of lunch. A cloud of steam rose when he removed the lid.

"Lunch is served. Where are your plates?"

"Here you go. I usually eat off paper ones, but this dish looks and smells too delicious."

Jesse handed Dash two plain china dinner dishes, and he served up the chicken and rice, making sure he got enough of the mixture on the plate so Jesse could taste the flavor. Jesse took their plates and set them on the table. Jesse's all-white kitchen was almost cozy with a built-in nook that held the table, and along one wall, a bench with bright-red cushions that matched the placemats—the only spot of color in the room. An island with a marble top took up the center of the room.

"Oh, I forgot the drinks. What do you want? I have water, soda, juice…"

It was cute how he bit his lip in an effort to please, and Dash wondered further about Jesse—if he'd ever had a serious boyfriend and what he did all day.

"Water's good."

Jesse took two tall glasses from the cabinet, filled them with ice and water from the refrigerator door, and brought them back to the table. Jesse took the seat opposite him, and Dash, fork and knife in hand, gestured to the food.

"Go ahead. You first. I want to know what you think."

Anxious, he watched as Jesse cut into the chicken and put a forkful in his mouth. His eyes widened in surprise.

"Oh, my God. This is amazing." He dug into the rice, and Dash could tell by his vigorous chewing that he wasn't saying it simply to be nice. Happy now, he ate his own food, sneaking glances at Jesse. A few times their eyes met, and Jesse turned a bit red. Dash's chest swelled, and he couldn't help a smile.

I wonder if he's a good kisser. His mouth…damn.

Dash brushed the thought aside as crazy. He was a porter, a poor kid from the Bronx, from an immigrant family. Jesse was white bread and upper crust. The man lived in the most well-known building in New York City and probably had a trust fund. What would Jesse Grace-Martin want with Dashamir Sadiko? Guys living with a view of Central Park didn't date guys who took the elevated train...guys from uptown with hard-to-pronounce names.

"Your mom's an amazing cook."

"Yeah, she is," he answered, his mouth stuffed with food. "She got this recipe from my grandmother. I've never met her. She still lives in Albania, in some small town outside the capital, Tirana."

"I don't know anything about Albania, but this food is delicious." As if to prove his point, Jesse scraped up the last of it. "Is there more?"

"Yeah, sure." He stood and took Jesse's empty plate to the stove to pile on more food. "My mother always makes a ton on Friday nights when my sister and her husband come over for dinner." He laid another cutlet on top of the rice and slid the plate in front of Jesse, then took his seat again.

"Thanks," Jesse said, and he ate that serving with as much gusto as the first. Damn, his mother would love Jesse. Dash wondered if he'd ever be willing to come up to the Bronx for a meal, and dismissed it almost immediately as another crazy thought. "Do you have any brothers or only a sister?" As he spoke, Jesse cut up the chicken and mixed it with the rice, then took a big forkful. It gave Dash pleasure to watch Jesse enjoying his food. He had a feeling everything about Jesse would be pleasurable.

"Only one sister. She's enough to handle. You?"

"I had an older brother who died as a baby. So yeah, I guess I'm considered an only child."

"Damn, I'm sorry. How old was he? Was he sick?" Dash bit his lip and cursed his stupidity. "I'm sorry. I don't mean to ask all these questions."

"It's okay. It was crib death. My mother said she put him down for his nap and he never woke up. It happened before I was born, so I never had a chance to know Henry." His eyes took on a faraway look. "Although it would've been nice to have someone to grow up with. It might've made things easier." Blinking rapidly, he ducked his head and stuffed another forkful of food in his mouth.

"Yeah, I get it. I mean, it's not the same, but being the boy was hard. My father worked long hours at a restaurant and was always at work whenever I was home, so my mother looked to me for everything. I've been taking care of things since I was fifteen."

"That's rough." Jesse's forehead furrowed. "You were still a kid. I didn't even know who I was at that age." He opened his mouth as if to say something, then shut it and pressed his lips together.

"I did, and I didn't like it. But we believe in family first, and I knew I had to take care of my mother and sister."

Admiration shone from Jesse's eyes. "It must be nice to be so close. I didn't think I'd miss my mom when she moved away, but..." He shrugged and dropped his gaze to his plate. "It gets lonely some-times."

"But I bet her house is awesome. I've seen pictures of those mansions. Does it have a pool and tennis court?" At Jesse's nod, Dash continued babbling. "Sweet. So you can go up there for the weekend and hang out and do nothing."

"Uh, are you finished?" Avoiding his gaze, Jesse stood abruptly, walked to the other side of the kitchen where the sink was, and rinsed off his plate, then put it in the dishwasher. "I'll take it whenever you're ready."

Another dumb comment. Over the course of their talks, Jesse had dropped little hints that he stayed inside or that he didn't go out. At first, when he'd heard the staff gossiping about the apartment owners, Dash hardly paid attention. It wasn't his business who was screwing whom and what kinky stuff people liked to do in the privacy of their own homes. He'd bet the staff did some pretty fucked-up stuff they wouldn't want anyone else to hear about.

Besides, Dash didn't care all that much about the other people, but Jesse Grace-Martin sure had wriggled under his skin. Maybe it was because Dash had been looking after his family since he was so young, but he always had a soft spot for the underdog, the person who needed a bit of help to make it. Jesse, despite his wealth, seemed almost lost. Whether it was from the unexpected death of his father or something else, Dash wanted to protect him and keep him out of harm's way.

"Yeah, I'm finished."

Plate in hand, he walked across the kitchen and handed it to Jesse. "I could wash them, you know. The plates, I mean. And the pot. It's no big deal."

"Why? That's what dishwashers are for."

"Well, you're looking at a human dishwasher. My mom doesn't have one at home, so that was always my job after my sister cleared the table."

"Oh. But this is easier." Jesse put his dish inside, next to the other one. "You can rinse out the pot, and I'll put it in here as well."

"Okay, but don't say the champion dishwasher of Belmont never offered." He struck a pose and flexed his muscles.

"Where's that? Belmont?" Jesse wrinkled his nose. "I know I've heard of it."

Dash expected that. If you weren't from the Bronx, you probably didn't know it. The only parts of the borough most people in the city were familiar with were Yankee Stadium or the zoo.

"It's in the Bronx, but in the East section. We have some amazing Italian restaurants, and it's got a large Albanian population. They call it Little Albania. That's the main reason my parents moved there."

"Oh, sorry. I only know Yankee Stadium."

Dash let out a chuckle. "Yeah, I figured. Maybe one day you'll come up, and I can show you around. Take you to one of the great Italian restaurants on Arthur Avenue."

Again, the longing Dash had seen previously filled Jesse's eyes. All he said was, "Maybe one day."

A quick check of his watch showed the hour had almost passed, and he needed to get downstairs and clock in from lunch or he'd be late. He took the pot off the stove, scraped out the leftover rice, and rinsed it clean. "Here. I hate to leave you to clean up after me."

"It's okay. I don't mind." Jesse bit his full bottom lip. "It was nice of you to offer to share your lunch." He put the pot down. "I'll let you out."

"Well," he said as they approached the front door, "it was nice talking to you."

Without answering, Jesse unlocked, then opened the door. "I really enjoyed myself. The food was amazing, and the company wasn't too shabby either." His face flooded with color. "Thanks again."

"I enjoyed it too. Being here beats sitting on a park bench fighting off the pigeons. And yeah." He smiled into Jesse's eyes. "The company was fine."

He left and walked down the hallway, aware that Jesse hadn't closed the door and might be watching. Dash hoped the man would be thinking about him, because he sure as hell would be thinking about Jesse Grace-Martin and how he could get to spend more time with him.

Chapter Five

"SO HOW WAS the weekend? Do anything fun?" Monday morning, Miranda poured them both coffee and sat on the sofa, ready for their usual chat. Only this time it wasn't the same old answer, "*Nothing new.*"

Lunch with Dash had remained on Jesse's mind the rest of Saturday and all day Sunday. He wondered if Dash worked every weekend and if he'd see him at all, but Jesse knew he was being foolish. The only way to accomplish that would be to go outside. He'd thought about it and had even gotten dressed, but when he put his hand on the front-door knob, the familiar wave of nausea and vertigo hit him, and he could barely make it back to the living room before he collapsed on the couch in frustrated tears.

But Miranda didn't have to know about that part.

"Um, yeah, kind of."

Already busy with her planner, Miranda's gaze shot to his. "Yeah? What? Tell me." She set the planner down, her eyes expectant.

"Well...I ordered a bunch of amethysts. You know how into them I've been lately, and the store on

Columbus said they could deliver them that day."

"Oh, yeah."

Jesse watched her face fall and guessed she thought he'd had something more interesting to tell her.

Okay, here goes.

"They sent it, and Dash—remember him?—he delivered it."

"Oh, yeah. He seemed…nice." Her eyes searched his.

"He is nice. While he was up here, I showed him my collection, and he was really interested. And then I burned my lunch."

"Wait, what?"

Grinning at Miranda, he left his spot by the window—was he hoping to catch a glimpse of Dash walking down the block from the train?—and stood in front of her. "That chicken you bought and left for me? I might've burned it."

Laughter bubbled out of her, and she clapped her hand over her mouth. "What? Oh my God, Jesse, how?"

"We got to talking, and I wasn't paying attention to the time." A smile curved his lips at the memory of him and Dash running into the kitchen to see the smoke. "It was a pretty ugly sight. But in the end totally worth it."

"And it looked like such a good chicken." She wiped her eyes. "Did you have anything else to eat? I guess you ordered in."

"Well…no. See, that's where it got interesting. Dash offered to share his lunch, and so he came up here and we ate together."

Wide-eyed, Miranda gasped. "No, you didn't. Jess, that's fantastic." She jumped up to give him a hug. "Tell me everything."

Oddly enough, he didn't want to. As much as he loved Miranda and trusted her, for the first time since he'd locked himself in his self-imposed prison, he had something he could call his own...that no one else helped him with. Her questions came from a place of caring and concern, but Jesse wanted to keep whatever he had with Dash as close to his heart and as private as possible.

"Nothing to tell, really," he said, shrugging. "We ate, talked a little, and then he had to go back to work. It was only an hour."

"Oh." Her disappointment was obvious. "But you'll do it again? Did you set another time?"

"We aren't dating." He frowned. "It was strictly a casual, one-off thing." Even as he spoke the words, his mind rebelled against them. He wanted to have lunch with Dash again and find out more about where he lived in the Bronx. He wanted to find out everything about him.

"It doesn't have to be." She gazed up at him, her eyes soft with sympathy. "He asked me about you."

Alarm mixed with excitement shot through him. "What? He did?" Like an eager kid, he pulled her down onto the couch to sit next to him. "Tell me what he said."

"After work that Friday when he helped us, he came up to me on the subway platform. At first I thought he was one of those weirdos who likes to talk to random women, but then I recognized him in his regular clothes. He stands out in a crowd."

"Yeah, he does." A person would have to be crazy not to notice. His thick dark hair, smooth olive skin, and muscular body were only the half of it. Dash's dark eyes shone with kindness, and his lips were quick to smile. Much of Jesse's recent nights had been spent restlessly tossing and turning in his bed, imagining what Dash's kiss would taste like. What his other parts would feel like.

"After he asked whether you were okay, he said if there was anything we ever needed in the apartment, we should call him. I'll admit I thought he was there to gossip about you."

"So what'd you do? You didn't blow him off, did you? He was really helpful." Hearing that Dash had asked about him sent a thrill through Jesse. It had been years since Jesse had such a strong attraction to anyone.

A guilty expression clouded her normally cheerful face. "I wasn't as nice as I could've been."

"Miranda." Jesse pounded his thigh with his hand, anger draining away the pleasure over Dash asking about him. "What did you do?"

"I'm sorry," she cried out. "I know you're going to say I'm overprotective of you, but I can't be sure."

Barely listening to her, he cringed at the thought of Miranda acting like a mother hen. "I'm thirty, you know. I may be crazy, but I can tell if someone's a decent person or not."

"You aren't crazy."

"Sure I am. What would you call someone who has a panic attack sitting on a bench in a private, heavily guarded courtyard?"

"Stop saying that. You have a problem, and you're trying to help yourself."

Witnessing her genuine distress, Jesse tried to soothe her. "I'm sorry. I know you hate when I talk like that. I'll try not to say it anymore."

Even though it's true.

"Have you called Dr. Mingione for a session? She should know. You have to realize how tremendous an accomplishment that was for you. It's been five years since you've been outside, and yet you went all the way to the courtyard with me." She hugged him close and whispered, "It's something to be celebrated."

Hearing her say it almost made him feel worse. "I'm acting like a fool. I want to go outside." He licked his dry lips. "Yesterday I tried. I got dressed and made it to the door, but when I put my hand on the knob, I couldn't turn it. All these horrible thoughts came crashing down on me. What if someone hurts me, or what if there's another attack and I can't get home in time?" Those last words were forced out in a whisper. "It's so big out there, and there are so many people. I couldn't do it. I didn't have anyone there with me I could trust."

Tears fell from her eyes and glided down her cheeks. "Oh, Jesse." Miranda gave him a squeeze. "It'll happen. When it's right. Call Dr. Mingione."

"Yeah, maybe I will."

✧   ✧   ✧   ✧

W̲HEN HIS THERAPIST heard what he'd done, she was more than willing to squeeze him in at the end of the day for a session, and the tightness in his chest eased. She could be counted on to give him practical advice, and he always felt better after seeing her.

He spent the rest of the day reading and setting up more of his gems and crystals in his display room. Miranda had done the weekly food shopping and they were putting away the groceries when the doorbell rang. He glanced at the clock on the stove.

"It's too early for the doctor." Nervous sweat broke out over him. "Who do you think it is?"

"I'll check and see." Miranda closed the refrigerator, and he banged a fist on the countertop.

"No. No. I can do this. I mean, I answer the door when you're not here on the weekend."

"Okay. I'm only trying to help." Hurt, she turned away from him and folded the reusable tote bags.

His anger melted away. "I'm sorry. I didn't mean to snap at you. I'm trying to take those baby steps you mentioned."

"Don't apologize. I know I'm a little overprotective. It's a habit I have to break."

Leaving Miranda in the kitchen, Jesse went to the front door and peered through the peephole. His trepidation turned to excitement when he saw Dash waiting. His hand slipped on the doorknob before he got a grip and opened it.

"Hi."

"Hi. I hope I'm not bothering you."

"No, of course not. Come on in."

Heels tapped on the wooden floor, and Jesse knew Miranda had left the kitchen and was waiting in the living room.

First glancing over his shoulder, Jesse opened the door wide.

"Are you sure? I don't want to interrupt."

"Not at all. We were putting away groceries, and then I was going to start a new assignment."

Still a bit hesitant, Dash came inside but remained in the foyer. A large plastic bag dangled from his hand.

"Well, when I told my mother how much you liked the food and that you lived alone…" He hefted the bag. "She made some extra for you and insisted I bring it."

Not in a million years would Jesse have ever guessed this would happen after their impromptu lunch. He gaped at Dash, who shifted uneasily from one foot to the other.

"If you don't want it, I understand. My mother can be very pushy. I tried to tell her you probably wouldn't, but—"

"Are you kidding?" The thought that Dash had even told his family about him and that his mother had taken the time to make him food? Jesse shook his head. Much as he loved his own mother, she'd never set foot in the kitchen and used to joke about how she barely knew how to boil water. "Is it your lunch hour?"

"Yeah. But this is separate. I ate mine and wanted to bring you this, but if you've already eaten…"

"No, no I haven't." He glanced back toward the kitchen. "Neither of us has."

"Oh, there's plenty for you both." That charming smile, the one he had dreams about, flashed, and Jesse found himself returning it. "If you knew my mother, she normally makes enough food to feed half a city block."

"Come on into the kitchen." Jesse started walking and waved for Dash to follow him. "Miranda," he called, even though he knew she was listening. "It's Dash. Remember him?"

"Of course. Hi, Dash."

"Oh, hi." His dark brows knotted, and lines furrowed his forehead.

Remembering Miranda's story of their meeting, Jesse understood Dash's wariness. He caught her eye and raised his brows as if to say, *Tell him you're sorry for mistrusting him.* Lucky for him, Miranda understood his signals and faced Dash.

"Hey, Dash. I want to apologize for the way I behaved on the subway platform. I should've known by how you helped Jesse that you wouldn't be the type of person to gossip. I guess I have to start trusting people."

"I don't blame you. You can't be too careful these days. There're a lot of weirdos around." Dash's forehead smoothed and he smiled, and Jesse feared both Dash and his smile might become addictive.

"How about we take a look at what Dash brought?" He rubbed his stomach. If the food was as good as what Dash brought on Saturday, he and Miranda were in for a treat. "I'm suddenly starving."

Dash laughed. "That's good, because I think you'll be eating this for a week."

"Lead the way." He hadn't felt this lighthearted in years, and he caught Miranda's wondering expression. Did it show on his face? Jesse wasn't sure he cared. He was enjoying himself.

Dash set the bag on the kitchen counter and rattled around inside it, taking out various plastic containers. When he finished, he opened them up and pointed to each one, explaining what they were.

"This one is *byrek*—I guess the closest would be the Greek *spanakopita*? It has the phyllo dough and spinach with *gjize* cheese. Then we have *tavë kosi*, which is like a quiche thing with lamb and yogurt and eggs. It's really good. For dessert, she made my favorite, *baklava*."

The array of foods boggled the mind, and Jesse couldn't take it all in. There were also grilled meatballs Dash called *qofte*, and a small cake—*trilece*—made of three different kinds of milk.

"I'm…stunned. It's too much. I can't wrap my head around the fact that your mother really made all this for me…a stranger." Jesse was so touched by Dash's mother's gesture, he was at a loss for words.

"My mother—most Albanians, in fact—believe visitors and strangers are as important as family. It is an honor for her to cook for you."

"Really?"

"Really."

Looking into Dash's eyes, Jesse knew he was telling the truth.

"And who knows?" Dash said. "Maybe one day I

can even take you up to the Bronx to meet her. I told her about your gem collection. All about you."

Instantly on guard, Jesse began to shake, and his heart fell. "Me? What did you say? That I was some guy you know who can't leave his apartment? That I almost passed out just from sitting outside?" His breath came in short pants, and his vision wavered. Miranda put a steadying hand on his back.

"Jesse, man, no. I don't know what you're talking about. You seem like a nice, cool guy. I like spending time with you, talking about different stuff. That's it."

Trembling, Jesse drew in a breath to calm down. "Sorry I overreacted." He pushed his sweaty hair off his forehead. "I'll remember that. It's part of something I'm working on."

Dash shook his head but said nothing.

"Should we heat up the food?" Miranda said brightly. "I love trying new cuisine, and I've never had Albanian."

"I can't stay, I'm sorry. I have to get back to work."

He heard the regret in Dash's voice, and it bothered him that they couldn't share all this amazing food. "Please come back later. I'll have the containers cleaned up for you to take back."

"You don't have to." Dash stuffed the plastic bag into the garbage pail.

"I know," Jesse said. "I want to. It's the least I can do since you can't even stay and eat with us. I feel bad about it."

Dash gnawed on his lip and hesitated. "It might be late, though. I don't get off work until eight thirty."

"It's okay," Jesse said. "It's not past my bedtime." A

slight smile crossed his lips, and Dash held back his own.

"I'll see you then," Dash said softly. "I can let myself out."

With a quiet smile, he left the kitchen, and Jesse remained lost in thought until the door clicked. At a tap on his shoulder, he jumped.

"Jesus, you scared me." His heart fluttered, and he put his hand on the countertop to brace himself.

Miranda frowned. "Sorry, but I've been calling your name and you didn't answer. What's going on between you two?"

"Going on?" he repeated. "What do you mean? Nothing's going on."

"Oh, come on, Jess. I see the way you look at him. You haven't been this...I don't know...*alive*, for want of a better word, since I started working for you."

No way would he share his feelings about Dash. Not that he had feelings. At least not ones he could talk to Miranda about. *Dammit.* Jesse ran his hands through his hair. "He's been nice to me. That's all. I mean, come on, he brought all this food his mother made for me. I have to be nice to him."

"That expression on your face didn't look like you had to force yourself."

"What is this? Why are you interrogating me?" Irritable, he took the food out of the containers and put those that needed to be warmed in the microwave. He picked up a piece of *baklava* and nibbled an edge. The sweet, honeyed flakes melted on his tongue. "I'm not a kid. I can handle myself."

"I never said you couldn't. I'm saying you don't

have to hide it if you are attracted to him." She turned and walked stiffly out of the kitchen.

Remorse flooded through him, and he chased after her. He found her sitting on the sofa, turning the pages of her planner.

"I'm sorry. I shouldn't have snapped at you. Maybe...maybe I do like his company. But I know I'm being silly. I mean, he's a normal guy who has a life outside this apartment building."

"It's not silly. I think the fact that you're having these feelings may be a sign."

IN THE LATE afternoon, when Dr. Mingione sat on the very same sofa, she stated something similar to what Miranda said.

"You know, Jesse, I've seen your restlessness as of late. You're testing your limits to see how far your body will go before the mind takes over."

"Not that far," he said grimly. "I tried this weekend and couldn't make it out the front door."

"And yet," she continued, her face serene and blue eyes sharp behind her black-framed glasses, "six months ago you barely spoke of leaving the apartment. A year ago it was a chore for you to speak to me here. Every time I see you now, there's more of a spark, more of the Jesse I believe is buried inside you. The Jesse that existed before the agoraphobia took control of your life."

"I do want it. I want it so badly." To be able to walk outside, go to the park again or browse in a bookstore? Shivers ran through him at the thought of sitting next to Dash on a blanket in the park, maybe having a picnic or listening to a concert. If it wasn't so pathetic, he would laugh at himself. Look at him, fantasizing about a guy he barely knew.

"So what's changed since our last session?"

Thinking on it, Jesse knew it wasn't Dash. He might be the impetus for the erotic dreams he'd been having, but Jesse had wanted to go outside before he'd met Dash.

"I've been more restless lately, thinking of my father more and everything we used to do together. But it makes sense because we're coming up to September eleventh, and I always think about him more around that date. I'm also tired. I'm tired of looking out the window and seeing everyone having fun and passing me by while I walk these rooms. I'm feeling like a prisoner in a multimillion-dollar jail."

"So you went out, and what happened?" She made notes as he talked.

"Miranda and I sat in the courtyard for a while— like fifteen minutes. I started to walk back toward the lobby, but that's when I began to feel the panic. One of the building workers helped me inside and into the elevator. Miranda was there too."

"So you sat outside and didn't experience any panic? You felt safe?"

"Yes. Until I tried to walk back to the lobby myself."

"That's fine. You don't need to accomplish everything at once. Think of what you have done: Gone outside. Breathed in the fresh air. Maybe seen and said hello to people walking by?" At his nod, she continued. "So what I want you to do is concentrate on the positives of your outings and of your interactions with people. If you want, write down your feelings when you're sitting outside or after speaking, and try and replicate those emotions when you're alone."

"You mean write in a journal?" He made a face, and Dr. Mingione laughed.

"Not a fan? You can make notes on your phone if you like that better."

"Okay. But I'm not sure. I know what sets me off. Being by myself, thinking that someone could come up to me and hurt me…" He ducked his head and picked at a thread on his jeans. "All that space for something to happen." Blinking back tears of frustration and shame, he forced his lips into a smile. "So as you see, nothing much has changed."

"No. I don't see that. What I see is you thinking of breaking free of what's holding you back. Slowly. And it's going to be scary. But." She set her notebook down. "Who said there has to be a deadline? You take this at your pace. If one day you can open the door and nothing else—then that's your accomplishment. Maybe the next day you'll step outside the door, and that will be enough. Try to talk to someone new." Her eyes twinkled. "My Italian mother-in-law, when she tried to teach me how to make her sauce, used to tell me, '*A poco a poco imparerai.* Little by little, you will learn.' "

If only it were that simple. But then he thought of Dash and how he'd like to talk to him every day if he could.

If only.

Chapter Six

O N A NOW-FAMILIAR path, Dash walked from the service elevator to Jesse's apartment, but this time he was in his regular clothes of shorts and a T-shirt. He'd managed to get to the time clock first to punch out, so he was right on schedule when he knocked on Jesse's door. It only took a few moments for the locks to turn and the door to open. Jesse's smiling face greeted him.

"Hey, come on in."

Dash stepped inside but remained in the wide-open foyer. "Hi. How did you like the food?"

The green in Jesse's eyes glowed, and his smile beamed bright. A tug of attraction curled around Dash's spine, and his skin prickled with awareness. If they'd been simply two men in a bar or at a party, he might've moved a bit closer and gotten his flirt on. But this was Jesse Grace-Martin. Prep-school graduate, son of an incredibly wealthy family, and grandson of one of the original residents of the Dakota. Untouchable in Dash's eyes, no matter how attracted he might be.

"Oh, I can't believe how good it was. I love all the spices." His eyes closed in appreciation and he licked his lips, and Dash's dick shifted in his shorts. He would have liked to taste Jesse's mouth right now, full of the spice and sweetness of the food and dessert. His pink tongue looked soft, and he imagined sucking it deep while they kissed.

"Uh." He coughed and slid his backpack off his shoulders to hold in front of him to hide his stiffening cock. "I'll take the containers if you have them ready."

"Yeah, yeah I do. And something else." Jesse hurried into the apartment, calling over his shoulder, "Come inside and have a seat." He disappeared into the kitchen, leaving Dash standing in the living room.

Looking around for the first time, Dash could see that while the apartment wasn't as grand as some of the others in the building, the rooms were large and airy with windows overlooking Central Park. Two pictures sat on the pristine white-marble fireplace, along with more of Jesse's quartz, and he walked over to look at them. In one, Jesse was a child, his parents on either side as they skated at Rockefeller Center; in the other, he was on the back of a camel at the Bronx Zoo, with his father standing next to him. He had the same sweet smile then as now, but his eyes were bright and his face shone with happiness. There was no hint of the present-day sadness that rested over him like a fog.

Footsteps sounded, and Dash hurried to the center of the room, not wanting to be caught prying. Jesse came in with a small shopping bag in one hand and the containers in a plastic bag in the other.

"I might've eaten all the *baklava*, it was so delicious." His eyes danced, and Dash had to restrain himself from glancing over at the pictures of young Jesse to see the similarity. "I saved the other cake for tomorrow."

"Did you like all the food?"

"I think I gained ten pounds from that meal alone." He patted his stomach.

"My mom will be thrilled. She's very old-school, and nothing makes her happier than knowing people love her cooking."

"Well, I want to let her know that, so would you give this to her?" He held out the shopping bag, but Dash didn't take it.

"What? What is it?"

"I wanted to give her something to express my appreciation for all the trouble she went to."

"Oh, but she loved doing it. You don't have to give her anything. She didn't do it for that. Her greatest pleasure is knowing she made something and you enjoyed it."

"That's really sweet, but I picked it out especially for her."

Reluctant, Dash still didn't take the bag. "I don't know."

"Please. I really want you to. I can't tell her myself, and this would make me feel good about accepting everything." He held out the bag. "Please? Come on, Dash."

Jesse could be damn persuasive, not the pushover Dash initially thought.

"Okay." He accepted the shopping bag, and at its weight, wondered what it was.

"Are you going to tell me what's in it?" He hefted it. "Is it a book?"

Those pretty eyes of Jesse's twinkled, and his smile gave Dash a warm, fluttery feeling in his chest.

"Nope. Guess you'll have to wait until she opens it."

"You're being so mysterious. Now I can't wait to go home and give it to her so I can see what it is."

"I hope she likes it."

Their eyes met, and Dash almost flinched at the yearning on Jesse's face.

"I'm sure she will. I'd better go. It's gonna take me about an hour to get home."

"I'm sorry. I shouldn't have kept you."

Unspoken words danced between them, and Dash wished he could hang out and talk to Jesse. It was so quiet—no noise from the outside filtered in. Not like in his neighborhood, where people kept the windows open and you could hear every argument on the street and smell the grease from the fried-chicken place on the corner.

Together they walked to the front door, and Jesse opened it. "Thanks again for everything." A struggle played out on his face, and then he said in a rush of words, "You know, I'm here all the time, so if you ever want to come and hang out on your lunch break, you have an open invitation." He stopped, his face red, eyes glittering. "Or even after work…"

"Wow. Really? Are you sure?"

"Yeah," Jesse said quietly. "I'm very sure."

It was against the co-op rules for residents and

workers to socialize, but Dash would be willing to bend the rules a little for a chance to spend more time with Jesse.

"That would be amazing. I mean, sometimes I like to take a walk or run errands, but it would be nice to have someone to talk to. It's probably best if I come after work—we could even go to the park and hang out."

"Yeah…sure," Jesse said faintly. "Maybe."

"All right. Thanks again. I guess I'll see you tomorrow."

THE TRAIN RIDE home, as predicted, took over an hour, and by the time he walked up the stairs to his parents' apartment on the third floor, he was exhausted. As always, he looked forward to the day he could make more money and afford to move them out of their cramped living space—a two-bedroom apartment above the dry-cleaning store on Pelham Parkway—and himself into something better than a second-floor studio apartment around the corner from them.

The aroma of Albanian spices mingled with Italian in the hallways, and he could hear the blare of the televisions from behind the various apartment doors. The Rhexas were having their nightly argument that would inevitably end up with Mr. Rhexa slamming out of the apartment and getting drunk at the bar down the block. Little wonder Dash enjoyed working at the Dakota with its hushed hallways and cherished the silence. Dash opened his parents' apartment door.

"Ma, I'm here."

"In the kitchen."

With a steaming cup of coffee in front of her, his mother sat at the table, listening to an Albanian radio station deliver the news. She'd left Tirana, Albania's capital, as a young girl, but still had relatives there and liked to keep up with the news.

"How are you? How was work?" Her eyes searched his. "You look tired. Are you sure you can keep up with everything? Working full-time and going to school?"

"Yeah, I'm fine. It'll be okay. I like working there." Images of Jesse flashed in his head. "I've met some really nice people, and the guys I work with are okay. And," he said, setting the shopping bag on the table, "the money is good, so I can't complain. Those people tip for everything, so I'm making some good cash."

"Tell me," she said as she turned down the volume on the radio and set aside her coffee. "How did your friend like the food? Did he eat it?"

He pulled out a chair and sat. "It was like Christmas. I've never seen anyone so excited. He loved everything." As he spoke, her smile grew wider and brighter. He hadn't lied to Jesse when he said nothing in his mother's life gave her more pleasure than pleasing others. Part of why his father treated her so badly.

"I'm so happy. Tell me which was his favorite."

"The *baklava*. He said he ate all of it."

Her eyes widened. "There were six pieces." She clapped her hand over her mouth. "He's going to have a stomach ache for sure."

Heat washed over him at the recollection of the peek he'd gotten of Jesse's flat stomach when he'd reached for a plate in the cabinet. Dash swallowed hard. "He'll be all right. But look." He pointed to the shopping bag. "He sent me home with this for you. As a thank-you."

His mother had been a runner-up in the Miss Tirana pageant when she met his father and was still gorgeous to Dash with her high cheekbones and deep brown eyes. Years of hard work and worry had scored deep lines in the soft skin of her face, but when she smiled as she did now, reaching for the bag, Dash saw that beauty queen again.

She lifted the tightly wrapped package, and Dash hitched his chair closer, eager to see what Jesse had given her. She pulled off the bubble wrap and gasped.

"Dashamir. What is this? It's beautiful." She held the crystal up, the purple sparkling in the overhead light. It was a large, natural amethyst crystal, as big as her palm. "It's the most beautiful thing I've ever seen."

Dash recalled telling Jesse that his mother owned an amethyst, and purple was her favorite color. He must've had this in his personal collection. Pleased that Jesse not only gave his mother such respect, but that he'd paid close attention to their conversation, Dash wanted to puff Jesse up in his mother's eyes.

"Jesse collects all kinds of crystals and gemstones. He has a whole room where all the pieces he's found himself, got from his father, or bought from a dealer are on display. You should see it, Mom. Rubies and emeralds and all kinds of gemstones in their natural state. It's so cool. I only mentioned to him in passing that you loved the color purple." He touched the glittering chunk of crystals. "I can't believe he gave you this."

With reverence, his mother set it down on the bubble wrap and cast an assessing eye on him. "You seem to talk a lot about this Jesse lately. How well *do* you know him?"

Dash flushed under her regard. "I don't know him at all, really. We've hung out a few times. Nothing special." He didn't like lying, because Jesse *was* special, but Dash wasn't ready to say anything out loud. It was new and tentative between them, and they were only friends. He was sticking to that story.

Her gaze cut to the amethyst, then focused on his face, her eyes dark with concern. "I don't know if I believe that. This isn't fake—it's real. It must be very expensive. A man doesn't give another man presents like this unless he might have feelings for him?"

"Mom, he gave it to you, not me. I'm sure he meant it as a compliment—a gesture of respect for everything you did. Jesse is a good guy."

She waved her hand in his face. "I hear things and know about these rich people. They're into drugs and drinking. They think because they have money, they can say and do anything they want. I don't want you to get caught up in a lifestyle you don't know about. You might work in a fancy building, but you don't really know the people who live there."

It would be hard to explain Jesse to her, as he barely knew the man himself, but Dash felt compelled to defend his new friend.

"Jesse isn't like what you've described, Mom. I mean, yeah, he's got money, but he doesn't act rude or obnoxious. He lives alone but doesn't go out much. Most of his time he's home reading and writing articles about gemstones for magazines." His lips tightened. "Jesse isn't a party boy. Not like the guys in the neighborhood here."

"I'm sorry. I didn't mean to upset you."

"You know I don't like stereotyping people. People think Albanians are all gangsters and thugs because of what they read in the news. Well, Jesse isn't some spoiled brat rich kid." Not that he'd seen, anyway. "He lost his father in the World Trade Center on 9/11, and now that his mother is remarried, he's alone. I think he's looking for a friend."

Ever the softhearted, his mother's eyes filled with tears. "Oh, that poor young man. He must've been a child when it happened."

"Yeah, he was thirteen. They were really close, and I'm not sure he's gotten over it."

"Losing a parent isn't something you can forget, no matter how old you are." Nodding at his words, she held his gaze, and her eyes took on a steely determination Dash had seen before. Her long fingers caressed the amethyst crystal. "No one should be alone. I'm going to give you some food for him again."

"You don't have to do that, Mom. He doesn't expect it."

"That's why it's special. The most unexpected things are the most important to the heart. And it sounds like you think he's special too. Am I right?"

For him to have this conversation with his mother would be considered odd in their culture, which respected domineering, rough men, like his father. But with his father ignorant of Dash's sexuality and out of the house so much, both working and socializing with his friends, there was no one else Dash felt he could trust.

"I've only spoken to him a few times, so I can't say if he's special. But I am intrigued by him. He's kind and sensitive, and I think he's got a lot going on inside his head that he hides from people."

"That sounds to me like you've spent a lot of time thinking about him."

"Come on, Mom." His face heated. The last thing he was about to do at his age was get into a discussion of his sex life with his mother. "We're friendly—not even friends yet. Lighten up."

"Okay, okay." She held up her hands in surrender. "Do you want a coffee before you go?"

"No, thanks. I have a busy night. Have to look up when I need to register for classes and figure out my budget with the books I have to buy or hopefully can rent online."

"Okay." Her face crumpled. "I wish we could help so you didn't have to work so hard. But to have you go to college and graduate…" She shook her head and sniffed, brushing at the tears on her lashes. "We're so proud of you."

"Thanks, Mom. I'll talk to you tomorrow."

"Don't forget. Come by to pick up your lunch and

your friend's."

"You really don't have to make him lunch, and I told you I can pick up something near where I work."

"Bah," she grumbled. "Why waste the money? I know you're saving all your pennies. It's no bother for me to make extra."

"Thanks, *Nënë*."

"I thought you'd forgotten all your Albanian."

"How could I forget the most important person in my life?"

A pretty pink blush stained her face. "All I wish is for you to find someone to make you happy."

"I know, I know. But right now, my pillow will make me the happiest man in the world. Right after I do my stuff for class."

With a kiss on her head, Dash left and walked around the corner to his apartment. It was an ugly place with thick metal bars on the two tiny windows and a musty smell. But it was cheap and close to his family and the subway. He didn't care so much where he lived as long as it was safe. The landlord was the father of a guy Dash had grown up with and was reputed to be a member of one of the big Bronx Albanian gangs. When he saw his friend Olsi driving around in a fancy red Mercedes, flashing diamond rings and a heavy gold watch, Dash assumed he'd joined his father. Dash stayed away from all that, and after numerous attempts by Olsi to get him to come work for his father and "forget the college thing," his friend gave up and left him alone.

Later that night, after signing up for his courses,

Dash lay in bed, trying to sleep while ignoring the moans of the couple next door as they had sex. The paper-thin walls let every sound through, and Dash wasn't sure which was worse: the squeals and smacks of them having rough sex or hearing them fight. He flipped the pillow over his head and fell asleep, dreaming of Jesse and the Dakota and all that beautiful quiet.

Chapter Seven

SLEEP ELUDED JESSE for most of the week. The previous day had been the anniversary of September 11, and unable to participate in the memorials downtown, Jesse had his own private mourning ceremony for his father. Miranda had gone on some errands, and around midmorning he called his mother.

"I'm happy…but always in the wings there's this darkness waiting. Am I making sense?"

Her confession surprised Jesse, but he understood. "Yeah. It's almost as if I'm afraid to ever be happy again, because if I am, it means something bad is going to happen to snatch it away."

"I'm happy with Harry. He's the best man, and I love him."

"I know, Mom. I'm glad you have him." But he also knew his parents had loved each other in a way people envied. They hadn't needed words—their smiles or simple touches were enough to show how deeply they were connected.

"I hope one day you'll find someone to love and take away your loneliness."

"Me too. I'll talk to you, Mom. Bye."

The rest of the morning he wandered about, staring at the pictures of their happy family, alternating between tears and frustration. At noon he received a call from Dash.

"Are you busy? Want to do lunch? I can't talk 'cause I'm on the phone in the break room."

Along with the emotions of September 11, Dash had been on Jesse's mind. He hadn't seen him for almost a week, and Jesse felt a bit slighted that he hadn't stopped by. He'd gotten a brief thank-you note for the gift to Dash's mother, but nothing personal. Nothing that said they'd see each other again.

Jesse's heart raced. "Sure. When do you want to come by?"

"I'll be there at two thirty. Gotta go."

Jesse supposed he'd get his answer then.

At a few minutes past two thirty, when Jesse opened the door, Dash greeted him with a smile and a raised shopping bag. "I'm sorry I haven't been by this week. Schoolwork's been kicking my butt."

"Come in." He held the door open, and Dash passed by him, bringing his spicy scent and all his heat. A slight shiver ran through him. "So you come bearing *baklava*?"

Dash grinned, and Jesse was swept away by emotions he didn't understand, so he tried to lighten the moment. "Okay. I can be bought by your mom's cooking. I'm easy."

"Good to know." Dash pushed a lock of his sleek dark hair from his face.

"I hope all this food means she liked the gift. I

know it wasn't much, but I had to thank her, so…" He trailed off and bit his lip.

Dash's eyes warmed, and Jesse found himself drawn into their inky depths.

"She couldn't get over how beautiful it is. Whenever I go over there, the amethyst is sitting in the middle of the coffee table. Like a prize. I wish I could've told you, but I had so much work, and when I realized I didn't have your phone number to text you or anything, I had to wait. I had a hell of a time sneaking a note for you past Eddie. I hung around and asked the mailman to stick it in your box."

"I'll give you my number if you want," Jesse blurted out, then, seeing Dash's eyes widen with surprise, felt the shame of humiliation at his overeagerness prickle over his skin. "It's okay. I guess it's silly. Why would you want my number? Forget I—"

"That'd be great." A spark of something kindled in Dash's eyes. "I, uh, don't want you to think I'm being pushy or anything. I know the staff aren't supposed to mingle with the owners, so…" He shrugged.

"This isn't the 1800s, and I don't really care what those snobs think. I can be friends with whomever I want."

His heated words brought a smile to Dash's face, but he said nothing further and handed over the bag. They walked toward the kitchen, Jesse hyperaware of Dash's presence next to him. It had been so long since he'd felt desire, and he didn't even know if Dash was gay or bisexual or just being nice to him. Not that it mattered anyway. He would settle for being friends with the man. He set the bag on the counter and delved inside.

"Be warned. My mother now plans on making extra food for you, but if you ever want her to stop, please tell me. And don't be afraid you're hurting her feelings. When I told her about you, she wanted to make sure you were taken care of. Today is the first time I've had a chance to breathe, so she made all this food and told me to bring it to you."

"You make me sound like a stray puppy." Unease crept through him. "What did you tell her?"

Dash nudged him. "Don't worry. Only good things. What else could I say?" His smile faded. "I know yesterday must've been hard on you. I mentioned to my mom about your father. I hope you don't mind."

Pain lanced through him. "I don't need people to feel sorry for me. I'm not a sympathy case."

"No, I didn't mean it like that. Shit, look." Dash ran his fingers through his thick dark hair. "I'm not explaining it right." A tinge of red stained his cheeks. "My mother doesn't know you, and she thinks that because you live here by yourself and have a lot of money, you must be living the life she reads about in the newspapers and sees on television."

"That's a joke. What would that be? *Lifestyles of the Boring and Lonely?* Could you imagine me on a reality show?" He caught Dash's eye, and they burst into laughter. "*Real Gen-Xers of New York City*—where everything is delivered so you never have to talk to a live person."

"Oh, my God, stop. I'm dying." Dash bent over

and howled with laughter. "It's perfect. I'm calling Bravo. That was the funniest thing I've heard in years." Dash took a napkin and wiped his streaming eyes. "But seriously." He faced Jesse. "She worries about me getting caught up in a life full of privilege and money to buy and do anything I want. My mother struggles every day, and we don't know from all…this." He waved his hand around, indicating the apartment, and Jesse once again found himself enraptured by Dash, this time by his passion and depth of soul. He remained silent and listened.

"I don't want to live their life. I'm going to college, and yeah, it's only online, but I'm going to get my CPA and get a job in one of the big firms. I want to wear that suit and tie and be respectable. I want to make money and live in a beautiful place like this, not one where there are bars on my windows like a prison and I have to wear earphones when I study and sleep so I don't hear my neighbors screaming through the wall every night." He broke off, his chest heaving.

"Everyone should have a dream," Jesse said with admiration. "I didn't know you were studying to be a CPA."

"I don't plan on sweeping the floors the rest of my life."

"I didn't mean to insinuate you did." The idea he'd insulted Dash, even unintentionally, sent a wave of panic through Jesse. "That came out wrong. I meant, you never mentioned it, so I didn't know."

What had happened? One moment they were laughing so hard they were crying, and the next Dash had his back up. It had all started when Dash had mentioned Jesse's father, and he wanted to get back to that easy place they'd shared.

The hard glint in Dash's eyes faded. "Sorry. I'm a little wound up. I haven't gotten much sleep this week, and I'm tired."

Jesse rushed in with his own apology. "I'm sorry I got all uptight about my father and everything. I have to learn to move past it, I really do. And I'm trying." He finished unpacking the shopping bag. "Wow," he said, surveying the various packages. "What did your mom do? Stay up all night cooking?"

"It doesn't take her long. And trust me, since my father works such late hours, she's always cooking for him and eating with my sister. This was a labor of love for her, knowing how much you enjoy her cooking. Plus, I hate to admit it, but she makes me my lunch almost every day."

"It's nice that you're close with your family. My mother escaped New York City because it reminded her too much of my dad. She almost never comes back."

Sympathy creased Dash's forehead. "That must be tough." With a glance to his wrist, Dash gave him an apologetic smile. "I hate to say this, but could we heat the food up? I don't have that much time left on my break."

"Oh, shit. I'm sorry. I forgot." Cursing his stupidity, Jesse took out some microwavable dishes and handed them to Dash. "I have no idea what gets heated and what doesn't, so you can take care of that while I get the forks and waters."

Dash scooped up a dollop of a creamy-looking casserole and set it down on the plates, then added several pieces of delicious grilled meat. He added potatoes and more of the spinach-pie thing Jesse recalled from the dinner he'd made of the leftovers.

"It all looks great. I can't wait to taste it."

The microwave whirred on, and Dash leaned against the island. "Where's Miranda? Is she working today?"

"Yeah. I needed her to go to the library and get some research I couldn't find online for an article I'm writing on the growing scarcity of tanzanite."

"Oh? I've never heard of that. Is it like diamonds or something?"

"No, not at all. It's actually even rarer than diamonds but nowhere near as expensive. Tanzanite is so rare because it is found and mined in a small area at the foot of Mount Kilimanjaro in the Manyara Region of Northern Tanzania." Realizing he sounded like an encyclopedia, Jesse bit his lip to stop rambling, but Dash folded his arms, his dark brows pulled together.

"Wow, really? So why isn't it more expensive?"

"Oh, you know how it is when the government sticks its nose in business. Everything gets screwed up. So my article is on the depletion of the mines and how it might mean the end of tanzanite."

"That's crazy. What does it look like?" The bell dinged, and Dash took two dinner plates from the cabinet and set them on the counter, then took the steaming dishes out of the microwave. It gave Jesse pleasure to see Dash acting so familiar in his kitchen.

"It's really pretty. If we had time, I'd show you my collection. I went to South Africa about ten years ago and picked some up."

They brought their dishes to the island, where they perched on the barstools and began to eat. Dash took a few bites, then set his fork down.

"You've been all over, I bet. Must be nice. I've never been anywhere but New York."

Finishing the food in his mouth first, Jesse shrugged. "It was." He bent over his fork and chewed, not tasting whatever he forked into his mouth. He knew Dash was staring at him, waiting for him to expand and talk about all the places he'd been. But he couldn't. That was another Jesse. The Jesse who lived like everyone else and wasn't afraid to walk outside. That Jesse was a dream Jesse, and he could barely remember him at all.

"Well, I hate to eat and run, but I don't want to be late and get docked." He held back a yawn and gave another apologetic smile. "I swear it's not the company. The lack of sleep from my noisy neighbors is catching up with me." Plate in hand, he stood and walked to the sink.

"You could study here if you want, after work."

"Here?" Sounding confused, Dash set the plate in the sink and glanced over his shoulder.

Hearing Dash's astonishment, Jesse tried to save himself from further embarrassment. "I said it before—you could hang out sometime. Maybe it was a stupid idea. It's just that it's so quiet at night, you'd get a lot of work done. But I know you have to get home."

"I really appreciate the offer. I don't want you to think I'm ungrateful. And if I had an earlier schedule, yeah, I would hang out every once in a while and do work, but I can't impose on you."

"It's not an imposition. I wouldn't have said it if it was. I'm here every night by myself after Miranda goes home. But I understand."

"I hear you. And thanks again for the invite." He picked up his backpack, and Jesse walked with him to the front door. "Um…but what about hanging out one night anyway? Maybe get a beer or something?"

At Dash's words, Jesse's breath grew labored and his heart climbed in his chest until he felt light-headed. A yearning grew inside him, and he physically felt the struggle between his heart's desire to be with Dash and his mind grappling with his crippling fear. He recalled Dr. Mingione's advice about trying, but he knew he couldn't go outside with Dash. Not yet. But could he tell him his secret? Could he trust him? He took the chance and stepped off the cliff into the unknown.

"I'd love to hang out. You could come here, and we could watch a game. Do you like the Yankees?"

Dash's eyes lit up. "Man, I'm from the Bronx. I bleed pinstripes."

This was working out better than Jesse could've hoped for. "They've got a home stand coming this weekend. A doubleheader on Saturday. You could come by, and we could have dinner and watch the game." As if to entice Dash further, he beckoned him. "I know you have to get back to work, but I want to show you something."

"Okay, but it's gotta be quick."

"It will be. Don't worry." The last thing Jesse wanted to do was get Dash in trouble. With Dash trailing a step behind, Jesse brought him to the study. It had once been his father's office, and though a throb of pain still hit him each time he entered the room, Jesse knew cleaning it out after the tenth anniversary of the disaster was the right thing for his questionable sanity.

"Oh, man," Dash breathed. "This is awesome."

Jesse had gotten a huge flat-screen television with all the bells and whistles, but the real highlight of the room for him was the set of two seats he'd purchased before they ripped apart the old Yankee Stadium. They were his and his father's season ticket-holder seats, and while he hadn't yet sat in them, having them there brought him a bit of comfort, like he had a small piece of his father there with him always. He'd placed them against the wall in the back of the room. One day he'd find the courage to sit in them.

A wide, soft-cushioned sofa sat in front of the screen, and a refrigerator was tucked away in the corner, where Jesse kept drinks and snacks so he wouldn't have to keep getting up during the game if he got hungry. A long marble countertop against the wall held a microwave and a collection of glasses and plates.

"It's not the Stadium, but if you tell me what you like to eat and drink, I can have it and we can watch the game. If you want to, I mean," he added in a hurry.

"Whooooa. That's gotta be like an eighty-inch screen." Dash walked inside the room to stand in front of the television, and Jesse held his breath.

He's going to say no. He'd rather go to a bar. I sound like a teenager, not a thirty-year-old.

"Are you sure? It'd be less trouble for you if we went out, wouldn't it?"

"Not at all. I'm kind of a homebody."

"Then heck, yeah. That'd be great. I never watched anything on a screen this big outside of the movies." Giving the set a lingering look, he walked to the door. "I gotta get back, or I'll get in trouble. The game starts at one, right?"

Still in shock that Dash agreed, Jesse could only nod.

"So how about twelve thirty? I'll bring some beer and chips."

"Yeah, sure."

They walked to the front, and Dash stopped before opening the door. "Thanks, Jesse. See you Saturday, if not before."

"Yeah, see you."

The door shut behind Dash, and Jesse waited a full thirty seconds before leaning against it and closing his eyes.

Holy shit. What the hell did I just do? And how will I be able to wait three days?

Chapter Eight

THE REST OF the week flew by. On Friday, Dash pushed his broom along the tiled hallways, hoping to catch a glimpse of Jesse, but his door remained frustratingly closed as it had the past few days. He knew if he showed up at Jesse's door with lunch again, it would be weird and kind of awkward, so he kept away. His mother had questioned him so much after he came home the last time, he made up a story that he had to take over someone else's shift and couldn't stop by to get his lunch.

His thoughts, however, stayed with Jesse. Dash set aside the broom, wheeled out the mop and bucket, and began the dip and swish while his mind drifted. He'd never had problems hooking up with guys before—not that he had a revolving door, but he'd had his share of sex in clubs and in cars. One thing he'd never do would be to bring a guy to his neighborhood. He kept his sexuality on the down low with his friends, and the last thing he needed was to get caught sneaking someone in or out of his apartment.

Jesse was different. Special. Dash warmed at the thought of spending an entire day with him instead of a rushed lunch. He swished the mop around, then squeezed out the dirty water. A door farther down the hallway opened, but no one walked out. From where the sound was located, Dash estimated it was the door to Jesse's apartment, and concerned when no one came out, he left the mop and pail and walked down the hallway to investigate.

Dash was correct that it was Jesse's apartment. When he reached the door, it was open, and Jesse stood in the threshold.

"Jesse…" Dash's voice trailed off. Jesse might be looking right at him, but he didn't see him. His gaze was fixed on a spot across the hall, and his chest rose rapidly, his breath stuttering out in short puffs. Sweat gleamed on his face, and his jaw was set in a hard line. From behind Jesse, Dash glimpsed Miranda, who watched Jesse with her heart in her eyes. When she caught his eye, she gave Dash a soft shake of her head, and the words died on Dash's lips.

After several minutes, Jesse's labored breathing steadied, and he blinked as if coming out of a trance. He turned his head, and seeing Dash standing there, flushed bright red.

"Dash. Wh-what're you doing here?" He licked his lips and bit them.

"I was mopping the floor, heard a noise, and got worried, so I came to see."

"And found the freak."

"Jesse, no." Miranda stepped behind him, and Jesse shuddered.

"Hey, I don't know what's going on, but if you

need me for anything, you should call me. Do you want my cell number?"

"That would be wonderful, thanks," Miranda said, and Dash spoke his number, watching Miranda enter it into her phone.

Jesse remained standing half in the doorway, half in the hall. He looked more relaxed, and when their eyes met, he gave Dash a tentative smile. "I didn't expect to see you until Saturday."

"Oh, well, I'm sorry I didn't come with lunch or anything. I didn't get to go to my mom's, and I grabbed a sandwich instead."

"You don't owe me an explanation. I mean, it was really nice of you to do what you did already."

"It's not a bother. I'm sure she'll do it again. I'd better get back. I don't want anyone to trip on the mop and bucket. See you tomorrow?"

Jesse braced his long body against the doorjamb. "Yeah. It—it's supposed to be nice weather."

"Yeah. Should be a good game. Okay. Take it easy."

He walked down the hall and heard the door shut. He turned back to an empty hallway, then reached his mop, picked it up, and continued to clean, whistling as he worked.

ON SATURDAY AT a little past twelve thirty and carrying two six-packs of beer in one bag and chips in another, Dash walked to the archway, but this time as a guest. He greeted the security guard, who gave him an odd look.

"Whatcha doin' here, Dash? Picking up an extra shift?"

On his subway ride in, Dash had debated what to tell his coworkers if they asked what he was doing back at the Dakota on his day off, but these guys only saw him for a hot minute every day and he figured the less said the better.

"Got some stuff to do." He shifted the heavy grocery bag, hoping Manny wouldn't ask to see what was inside. "Catch you later." Without waiting for an answer, he hurried through the gate and into the courtyard. As usual, it was a hub of activity with gardeners mowing the grass and trimming the bushes, and cars waiting for pickups.

He hefted the bags and entered the lobby, plastering on a smile when he saw Eddie at the front desk.

"Dash, whatcha doing here? It's your day off."

"Got asked to help fix some things, so I said why not? Make some extra cash."

"Nice," Eddie said. "Hope she's good-looking?" He winked and cackled with laughter, but Dash gave him a pained smile.

"Uh, it's cool. I'll catch you later." Hurrying, Dash managed to catch the elevator, and several moments later he stood in front of Jesse's door, rapping on it with his knuckles. It opened almost immediately, as if Jesse was waiting on the other side.

"Hi, I wasn't sure if you were coming."

Puzzled, Dash handed him the bag with the beers.

"Why wouldn't I? I said I was, the last time I saw you."

"Yeah, but it's almost twelve forty-five, so I thought maybe you were blowing me off."

"I wouldn't do that. I've been looking forward to today since you invited me. You know how it is with the trains. They're horrible lately."

"Yeah, right. Well, let's get this in the fridge." Jesse gave him that wide, transformative smile, and prickles of awareness swept through Dash.

"Okay." Something smelled delicious, and he sniffed, his mouth watering. "Mmm, what's that cooking?"

"Oh, I started heating the chicken wings. I figured we'll get those set up with the chips and beer, and then I can pop the hot dogs and sliders in after we finish."

"Damn, man. This is better than the Stadium."

He took a cold beer from Jesse and drank it down. "Ahh, that's good." Jesse took only a sip from his bottle, then took a bowl and handed it to Dash. "Pour the chips in here."

"Sounds good." He ripped open the bag and dumped the chips into the bowl while Jesse opened the oven and slid the wings from the baking pan onto a big serving platter. Fragrant steam rose from them, and Dash's mouth watered.

"Ready?"

"As I'll ever be. But what're you gonna eat? Ha-ha." He followed Jesse to the television room, admiring the man's firm butt and lean physique in his soft faded jeans and T-shirt. Guys like him didn't hang out with guys like Jesse, but there they were, sitting on that big comfy sofa, sneakers kicked off and beers in hand.

"They're doing great this season, so I keep waiting for something, like a string of injuries or the bullpen to fall apart." Jesse picked up the remote and turned the set on, clicking until he found the pregame show. "That's what usually happens with them."

Chicken wing in hand, Dash nodded. "Yeah. I mean they survived Mariano retiring, but can they hold up? I don't know. Their bullpen hasn't been the same ever since." He took a bite of the wing. "Umm, these are good. I could eat a bucketful."

"I have a bag of fifty more in the freezer. I get them from the wing place on Amsterdam. Can't be without wings during baseball season."

Gnawing on the bone, Dash nodded. "Yeah. I haven't been to the new stadium yet. Too pricey for my blood. But when I was a kid and we'd go? Always had to have a hot dog. Lots of mustard, sauerkraut, and onion. Mmmm." He closed his eyes for a moment, remembering. "Nothing like a dog and a beer at the Stadium."

Staring at the TV, Jesse's eyes had a faraway look. "Yeah. I haven't been to the new stadium either. Maybe one day…" His voice petered off, and he looked so damn forlorn that without thinking, Dash put his hand on Jesse's shoulder and gave it a squeeze.

"Maybe we'll go together. Catch a game."

Those big sad eyes of Jesse's brightened. "Yeah. Maybe."

Loud cheering began as the Yankees took the field, and Jesse turned up the volume. "Here we go."

There was something endearing about Jesse's excitement, and Dash found himself getting more into the game than if he were at a bar with his friends. Jesse knew each player's stats, and they both agreed that Girardi should've been out years earlier.

Jesse waved a wing in the air. "I'm glad you get it. I mean, I know they wanted to give Girardi a chance, but if George Steinbrenner were still alive, he would've been gone."

"Oh, hell yeah. I heard stories about the fights that used to go on."

The first two innings went by quickly, and they'd soon depleted the wings. At the commercial, Jesse picked up the almost empty platter. "How about I get some sliders and the hot dogs going?"

Well into his second beer, Dash leaned back on the sofa. "Yeah. This is the life, ya know? Hanging out, watching the game. Good food, good company. Makes everything else you got going on fade away for a little while."

"I'm a good listener, if you need to talk about anything."

"I wouldn't want to bore you." He tucked his feet up under him. "You know how it goes. I'm working this job, going to school at night online. Helping out my mom when I can."

"You've got a lot on your shoulders." He set the platter back on the table in front of them. "You want to be an accountant, right?"

"I want to be a CPA. But the exam is a killer. It's gonna take me some time, but it's all I ever wanted to do. I love working with numbers and seeing everything add up. I was always like that as a kid. I don't like when things are out of balance or messy."

He noticed how close he and Jesse were sitting. Close enough to hear Jesse breathe and see the flare of desire spark in his eyes. Maybe if he hadn't had the two beers in quick succession, Dash wouldn't have felt so reckless. Instead, he reached over and dragged the pad of his thumb over a spot of sauce clinging to Jesse's bottom lip.

Jesse froze, his breath hitting Dash's finger.

"You have some hot sauce…right there." Taking a risk, Dash slid the palm of his hand to cup Jesse's cheek. "It looked messy." He ached to taste Jesse and had dreams about what those full lips would taste like. "Jesse," he breathed. "Can I kiss you?"

Wide-eyed and trembling, Jesse nodded, and Dash leaned forward. Sensing Jesse's skittishness, Dash didn't grab him and mash their lips together but instead feathered light, whispery kisses along Jesse's mouth, licking the fullness of his lips. Jesse's raspy breath stuttered against his cheek, but he didn't pull away.

This wasn't a quick hookup at a club with a guy he'd never see again. This was sweet Jesse, whom Dash had been thinking about since the day they'd met and liked more than he cared to admit. Dash wanted more of him, his soft mouth, his silky tongue. His gasping, needy sounds.

"Mmm." He shifted closer, the blood rushing hotter through his veins as his cock thickened. "You taste so good. Better than I imagined."

To Dash's surprise, Jesse slid his arms around Dash's neck. Warmed by his response, Dash grew bolder and covered Jesse's mouth with his. Jesse tasted of the spicy wing sauce, and Dash couldn't help but suck that full, pouty lower lip into his mouth.

"Ohhhh." Jesse sighed, sliding his hand up to clutch at Dash's hair.

Their kisses grew more fervent, and Dash pressed his tongue against the seam of Jesse's lips, demanding entrance. With a whimper, Jesse opened to him, and Dash slipped inside, finally tasting the velvety sweetness of his tongue. Jesse's hands gripped his shoulders, straining toward him.

Heat built within Dash as their mouths and lips pressed together, and a shiver ran through him as his hands caressed the soft skin of Jesse's neck. Dash trembled and he stopped, flustered by his uncertainty while his body pulsed with hungry desire. Jesse's eyes glowed, their gaze unfocused and dreamy. Red patches stained his cheeks, a slight smile rested on his lips, and he looked adorably and completely unsettled.

"I'm sorry. That shouldn't have happened." Dash ran a slightly shaky hand through his hair, hoping his heart would stop thumping in his ears. The ache reached through him, and he wanted to gather Jesse in his arms again and kiss him until they both couldn't see straight.

"Oh…" Jesse said, pulling away from Dash. "Why not?"

Surprised, Dash rubbed the back of his neck. "Well, I didn't want you to think I came here only for sex. I can get that anywhere."

"I'm sure you could." Jesse's lips twitched, but then his smile faltered. "I'm not sorry. It was a wonderful kiss."

Dash could've smacked himself in the face. "I'm saying this all wrong....I knew I would. The kiss was great, but I didn't want you to think I came here only to jump your bones. I like you, I think you're cool to hang out with, and I'd like us to be friends."

Darkness shadowed Jesse's face. "I'd like that too. But before you say that, I think there are some things you need to know."

Chapter Nine

LISTENING TO DASH say he liked him, Jesse felt like Sally Field giving her Oscar acceptance speech for *Norma Rae.* "*You like me. You really like me.*" But before he could allow Dash further into his life, Jesse knew he had to tell Dash the truth about his anxiety and agoraphobia.

A huge roar sounded, and Dash bounced on the sofa. "Oh, damn. A grand slam. Yeah, baby."

"Holy shit. That's awesome. Now they're up by six." They high-fived each other, and when the game went to commercial, Jesse jumped up and grabbed the platter. "I'm gonna go heat up the other food."

He hurried into the kitchen, slid the fries, hot dogs, and sliders he'd ordered the night before into the oven, then went to the refrigerator and took out the tub of guacamole, dumped it into a serving bowl, and grabbed a bag of taco chips. He swiftly returned to Dash and stopped at the doorway to watch him drain the rest of his beer.

Was he ready for this? Exposing himself to Dash might mean the end of their budding friendship. After all, who wanted to be saddled with someone who had an anxiety attack at the thought of going outside? And yet…Dash settled the rising panic bubbling under Jesse's surface. He made Jesse yearn to try, to take the chances waiting for him, because the reward might be incredibly sweet and everything he'd ever hoped for.

"Did it start again? Did I miss anything?" He placed the bowl and chips on the table in front of them. "The food has to heat up. I'll get it at the commercial."

"Cool." There was a certain wariness to Dash that hadn't been there before. "They've replayed it about four times from every angle. Now the Rays pulled their pitcher, and they're going to the bullpen, so we'll have to wait for him to warm up."

"Okay." His knee jiggled, and Jesse knew it was confession time. "So…you might've figured out I'm kind of an anxious person."

Dash shrugged but remained silent, so he continued.

"It goes beyond the normal, like what everyone feels before a test or speaking in public. Anxiety can manifest itself in many ways, and with me…" His voice wobbled a moment. "It's made me a prisoner, both of my mind and in my life."

Dash's brows knitted together. "I kind of understand, but not totally. I mean, I'm not gonna lie and say I never noticed anything, but what do you mean, exactly?"

Unable to meet Dash's eyes, Jesse focused on a dropped potato chip on the floor and swallowed hard. "I, uh…" The words stuck in his throat, and he held on to that kiss they'd shared as a memory of the day because Jesse was certain once Dash knew, he'd find any excuse in the book to leave. "I haven't been out of my apartment in over five years. When my father was killed on 9/11, I began to see the world as a terrible, dangerous place, full of people waiting to do something bad. Everywhere I went, I imagined someone was going to hurt me. I tried to go on with my life, and for a while I managed. I traveled, did some collecting, and even went to school to get my masters…" His voice dwindled. "But inside I was dying a little each day from fear. I kept trying. Really. Eventually, I started only going out very early in the morning when there were less people and I could see around me and not be in a crowd. But even that failed when one morning I left here at around five a.m. to go get coffee."

This time Jesse's voice didn't wobble. It broke, and he cringed, hating how weak he sounded.

Dash put a hand on his knee and squeezed. "Hey, if it's too much, you don't have to tell me. I'm not here to put pressure on you."

"No, I want to. It's been years since I spoke of it. It would be refreshing in a way, since I've buried it for so long. Miranda doesn't like to hear about it because it upsets her too much, but it'll be good to get new insight…maybe." He gnawed at his lip, worrying it was too much to talk about. Too soon.

"Okay, whatever's best for you."

Was he real? Jesse had to wonder, because Dash was everything he'd ever hoped for in a friend.

"I was walking up 71st Street past Amsterdam with my coffee. It was five thirty in the morning, and there were some people around—mostly dog walkers, but not many. Even New York City can be a little deserted, especially on a not-too-busy side street. Anyway, someone came up right behind me, and I felt a sting in my side and a hand push in my pocket. When I jumped away, I discovered he'd grabbed my wallet. Then I saw the blood and realized I'd been cut."

The game forgotten, Dash shifted closer. "Oh, my God. You got stabbed? What happened? Were you hurt bad?"

Jesse remembered his panic and how he sank to the ground, unable to take another step. When the paramedics came, he freaked out so badly, they had to strap him down and take him to the hospital, where they called his mother.

"Physically, no. It was a minor flesh wound. But something snapped inside me. When I returned home, I barely spoke for a month."

"But you're okay now."

Jesse forced a brittle smile. "Yeah? I'm not so sure. Since that day, I haven't been out of the house. At all. That day when you saw me sitting in the courtyard was the first time since my hospitalization that I'd walked outside and breathed fresh air."

"Five years?" The disbelief in Dash's voice made him wince. "You haven't left this apartment in five years?"

"Yeah." Now he waited for the withdrawal and excuses. Dash would pretend for a while longer everything between them wasn't different, but in the end he'd drift away and Jesse would be alone again.

Like in one of those cartoons, a lightbulb seemed to click over his head, and Dash nodded slowly. "So Miranda does everything you need on the outside. That's why she's always running errands instead of you doing it?"

He shrugged, his face hot with embarrassment. Hearing Dash say it made his life sound even more pathetic than it was.

"But you have a job, right? You said you write articles?" Dash ran his hand through his hair. "You can tell me to shut up if I'm being too nosy."

"It's okay. I mean, I can function. I take medicine which controls my panic attacks from the anxiety. And I work remotely, so I can send in my articles from anywhere. And no, you're not being too personal at all. I just dumped a shitload of my mess on you. I should be the one to say sorry. You're actually one of the few people I've talked to about this since it happened. I had a boyfriend at the time, but it didn't work out." Jesse picked at a hole in his jeans. He hadn't thought about Sean for a while now and wondered if he'd found someone else who could give him what he wanted.

"Someone you were seeing before the mugging?" Dash's brow furrowed. "You mean he didn't stay to help you?"

"No." Jesse swallowed his humiliation. "We broke up right before I got mugged. But it was for the best. We met in grad school. In the beginning, I wasn't like this. I could still go out for short periods of time. I managed to hide my problems from Sean, but when the anxiety progressed, I wanted him to stay over here all the time instead of going to his dorm. We both went to Columbia," Jesse explained. "Sean lived on campus up in Washington Heights."

"And he didn't want to stay here in the Dakota instead of some ratty-ass dorm? This place is gorgeous. If my boyfriend asked me to stay with him here, I wouldn't say no."

Jesse stared at him, and as if realizing what he'd said, Dash blushed furiously and avoided his gaze. "Well…you know what I mean."

"Sean didn't see it that way. He wanted to go to parties and clubs and movies and be a normal twenty-five-year-old guy. I couldn't fault him for wanting to have the full experience of living away from home and going to school. Why should he be saddled with a neurotic boyfriend who's afraid to walk on the street?"

"Maybe because it's the right thing to do? If you care about someone, you want to be there to help them. He should've tried to help you."

Was this man real? Jesse's lips tingled. Oh yeah, he sure was. The pressure of Dash's mouth from their earlier kiss still left him weak.

"Um, yeah. But he has the right to live his life too."

Their last interaction hadn't been ugly, but rather sad, and Jesse couldn't forget it.

Sean had him by the arm and tried to pull him toward the door. "Come on, Jess. We can even walk there—it's only on 80th and Columbus. We'll have a great time. I promise to stay by your side all night."

Jesse didn't want to see the disappointment in his boyfriend's eyes again, so he agreed, even though the night suffocated him and he couldn't stop thinking he'd be hurt or attacked all the way to the party.

After only two blocks, Sean stopped. "This isn't going to work."

"It's okay," Jesse managed to grit out. "I can do it."

With his hand clamped on the crook of Jesse's arm, Sean turned around and pulled him along. Jesse stumbled after him, repeating over and over, "I can do it. I promise." They passed through the front gates of the Dakota and were inside his apartment within five minutes. Calm settled through Jesse once the familiar walls of his apartment surrounded him. Safe. He was safe. Sean, on the other hand, paced the floor of the living room, growing angrier and more red-faced as the minutes passed.

"I've put up with this for a long time. It's been years already, and not only are you not better, you're getting worse. I'm only twenty-five, dammit. I want to go out and have fun. I wanna go dancing and to parties with my boyfriend, not sit in his apartment every night and stare at each other or the TV."

"I'm sorry," Jesse whispered. "I'm really trying."

With a mixture of exasperation and sorrow, Sean sighed. "It's not enough for me. I think I need a break. And you need help." He shoved his hands into his pockets and pursed his lips as if he was about to say something further, but then shook his head and walked out.

Thus ended Sean and Jesse. His first and only relationship.

With his story told, Jesse wanted to run and hide. The afternoon of baseball and fun had vanished with the sad story of his life. But once again, Dash surprised him and gave an encouraging smile.

"The first time I saw you, you were sitting outside.

And then you were in the hallway the other day. So you *are* improving."

"I know, whoopee." Jesse's lips thinned in disgust, and he twirled a finger in the air. "I made it outside my door all by myself. Give the man a medal."

"Ah, man, don't be so hard on yourself." Dash hesitated. "Can I ask you something?"

"Sure, go ahead." He stared at the television screen, and though the game had begun again, nothing much was happening. Three up, three down. Gardner struck out swinging. Sort of like Jesse's life. A strikeout.

"You had a lot of terrible things happen to you. Are you seeing anyone, like a doctor?"

"Every week. And my therapist says I should consider each step an accomplishment, like a brick in the wall, no matter how small or insignificant it might seem, because whatever I do, it's more than I managed the day or week before."

A smile warmed Dash's brown eyes. "You have a very smart therapist. That's what I was going to say. Why put pressure on yourself? You're working on your problems, and eventually you'll do what you need to do."

"But—"

Dash placed his fingers over his mouth. "No buts. I'm right, and that's all."

It would be easy to agree with Dash and brush it off, but Jesse didn't want that. He wanted it exposed to the light. No secrets. "It's not that simple. I do want to change. But what if I can't?" Frustrated, he clenched his hand into a fist. "What if no matter what I do, I'm stuck like this the rest of my life?"

Chapter Ten

THE CONVERSATION HAD turned into something much heavier than Dash had anticipated talking about today. When he arrived that afternoon, all Dash had expected was some good food, a little chitchat, and hopefully some heavy-duty flirting. That kiss had sent everything veering off course at one hundred miles an hour. Holding Jesse in his arms rocked his world, but Dash knew not to push. Jesse was too vulnerable.

Dash sniffed the air. "I think the food is ready."

"Shit." Jesse scrambled off the couch and ran, but Dash stayed put. He needed a moment to process everything Jesse told him.

Damn. He'd known something was off the first time he met Jesse. That panic attack in the courtyard was the first sign, but then the other day in the hallway when Jesse stood frozen with fear, drenched in sweat, Dash knew the man had serious issues. What he didn't figure on was the extent to which Jesse had withdrawn from life. It saddened him, but it infuriated him even more. How could Jesse have been left alone to fend for himself?

Like a lamb and the big bad wolf New York City.

Hearing Jesse's footsteps, Dash made sure to school his features into a neutral, untroubled mask, even though inside he seethed with anger at the people who'd let Jesse down. That ex-boyfriend, who couldn't be more selfish than to leave someone in distress. If he'd been with Jesse, even if they'd broken up, he'd make sure to stay in touch and check up on him or at least encourage him to get help.

But the person Dash had the most anger toward was Jesse's mother. Who could abandon their own child to live inside his mind? It was hard to imagine coming from a mother such as Dash's own, who would give anything to see her children happy.

"Good thing you called it." Jesse walked in with a steaming platter piled high with sliders and hot dogs. Bottles of ketchup and mustard teetered on the end, and Dash sprang up to help, grabbing the condiments and setting them on the table. "Another five minutes and they would've been dried out. Now they're perfect. I've got buns and lettuce and pickles and onions if you want."

"Sounds good."

Except for the occasional "Pass the ketchup" or "Do you want the pickles?" the next few minutes were spent in relative silence as they made their food and ate. The Yankees hit a few more home runs, and at that point it was time for the seventh-inning stretch. Dash popped the top off two more beers and handed one to Jesse.

"Can I ask you something—and you can tell me to shut up if I'm way out of line. I won't get offended."

"I don't ever say shut up to anyone. I think it's really disrespectful."

Jesse spoke with such earnestness, Dash could almost see him as a young boy, promising he'd always be a good boy.

"Well…I don't understand. You say you and your mom have a good relationship, yet she moved away to Connecticut and you never mention her. Do you talk to her or see her? Doesn't she come to visit?"

The flash of pain in Jesse's face had Dash instantly regretting his words. "I'm sorry, man, I shouldn't have said anything. Forget it."

"No. It's okay." Jesse's long fingers played with the tassels of the small sofa pillow he hugged to his chest. "It was hard for her, you know? Losing my dad so suddenly. One morning he kissed us good-bye and said he'd be home before dinnertime so we could go to the park, and the next…" His eyes grew shiny-bright with tears. "She didn't get out of bed for days. My babysitter took over everything—cooking, taking me to school and picking me up. Rosa was a lifesaver in the most literal sense of the word."

"I can't even imagine. My father knew some of the dishwashers who worked at Windows on the World and died. It was horrible."

"Yeah. I'd only been there once. My parents took me there for my tenth birthday."

Another example of the great divide between someone like him, a guy from the Bronx, and Jesse, who had the world at his feet.

"So," he began hesitantly, "eventually your mom

remarried."

"She did. After many months passed, she pulled herself together. But it was never the same. From the day my father died until she left the city, I don't think she ever went downtown again. But I don't begrudge her that happiness. I wouldn't expect her to never fall in love again. She was young and beautiful and very loving."

Right. So loving that she left her son alone, knowing he couldn't leave his apartment, and never came to visit. "And you like the guy?"

"Yeah, sure. Harry's fine. I mean, he's not my dad, but he never tried to be. I wish…" He glanced at the game, but the Yankees were ahead by eight now. Not much of a game. "I wish they didn't leave the city. When they got married, she moved in with Harry. I was in grad school and living here."

"So she left you by yourself?" It seemed unfathomable to Dash, who lived in the lap of his family at thirty, to be alone at that young an age.

"I mean, she only moved a few blocks away, but yeah."

Dash could see Jesse had become a bit more agitated. He'd wrapped the fringes of that pillow around his fingers.

"But I was okay then, for the most part. I mean, I started seeing a therapist after my dad died, which was normal for a kid who'd lost a parent during a crisis. I went out with friends and attended classes. But there was always this grayness around me, and it started creeping closer and closer."

"What did your mom do?"

"Well...she was busy with her new marriage....I didn't want to bother her."

You are her son. You were hurting. Children should never think of themselves as a burden.

But Dash kept his opinions to himself. At least for now. He wanted to learn more about Jesse—as much as he could.

"And she moved to Connecticut? How long ago?"

"Oh, about five years, I guess." He let go of the pillow and grabbed another beer. "Want one?"

Surprisingly sober for having had three beers already, Dash reached for a water instead. "I'm good, thanks."

"Can we table this for another day? I really want to relax and watch the game. This one's almost over, and we barely followed it," Jesse appealed to him, then settled back onto the sofa, eyes trained on the set.

Not wanting to push, Dash gave him a thumbs-up and felt a little guilty watching the relief on Jesse's face. "I'm sorry. I'll back off. Promise." He made himself more comfortable on the sofa. At Jesse's smile, a tug of lust coiled around Dash's spine, and he shifted a bit closer. "I can think of other ways to get to know you better."

Jesse's lips parted, and his face flushed. "Oh, yeah?" His eyes glittered, and Dash wanted to catch Jesse's heated breath with his mouth and drink him in. "Like what?"

"Like this."

In one swift motion, Dash grasped Jesse by the

neck and kissed him, loving how Jesse's lips softened against him. This time it was Jesse who pushed his tongue into Dash's mouth, sweeping over his teeth and inner cheek, then coming back to flirt with Dash's tongue, stroking along its length.

"Mmm," Dash hummed and wound his arms around Jesse, pressing him back against the sofa cushions. "I like you. A lot."

"Me too." Jesse's breath rasped against his cheek, and he moistened his lips, spiking Dash's lust. He knew if he pushed Jesse, they'd end up naked and probably fuck. And as much as he wanted to rip Jesse's clothes off, and as much as his hard dick throbbed, pushing against the zipper of his jeans, Dash knew that would be a disaster. He smoothed the tumbled hair off Jesse's brow and kissed him, rubbing their cheeks together. "Dash, I've never met anyone like you."

"I'm nobody special." He smiled into Jesse's face. "Just a guy."

"Don't say that. You saw me when everyone else looked through me. So you're special to me."

"That's nice to hear. You're becoming special to me also. I like sharing my lunch with you."

"I do too." Surprising him, Jesse reached up and cradled his jaw, stroking his fingers up and around the bones in his face. "What does your name—Dashamir— mean?"

"Kind and benevolent."

Something in his face must've conveyed his displeasure, because Jesse grinned. "Not good enough?"

"When I was a kid, I wanted the name of a king or

a warrior. That would mean I was strong and fierce. *Kind* meant weak." At least that was what his father said, but he was named for his mother's father, his *gjysh*, and his mother refused to back down.

"That's bullshit. It's easy to be a bully and have a loud mouth. Haven't you noticed the people with the loudest bark are often the ones you want to hear the least?" The pads of his fingers traced Dash's lips, and he had to bite back the moans of pleasure threatening to spill from his mouth. "It's much more important to be kind." His index finger played along the seam of Dash's lips, and Dash touched the tip of Jesse's finger with his tongue.

"It's easy to be kind to certain people. Like you. I like being nice to you."

Hearing the hiss of Jesse's indrawn breath, Dash licked, then sucked Jesse's finger into his mouth. He twirled his tongue around and around, then drew it up and down its length, tasting the flavor of Jesse.

"Dash." Jesse expelled a sigh so intimate and full of longing, he couldn't move. Jesse's lashes swept down over his cheeks, and he whispered, "I think you're nice too. I'm glad you're here. And that you still want to be my friend."

How sad that so much of Jesse's life had been shadowed by tragedy, especially when he had a face made for sunlight and laughter.

"Nothing's changed. I'm glad you feel strong enough, secure enough, to share something about yourself."

"The years have been lonely, I'll admit." Braced on

his elbows, Jesse's gaze was as open and unguarded as Dash had seen since the beginning of their friendship. "Everyone told me to try, to take a chance, but it's not as simple as that. There's nothing more I would've liked to do than go to a bar with you today and watch the game. Or take a simple walk in the park."

"But you can't?"

"No." Jesse slumped back to lie flat on the sofa. "People don't understand. They think it's simply a matter of me trying harder. But it's more than that." He turned his cheek to face the television, but Dash suspected it was deliberate, to break their eye contact.

"I know," Dash said, brushing his knuckles against Jesse's cheek, surprised by the rush of conflicting emotions sweeping through him. He wanted to hold Jesse and protect him, yet he admired the fierce and independent streak the man had in refusing to give in to his fears. "You don't need to justify yourself to me. Only you know how much or little you can handle. I'll never push you. You wait until you're ready. And you're right—we should be relaxing and enjoying the game."

"Now that they blew the Rays out in the first game, they'll probably lose one-nothing in the next."

Dash huffed out a laugh. "Ain't that always the case."

Jesse rolled to his side and stood. "I'm going to clear this all up. Are you still hungry?"

"Nah. Are you?"

"Not at all. Next game we'll actually watch. How's that?"

To be honest, he'd rather kiss Jesse, but he respected his wishes and pushed himself up and off the sofa to help him clean up. He followed Jesse to the kitchen and handed him the platters to put in the dishwasher.

"Teamwork makes the dream work." He crossed his arms and leaned against the counter. Jesse snapped the door shut and pushed some buttons to start the cycle running.

"I'm usually alone on the weekends and in the evenings. It's—it's nice to have someone to spend time with." Red patches stained Jesse's cheeks, and Dash recalled his invitation to hang out and study in the apartment, now recognizing it not only as a help to Dash, but as a way to ease Jesse's own loneliness. He couldn't even imagine Jesse's isolated world, and if he could draw him back into life, he'd be his good friend.

"You know what? Maybe I will take you up on studying here. I'm on early shift on Tuesday and get off at four. If I could get in some good solid hours, that would be amazing."

"Yeah?" Jesse's eyes brightened. "Anytime. Come over when you're finished. Let me know ahead of time 'cause sometimes Miranda will be out and I'll have headphones on when I'm writing and I can't hear the bell."

"You never gave me your number. I have Miranda's but not yours." Dash pulled out his phone. Jesse recited it to him, and Dash texted him back. "There. Now you have mine. And if I'm coming on Tuesday, then I'm bringing dinner."

Jesse glanced at the clock on the stove. "Second

game should be starting soon. Let's go back." As they walked, Jesse continued their conversation. "And you don't have to bring dinner. We can order something in."

"Hell no. I'll tell my mother." He slapped Jesse on the shoulder. "She'll love to cook for us."

They shared a laugh, and he and Jesse sat on the sofa, not close, but not far apart either. Then he realized the implication of what Jesse had said earlier. That he hadn't left the apartment in five years. More than likely, it also meant he hadn't been with another man since then, and that fact freaked Dash out more than he cared to think. Time to slow things down before they got out of hand, because Jesse Grace-Martin wasn't a once-and-done type of guy. If ever anyone had boyfriend written all over him, it was Jesse.

Flirting with Jesse was fun, but that was as far as it would go. The last thing Dash needed was to get involved with someone.

Chapter Eleven

"TELL ME SOMETHING new since our last visit." Dr. Mingione's brightly tipped nails clicked on her laptop's keyboard as they spoke. "Have you been out of the apartment at all?"

Jesse had high hopes that the past Saturday spent with Dash would've helped make it easier for him to move forward. But once again, he'd tried and failed. On Sunday morning, he'd opened the door, stepped into the hallway, and frozen. The dark-paneled walls closed in on him, looking menacing, and with his heart pounding, he'd taken a step back and shut the door. Furious with himself, he'd gone back to bed and stayed there all day, ignoring a phone call from his mother and even a text from Dash, "checking in to say hi."

While Dr. Mingione wouldn't be angry with him, Jesse knew how much she wanted him to try. "No, not really. I mean, I stepped into the hallway, but I still didn't go outside. I thought I could 'cause I had my friend come watch the game on Saturday. Somehow that built up a fantasy in my head that if I could do that, going out would be the natural next step."

"So what happened?" Dr. Mingione stopped typing, her eyes wide with what Jesse could see was curiosity. "And who is this friend? You've never mentioned anyone. How did you meet them?"

Suddenly shy, Jesse dipped his gaze to rest on a fascinating spot on the floor. "He works in the building. His name is Dash, and he's a porter." The last part he stated a bit defiantly, almost daring Dr. Mingione to ask more questions. "Dash is short for Dashamir. He's Albanian."

"Does he live in the Bronx? My doorman's Albanian, and that's where he lives."

"Yeah." A whole world existed outside the confines of his self-imposed prison of luxury. For while there were thousands of people dying to step inside the rarified gates of the Dakota to see where the rich and famous lived, Jesse now longed to join them on the sidewalk, shoulder to shoulder, but couldn't figure out how to take that step and make it happen. "He goes to college—takes classes online so he can work—and I told him he could come here after his shift to study. I think that might help me get up the courage to go outside."

"And how do you figure that? I'm not disagreeing with you. I'd like to hear your thoughts."

"Well…" He paused to consider his words. "Dash has come over a few times, and we've talked about his life. We spoke about the new Yankee Stadium, which I've never been to, and all the new restaurants that have opened up in the city. It made me more aware of everything I've missed by hiding away inside this apartment. And another thing."

"Yes, tell me." Her laptop now forgotten, Dr. Mingione leaned forward.

"I once used to think of this apartment as my refuge. My shelter. But now, more and more every day, I think of it as holding me back, almost as a prison."

Her eyes shining, Dr. Mingione nodded. "This is what I was waiting for. I—all of us—can only talk so much about you being ready, but it has to be up to you, for your own reasons. You're ready, Jesse, to take the step. You know it, and that's part of your fear. But you also want to. And if it's because you found a person you want to explore the world with or simply because it's time, it doesn't matter. What matters is that it's on your own terms."

Excitement, fear, and a touch of nausea bubbled up inside him. "I haven't wanted it this badly in a long time. Maybe ever."

Not normally demonstrative, Dr. Mingione reached over to give his hand a squeeze. "You can do this. You're more alive than ever before, like a flower slowly unfurling to the sun. Tell me. Have you told this man about your agoraphobia?"

"Yes."

"And?"

He couldn't hold her gaze for long. "He didn't say anything. He asked me a few questions and seemed a little freaked out, but then we got sidetracked and it never came up again."

"I'm glad you told him, but do you have stronger feelings than mere friendship for him?"

Heat swirled low in his belly, but he thrust that

aside. His feelings for Dash were complicated. More than friendship certainly, but Jesse knew, without the doctor telling him, that he wasn't ready for anything further. Not the way he was.

"No, not yet. I enjoy spending time with him, but we're only learning about each other. He's as wary of me as I am of him."

"Why is that?"

"I think he's a little uncomfortable with all my money. He's a regular guy, you know? And close with his family. His mother thought I was one of those party guys she reads about in the paper."

"Well, it sounds like both of you have your heads on straight and you're taking it slow." She pulled her laptop on her knees and made a few notes. "I'll be back next week, and I hope to hear you've made even more progress. We can discuss lowering the dosage on your medication. I think it's time."

"Thanks, Dr. Mingione."

Miranda entered the living room. While he had his sessions, she did her work in the television room. "Would you like some tea, Doctor?"

"No, I'm good." She stood, and he accompanied her to the door. "Maybe soon you'll walk with me to the elevator."

His heart kicked up a notch. "Maybe."

She opened the door and left, and he peered after her. Her footsteps tapped on the tiled floor and faded as she turned the corner. In the distance he heard the elevator door open. He shut the door and leaned against it with a sigh.

"Everything okay?" Miranda stood before him. "You want something before I leave for the evening?"

"Nope. I'm good." He strode back into the living room to get his phone and saw several missed calls from his mother and a few texts from Dash. First he checked the messages from Dash.

"Dammit." He swore softly. Today was Tuesday, and he remembered that on Saturday he'd told Dash to feel free to come over and study because he got off shift early. He checked his watch. Five thirty. "Shit." His fingers flew as he typed out an apology and told Dash to come over. Now, if possible.

He waited anxiously for the text to turn from *delivered* to *read*, but after staring at the phone for what seemed like five minutes but was truthfully more like thirty seconds, when nothing happened, he decided that Dash, having tried and failed, had given up and went home. Maybe he was on the train and couldn't get service.

He gnawed on a cuticle, and then with a sigh, pushed Return Call for his mother.

"Jesse, what's going on? I've been worried sick."

His eyes rolled so hard, it hurt his brain. "I'm fine, Mom." She was so "worried sick," she called him once.

"Why didn't you call me back earlier?"

"I've been busy."

"You have?" Caution edged her voice. "Have you been out of the apartment?"

Even though she couldn't see him, Jesse lifted his chin. "Yes, I have."

"What?" Her shriek hurt his eardrum, and he

winced. "You went out? Why didn't you tell me? Where did you go? What did you do?"

"I sat in the courtyard with Miranda. And then on the weekend, I walked into the hallway." Jesse didn't speak of the failed attempts or how shaken he'd been afterward.

"Oh." The disappointment in her flat tone spoke volumes.

"You thought it was more, didn't you?"

"I'm not going to lie and tell you no. I am disappointed. You're still seeing the therapist, right?"

"Of course."

She knows me better than you do. Sometimes I think she likes me better too.

"And what does she say? Is she happy with your progress?"

"In the beginning, there were days I couldn't get out of bed. After I could, I refused to walk by the windows, fearing someone could see me inside." He breathed deep, willing his voice to remain strong and unbroken. "So for me, going outside to sit in the courtyard is huge. Windows no longer frighten me, and I can look outside with no fear. Plus, I'm happy the doctor has decided to reduce the dosage for my medication. So to answer your question, yes, I've made progress. A hell of a lot of progress. And maybe if you ever came to see me more often than once a year, you'd notice."

"You know Harry and I moved to Connecticut so I could get away from New York. I'm not sure I can handle being there."

Pain rippled through him. "I'm here. Isn't your son enough of a reason? Don't you miss me?" The moment the words left his lips, Jesse regretted them. He wasn't sure he wanted to know the answer.

"I do. You have no idea….It almost killed me when I lost your father."

"I remember."

"You look exactly like him. You have his eyes and that same sweet, beautiful smile."

"Is that why you stay away from me? Because I look so much like him, it's too painful?" If it was true, it would hurt, but Jesse could understand.

"I watched you grow and loved you so much, yet it hurt to see you and hear your voice. I hated what was happening to you and to myself. I know if your father had lived, we would've been married forever. I loved him with everything I had."

It hurt to hear what she had to say, but the sheer crippling pain of earlier years had dulled to a soft ache.

"Do you still miss him?"

Several beats of silence passed. "Yes. I'll always miss him, Jesse. I never had a chance to say good-bye or say I love you. He'd already left for work by the time I came home from my morning Pilates class. There I was, foolishly thinking my life was perfect, laughing with my friends, while he…" Her voice drifted away.

Remembering, Jesse lay on the sofa and stared up at the ceiling. "He gave me a kiss and said, 'See you later, kiddo. I'll try and make it home early.' "

"You were his greatest joy."

Strangely enough, those words brought a smile to

his face instead of the usual rush of tears. "I still miss him so much. Every day. But this past year, it's gotten a little better. You may not think I'm improving, but I know I am. I'm not sure how far I'll progress, but I know I'll be walking outside soon."

"I hope so. And please, never for one second doubt that I love you. I'm glad we've had this talk. I'll try and be better about staying in touch."

It went both ways, Jesse realized later that evening. He could fault her for them not being closer, but he was equally negligent in calling her to talk or check on how she was feeling. Somehow he'd forgotten he wasn't the only one whose world had been ripped from underneath them.

Speaking of checking in, Jesse pulled out his phone, hoping to see something from Dash. His inbox remained empty, and after staring at the screen for a moment, Jesse figured no harm no foul, and shot off another message to Dash.

Yanks-Twins Friday night. Wanna watch?

He hit Send, and this time the message changed from *delivered* to *read* in a moment. And Dash replied: *Sorry. Had class tonight and lots of homework to catch up on. Not sure yet about Friday night.*

His stomach sank, but he sent the next text anyway. *I'll have more of those wings.*

Jesse stared at the screen until his eyes blurred.

I'll let you know.

And that was that. No "Talk to you soon" or "See you around." Angry with himself for acting like a high-schooler with a crush, Jesse picked up his computer and for the next hour, he worked on an article he had to turn in by the end of the week. At a break, he walked to the window and looked down at the street below. Horse-drawn carriages waited for riders, the horses shifting from hoof to hoof, their manes braided with multicolored flowers. It must've been another steamy summer night, because both men and women wore tank tops and shorts, and Jesse could see many with ice cream or cold drinks in hand. He wanted that normalcy, that intimacy of walking with a lover on a warm summer night.

His jaw set in a hard line, Jesse turned his back to the window. "Now or never," he muttered to himself and left the living room to stand by the front door. The voices in his head yelled, *Not safe, not safe*, but he thought of his conversation with his mother. Of moving forward. He thought of his father's gentle smile. He wanted to walk among the living now instead of hiding with the shadows of those who passed.

Maybe his problem was that he thought too much. He wrenched open the front door, and concentrating on his breathing, he took a step over the threshold. And then another. And another. Before he knew it, he'd crossed the hall and stood swaying and gasping a bit, but he'd done it.

Five years. It had taken him five years to get to this step, and he pulled out his phone and snapped close to a dozen pictures. He pulled one up and sent it to Miranda first, with the caption: "Look at me." Then one to Dash that stated, "I'm on my way."

His phone rang, and it echoed loudly in the silent hallway.

"Hello."

"Jesse. Where are you? Oh, my God. Are you out in the hall by yourself?"

He laughed at Miranda's rapid-fire questions and leaned against the wall. "Yeah. I decided I had to do it. It was time."

"I'm so happy."

"I guess that's why you're crying, huh?" He knew he had a crazy, cheesy grin on his face, but he didn't care if everyone in the building saw him. He felt free like a bird, and he wanted to soar.

"Oh, you be quiet." She sniffled a few more times. "I'm so proud of you. I can't wait for tomorrow."

"Me either. I'll see you then. Night."

"Good night."

He checked his phone to see if Dash had answered, but he hadn't, so he put the phone back into his pocket, unwilling to let anything diminish the moment for him.

With his hands touching the walls, as if he needed their solidity to hold him upright, Jesse walked back to the apartment. He shivered and was surprised to find his shirt soaked through with sweat. His heart pounded, and his legs trembled, allowing him to make it to the sofa before giving out beneath him, and he sat staring into nothing.

"IT'S BEAUTIFUL TODAY. Do you want to go outside? We could see about going for a walk." After greeting him with a hug and a kiss the next morning, Miranda handed him his coffee and bagel. "I'm so happy for you, Jess."

He gave her a thin smile but didn't answer. The night had been hard, with his sleep interrupted by nightmares of people chasing him and secret plots against his life exposed. He'd been lying awake since four a.m. without any energy to get up.

He drank the hot coffee Miranda had given him. "Thanks. I didn't have the best night."

Concern darkened her eyes, and she frowned. "Are you getting sick?"

"No." Maybe a little heartsick. He'd never heard back from Dash and assumed the man had written him off as too much trouble.

"So what's wrong? You should be celebrating this morning. You did something you haven't been able to for five years. That should make you want to swing from the ceiling and open the windows and shout it out loud."

"I'm thinking it's not as easy as that. Five years don't disappear in five minutes."

"I know." She took a seat next to him and squeezed his arm. "I'm not pushing you. I hope you know that. Just wanted you to know how excited I was for you."

"Thanks. I'm going to finish up my article and then maybe see if we can go to the courtyard. Did you have anything planned?"

"Nothing that can't be put off. You tell me when, and I'm there."

"Okay." He popped the rest of his bagel into his

mouth and brushed off his hands. "I only have a few more research points to check, and then I'll be ready." He jumped up and grabbed his laptop. He liked writing at the dining table as the light wasn't too bright.

Two hours later, Jesse stretched the kinks out of his back and yawned. "Miranda?" He rubbed his eyes. "I'm done."

She glanced up from her iPad. "Okay. I was entering your monthly expenses on the Excel spreadsheet and just want to finish this last bit. It's time to schedule your dental appointment. Do you still want to use the in-home dentist like you have been?"

Jesse wanted to say no. He wanted to be able to hop into a car and go to an office. But he couldn't. Not yet.

"Let's wait and see."

He paced the kitchen, stopping briefly to get a bottle of water from the refrigerator. Dash had sent him a clipped answer: *Happy for you. Busy today.*

Okay…Jesse worked it out in his head. What more could he expect or want from Dash? They were new friends, certainly not lovers.

Sorry. I won't bother you.

To his surprise, Dash answered right away. *Lunch? My mom cooked.*

And damned if his heart didn't leap at those words staring up at him from the screen.

Sure.

Great. C U at 2:30.

The mixed messages from Dash made Jesse's head spin, but he couldn't hold back his smile.

"Good news?" Miranda stood before him, and he

hadn't realized she was even there.

"Dash will be here for lunch. That's all."

She gave him a funny smile. "That's nice. I finished the numbers. Do you want to go outside?"

It was all getting real now. This was what people did. They woke up, ate breakfast, did a few things in the house, and left for the day. His throat dried.

"Sure." Jesse pressed his lips together. He could do this. He *would* do this. "Let's go."

"Jess." Miranda placed a hand on his arm. "This isn't a prison sentence. You don't have to prove anything. Take it at your own pace."

But he did have something to prove. To himself. "I want it."

He grabbed his keys from the bowl and put his hand on the cool knob of the front door. The sweat on his hand made his palms slippery, and it took two turns of the knob before he could open the door. Immediately, the sight of the wide-open hallway stretched out in front of him like a road not traveled. Heart beating madly, Jesse tried to remember the joy of last night, when he made it to the hallway and thought he owned the world.

"One foot in front of the other. That's all. One at a time," he muttered to himself. "One. At. A. Time."

With Miranda hovering behind him, close enough that he could hear her breathing, he walked. She put her hand on his, but he shook it off. "I need to do this alone. Please." A quick glance revealed the hurt in her eyes before she turned away. Guilty over his snappish behavior, Jesse stopped. "I'm sorry. I didn't mean to bite your head off. I want you here with me. I just have to prove to myself I can really do this without always leaning on you."

"I understand. I'll always be here for you."

As they talked, they kept walking, and when he stopped to catch his breath and put his hand on the wall, Jesse realized they had not only passed the place where he'd stood the night before, but had turned the corner. The elevator was now in sight.

"Are you going outside?"

Grimly determined, Jesse nodded. "Outside to the courtyard. But not only to sit. I want to walk around."

Her eyes widened. "You want to go out? On 72nd Street?"

"No. I'm not ready," he said quickly. He couldn't think about going outside the gates. Brushing against people. Having them close to him. "Just around the courtyard." He held her gaze. "That would be good, don't you think? That's still progress." He'd worn a light-colored shirt so his sweating wouldn't show through, and he shivered, feeling the moisture roll down his back.

"Of course it is. I hope you don't expect to simply walk out and be able to mingle with people after five years of being inside. But this is only the beginning for you. I feel it. Should I push the button to go downstairs now?"

"I love you, Miranda." He hugged her tight, burying his face in her hair. "Thank you for always being there for me." He straightened and punched the button himself. "Let's do this." He and Miranda stepped into the elevator cab.

People who didn't have issues never gave a second thought to the little, everyday things like riding down an elevator or facing the wide-open space of being outdoors. Jesse swallowed his urge to bolt, holding himself rigid. The doors opened, and Miranda's hand crept into his and gave a squeeze. Grateful to her as always, he laced their fingers together, and they walked out through the lobby and then into the sunny courtyard.

The warm breeze hit his face, the smell of the various flowers teased his nose, and he could hear the faint sounds of traffic. He lifted his face to the sun and closed his eyes. Miranda remained silent, allowing him to soak it all in. After several moments, he opened his eyes.

"Let's walk." Their hands still clasped, they took a turn around the perimeter of the oval-shaped courtyard, and Jesse stopped at each of the four green-awning-topped entrances to say hello to the doormen. He took it slowly, noting the surprise and genuine happiness of each man, most of whom he'd known since he was a baby.

When he checked his watch, Jesse was surprised to discover an hour had passed. Cars and limos had driven into the courtyard, picked up and discharged passengers and left. The center of the courtyard had been redone, and now boasted two fountains, one on each side. There were bushes and flowering shrubs, and Jesse, still with Miranda by his side, walked onto the red-bricked median and sat on a bench. Once again, he closed his eyes and lifted his face to the warmth of the sun.

"You're doing amazingly well. Do you realize how long you've been outside?" Miranda sat next to him, and he kept his eyes closed, enjoying the scents and sounds of the outdoors. He could hear the chickadees peeping and the traffic noise from the street. Listening and not looking was a good beginning. The first time he'd gone outside, he'd been so sick to his stomach with nerves, he hadn't been able to enjoy everything going on around him.

"An hour. And yeah. It's different than it was the other time. I'm feeling more confident."

"But not confident enough to step outside the gates, right?"

Panic swelled inside him, and his eyes flew open. "N-no. Miranda. I'm not ready. Please don't push me."

"I'm not. I wanted to make sure. I think you're remarkable."

Reassured, Jesse drank in all the blue sky and gazed around. At the far corner, he watched several mainte-nance people from the building begin to power-wash the brick walkway. Another man walked by them with a hose, and Jesse's skin prickled with awareness. *Dash.* He'd recognize that fit, muscular torso anywhere, and his gaze roamed hungrily over the man's biceps as he hauled the hose toward them.

"He's very good-looking," Miranda murmured.

"Shh. He'll hear you."

"Don't be ridiculous. He's too far away."

Jesse tensed, recalling their strange interaction when they'd texted the evening before. He really liked Dash and hoped their mixed signals could be worked out.

As he approached, Dash's brows rose in surprise, and a tiny smile teased his lips. "Hey. You're outside. That's fantastic. An even bigger step than the hallway. You looked great in those pictures you sent last night."

Dash seemed genuinely happy to see him, and Jesse breathed easier, relieved they were on the right track again.

"Yeah, well, I realized it was probably stupid to send them to you after you said you were busy. I got excited."

A frown marred Dash's smooth forehead. "Don't apologize. I was psyched to see it. It made me happy for you."

"It's nothing. Silly really to get so worked up about walking down a hallway." Seeing Dash before him, so masculine and real, made Jesse feel weak. What was there to celebrate—walking in a hallway? Sitting outside? Why would someone so obviously confident and good-looking want to be around him? As far as Jesse could tell, he brought little to the table.

"Nah, Jesse, man, why're you downplaying it?"

"Because I see how natural it is for you all, and struggling to do the simplest of things makes me feel pathetic."

"I gotta work while I talk, or I'll get in trouble, but hold on a second." Dash unrolled the hose and connected it to the spigot in the ground by his feet, then turned on the water and began to spray the bushes as he continued to speak.

"I think it takes a strong person to first admit they

have a problem, and second, take it head on and try and overcome it. I can't pretend to understand what you feel. But you're already like one hundred times better than you were the first day I met you, when you couldn't sit for more than a few minutes before you had a panic attack and ran inside. Cut yourself some slack."

He supposed Dash was right. And maybe one day in the not too distant future he'd step outside the gate and onto the sidewalk. He trembled at the thought but thrust it out of his mind for the moment.

"Are we still on for lunch?"

Dash waved the hose back and forth to give each tree and bush an equal soaking. "Absolutely. My mom went crazy again. I have enough for all three of us, if you want, Miranda."

"Oh, that's sweet, thanks, but I have some errands this afternoon, so I was planning on grabbing something while I'm out running around."

Not that he didn't love Miranda, but Jesse looked forward to having some alone time with Dash. He caught Dash's eye, and when he received a wink, a warm glow enveloped him.

"I better go deal with the other side, so the plants don't die of neglect. I'll see you around two thirty?" Dash turned off the hose and unscrewed it from the spigot.

"See you then."

Dash walked out of earshot.

JESSE PLAYED AROUND on the Internet, and seeing a beautiful leather jacket he knew would look great on Dash, bought it for him, paying for expedited shipping to get it delivered the next day.

Miranda leaned over and whispered in his ear, "You better save me something from what Dash brings and not eat all the food. Tell me how long you want me to stay out."

"You're crazy," Jesse whispered back. "I'm not asking you to stay away."

"Okay." Her eyes sparkled. "Then I'll stay."

"You're fired." He snickered at her pretend squeal of outrage, then lowered his voice. "Thanks, I owe you one."

Her expression softened. "Who am I to stand in the way of true love?"

"Don't be ridiculous." Jesse's heart beat a bit faster. "It's only lunch."

Chapter Twelve

"I T WAS SO nice outside. I almost didn't want to come back inside." The microwave dinged, and Jesse handed Dash a plate piled with delicious-smelling food. "And I can't believe I just said that."

Leaving his plate untouched, Dash braced his elbows on the table. "How did it feel? Do you think you're gonna be able to get out more? I hope you don't think I'm asking too many questions." It had given him a jolt seeing Jesse sitting outside with his face upturned. He seemed happy and carefree and utterly desirable, and though Dash had hoped his feelings had changed, the tumbling of his stomach proved otherwise. There were so many reasons why he shouldn't get involved with someone like Jesse, but like a shooting star, Jesse had a magical quality, a sweetness Dash found impossible to resist.

Jesse toyed with the food on his plate, then set his fork down. He blew out a breath. "I'm not sure. It shocked me how much I enjoyed it. I don't know if I can do more. Yet." He picked up his fork, and they began eating, but then he set it down again. "Before the weather starts to get cold, it might be nice if maybe we could eat lunch outside one day in the courtyard."

Dash finished chewing. "I wish. But I don't think it would be a good idea. They don't want us hanging around with the residents, remember? I mean, I'm sure I'm probably violating a million rules right now by being here with you."

Jesse's mouth tightened in anger. "Let them say something. I'd like to see them try."

"I wouldn't. I need this job to pay for rent and school. I can't afford to lose it."

"That would never happen. I wouldn't let it." His eyes shot sparks, and Dash had to admit it was a bit of a turn-on to see Jesse hot with anger. He wondered what he'd be like in bed, spread out naked underneath him.

Shit. Dash shoved more food in his mouth. He'd better stop. A few kisses didn't mean they were going to sleep together. He didn't need a boyfriend; he needed to focus on school.

"I wanted to apologize."

Drawn out of his musing, Dash jerked his head up from staring at his plate. "Huh? What? Apologize? Why?"

"I forgot I'd given you an invite to come and study here on Tuesdays after your early shift ended. I'm sorry."

He was glad Jesse brought it up because he never would have. He'd texted Jesse about coming up to the apartment to study, but when he didn't receive an answer, he left for home, feeling a bit slighted. "I'm sorry too."

"I had a session with my therapist, and when we

finished and I saw it was five thirty, I texted you right away, but you'd already left for home."

That explained it. "Yeah, my shift ends at four, remember?"

"Damn. Well, that was a big fail on my part. But next week, just come upstairs. You don't have to ask beforehand. I'll put it in my calendar and even have Miranda make a note of it."

"Okay. We'll see how it goes. And you mentioned something about Friday night and the Yankee game?"

Jesse's eyes lit up. "Yeah. The game starts at eight. Are you busy?"

Feeling better about the way things stood between them, Dash teased, "You asking me on a date?" He held his breath, waiting to see how Jesse would respond.

Jesse licked his lips, his face aflame. "Uh…I guess."

Dash stood to dump the remnants of his lunch into the garbage pail under the sink, then turned back to Jesse and framed his face between the palms of his hands. Jesse's breathing sped up, and before Dash knew what he was doing, he bent and kissed him.

"Ohhh." Jesse wound his arms around Dash's neck and molded his lips to Dash's, melting into him. Dash's hunger spiked, and with Jesse still clinging to him, he picked Jesse up and sat him on the island, kissing and licking his soft, full lips. He couldn't get enough of Jesse's mouth. He'd dreamed about those lips wrapped around his cock, sucking him into oblivion.

"Mmm, you taste so good." He pushed his tongue inside Jesse's hot mouth, drinking in his heat, while his hands slid under Jesse's T-shirt, touching all that soft skin. Dash wanted to swallow him whole, lay him down and lick him from head to toe. He smoothed his hands over Jesse's chest, tweaking the pointy nipples, loving his little whimpers and cries. "Anyone ever tell you how fucking sexy you are?"

Jesse moaned and buried his face in the crook of Dash's neck, sucking at his skin. "N-no."

"Good. I like being the first." He grasped the hair curling at the base of Jesse's neck and took his mouth again in a hard kiss, sucking Jesse's tongue. Jesse whimpered and held him tighter, and Dash wished he could pick him up, carry him to bed, and bury himself in that tight ass. Gathering his shaky control, he pulled back, both of them breathing heavily, staring at each other.

A bit dazed from the intensity of their kisses, Dash ran his hands through his hair. "Sorry."

"You are?" A teasing smile curved Jesse's lips. "I'm not sorry. Not one damn bit."

The redness of Jesse's lips and cheeks were a picture Dash wouldn't soon forget.

"I didn't mean I'm sorry for kissing you. I like kissing you. A lot." He stepped back, hyperaware of the desire between them. It could go very wrong, very fast, and Dash refused to give in to the temptation of Jesse Grace-Martin. "Too much in fact. I'm still an employee here, and I'm on my lunch hour."

"I get it." Jesse reached out and swept the tips of his fingers across Dash's jaw. "I wouldn't want you to lose your job. But Friday night? Are you working on

Saturday?"

"Yeah. I have the twelve-to-eight-p.m. shift." He picked up Jesse's plate and walked to the sink, where he ran the water over it. "I'll dump this and leave it in the sink for you to put in the dishwasher. I gotta get going in a few."

"Um, to make your life simpler so you don't have to take the train back and forth, if you do come to watch the game, you could stay over…if you wanted to." Jesse spoke in a rush, and despite his words, Dash knew how hard it was for Jesse to push himself.

"That's very thoughtful of you. But I knew you were a giving person." He dried his hands and returned to where Jesse still sat on the island.

"Yeah. I'm all about giving, especially to you."

At his approach, Jesse's breathing sped up, and Dash liked how his presence affected Jesse. It made him feel wanted. He took Jesse's hand and played with his fingers. "I may take you up on that offer."

"I like spending time with you and getting to know you."

True honesty in a person wasn't something Dash encountered often. Certainly not in his past sexual partners—there was never any depth to their meetings. It was simply a joining of their bodies, never their hearts. Dash had never met anyone like Jesse before.

"I like that too."

They gazed into each other's eyes, and Dash leaned forward, ready to kiss him again, when he heard the front door open and Miranda called out, "Jess, where are you?"

Disappointment flared in Jesse's eyes. "In the kitchen."

Dash circled around the center island to pick up his phone and the building's walkie-talkie he had with him at all times. "I better leave."

"I'll see you Friday, then?"

He nodded and slipped the phone into his pocket. "Yeah. Definitely. Don't forget the wings. They're really why I'm coming."

"Idiot."

Miranda entered the kitchen and looked from Jesse to him, a slight smile on her lips. "Did you guys have a nice lunch? It smells delicious in here."

"Yeah, and I'm sorry to say hi and bye, but I'm going to get reamed out if I'm not downstairs in five minutes. I have to make the package deliveries, and there's a ton that came in today."

"Go, go," Jesse said. "Let yourself out."

"See you Friday."

He hurried off, hearing Miranda ask Jesse, "Friday? What's happening Friday?"

The door closed behind him with a *click*, and he made tracks to the elevator. He got downstairs with a minute to spare. Emilio, another porter who was assigned to work with him that afternoon, wheeled one of the dollies over with the boxes. He held a clipboard in his hand Dash knew had a list of every apartment they needed to visit. "Thought you were gonna be late."

"Nope. I'm here." He turned on his walkie-talkie and took another loaded dolly. "Ready?"

At Emilio's nod, they exited the package room and walked to the elevator.

"Where'd you go for lunch?"

Dash remained deliberately vague. "I brought mine."

"Smart. Still warm enough to go eat in the park and watch all the sexy ladies walk by, know what I'm sayin'?"

Giving Emilio a faint smile, Dash held open the door of the service elevator. "Where's our first stop?"

"The old ladies on the third floor. They got three boxes. Every week they get three boxes. What the hell do they got in there?"

"I got no idea. Not my business."

"Paul thinks it's sex toys." He snorted. "They ain't never had a man, far as anyone knows. They gotta get their jollies somehow, ya know?"

The two women Emilio talked trash about were nothing but polite and nice to Dash. They weren't so old either. Probably around his mother's age.

"That's gross, man. They're ladies. I don't like to think about women like that."

"Like what? Having sex? You got a girlfriend?"

"No." He prayed the elevator door would open soon so the conversation would end.

"Lucky. Take your time. Don't get tied down. There's enough who'll give it up for free, so you don't gotta put a ring on it."

"Whatever. I mean, I respect women. And those ladies could be my mother. So cut it out."

They finished their deliveries and returned to the

package room to take a break before heading out again. Leaning up against the desk in the corner, Emilio drank from a bottle of water, and Dash shifted under his assessing stare.

"What? You're giving me the weirdest look."

"You're friendly with that strange guy on the seventh floor, the one who never comes out of his apartment, right?"

"We've talked a bit, yeah." Careful to keep his face schooled, Dash reached for a bottle of water for himself.

"What's his deal?"

"No deal. He's a nice guy, that's all."

"C'mon." His eyes narrowed. "Ain't nobody stays in their apartment all by themselves without something strange going on."

"Not my business." He sent Emilio a sharp glance. "Or yours neither."

"Don't be so touchy. Not like you're friends or nothin'." He snickered. "Guy's a fruitcake for one, and I hear he's gay. You're a real man."

Bile rose in his throat, and there was nothing Dash wanted more than to punch Emilio's stupid, grinning face, but that would get him fired. Dash set his water bottle down. "Hey. Don't pull that shit talk on me. I don't go for it. I'm cool with everyone. Got it?"

"Yeah, yeah, whatever. Chill out, man. I don't got nothin' against nobody as long as they leave me alone."

"Don't think you gotta worry about that."

After that, they spent the afternoon barely speaking, and it put Dash in a pissy mood for the remainder of his day and well into the evening. It affected his ability to concentrate on his two classes that night, and unable to work on an outline, he threw down his pen in disgust. The assignment would have to wait.

Restless and annoyed that he'd let some asshole get the better of him, Dash grabbed his phone and texted Jesse.

Hey, what's up?

His response was almost immediate. *Nothing. Hanging out watching something on Netflix.*

Netflix and chill? He added a grin emoji.

Not likely.

Dash chewed on his lip a moment, then sent back: *Good. I wouldn't want to think I had any competition.*

None at all.

Thinking about Friday night.

So you're coming?

I'd like to.

But? I hear a but.

Not sure if I should stay over.

Yes, he wanted Jesse. Badly. Having a whole night to share a bed together, getting to kiss those soft lips, hear his breathless sighs, and touch all that silky skin would be a dream. But if he stayed the night with Jesse and they slept together, that would take their friendship to a place Dash wasn't sure he was ready to visit. Not yet, at least. The last thing he wanted to do was hurt Jesse, and Dash imagined that sex for Jesse would mean commitment. Dash, having no experience with someone who would expect more than a one-night stand, knew that when he and Jesse took that step together—*if* they did—he wanted to be sure.

Guess we'll take it one step at a time.

Sounds like a plan. Gonna go back to studying. TTYL.
Jesse sent him a thumbs-up emoji.

With that resolved, Dash picked up his pen and, chewing on the edge, set to tackling the outline. It flowed easier now, and at midnight he put his pen down, stretched out the kinks in his neck, and after brushing his teeth, went to bed.

Vivid dreams, dreams of Jesse and him naked in bed together, left him restless and edgy when he woke up in the morning. The day passed by in a blur, and Dash wasn't able to spend his lunch with Jesse, nor did he see him sitting outside, but they did exchange a few texts. It surprised him how much he missed talking to Jesse. He thought long and hard about spending the night and decided that if Jesse asked him again, he'd say yes.

On Friday morning he stopped by his parents' house, only to find his mother and sister gathered in the kitchen, his mother weeping.

"What's wrong?" He dropped his knapsack by the front door.

"Your father. He-he wants a divorce. He's in love with someone else. Sh-she's having a b-baby." A fresh wave of tears streamed down her cheeks, and his sister, Drita, held her close.

"Oh, *Nënë*." He didn't know whether to cry for her obvious distress or be happy that she would finally be free of a man who'd never held her in the regard she deserved. "I'm sorry. He never deserved a woman like you."

"The shame of him, to do this to his family. A

woman less than half his age."

It didn't surprise Dash. His father spent all his free time at the restaurant where he worked, at the gym trying to stay young, or hanging out with his buddies. He couldn't remember when he'd last seen his parents together, except during a major holiday. And even then, his father was always on his phone, disconnected from the rest of them, nothing more than the stranger he'd always been.

"You know who she is?"

She nodded. "Some girl he met in the gym. She's only twenty-two—younger than both of you. How can he not be embarrassed?"

"It's a man's world," Drita said, her mouth set in a firm line. "Especially for someone like *him*, who holds on to old-world ways." She held their mother close. "You'll come out of this stronger. Finally you can go to school and get that high-school diploma you always wanted. Right, Dash?" Drita stroked her shoulder and poured her a steaming cup of tea.

"Yes. We'll help you. Whatever you need."

"I don't want to be a burden." She sniffled and blew her nose. "You don't need to worry about me." Her red-rimmed eyes gazed back at them.

"You're our mother. You can't ever be a burden."

"I told *Nënë* that we would come for dinner tonight."

"Tonight?" His stomach sank as he thought of his plans with Jesse. But family came first.

"You have plans? It's fine. You don't have to come. Drita and I will have a nice dinner together."

"No, it's fine. Nothing I can't change."

"Are you sure?" Her hand trembled as she lifted the teacup to take a sip. "I don't want to interfere, especially if it's important."

"Nah, I promised a friend I'd come over to his place and watch the game. Nothing big." Imagining the disappointment in Jesse's eyes, Dash's stomach tied in knots. But his mother needed her family around her. Jesse would understand. "Of course I'm sure. I'll be home tonight, and we'll have a nice dinner."

At his mother's happy smile, Dash's head knew he'd done the right thing, but his heart? That was a different matter.

Chapter Thirteen

"**O**F COURSE I understand." Jesse slid a bottle of water across the island. He'd just ordered delivery for lunch when Dash had shown up, red-eyed and weary, obviously upset. Hearing the story of Dash's father's betrayal overrode Jesse's own disappointment in not being able to spend the night together or even watch the game. "Family is the most important. There will be other games. And other nights."

"Yeah, so about that. I was thinking. What about Sunday? There's a four p.m. start at the Stadium. If you don't have plans, maybe we can do it then? And see how the night goes…?"

Dash bit his lip, and Jesse wanted to kiss him and take the hurt away. It had to be devastating, even with the almost nonexistent relationship Dash had explained he and his father had, to find out about his betrayal. His parents had to have been married for over thirty years.

"Let me think…plans?" He tapped his chin. "Oh, yeah. I was planning on a run through Central Park and then taking the train down to 34th Street to do some shopping at Macy's." He snorted. "Of course I have no plans. It's me, remember?"

Dash's brows drew together, darkening his normally open expression. "Don't joke about yourself like that. You're trying."

Seeing that Dash wasn't in the mood to joke, Jesse didn't think twice about leaving his seat to give the man a hug. "I'm sorry. I didn't mean to make light of the situation. I can't imagine how hard it was to hear that."

To his surprise, Dash snorted but leaned into Jesse's arms, his muscular back pressing against Jesse's chest. "I barely see my father more than once a month. It's the *why* of the divorce. He's having a baby with a woman younger than both my sister and me. My mother feels such shame."

Holding Dash distracted Jesse, but he wanted to be there for his friend. "Your mother should only know that it's pretty standard in the circles I grew up in. What I remember is how my friends' parents would divorce and their dads would marry much younger women and start new families. They'd be graduating college with a two- or three-year-old little half brother or sister."

Dash rested his cheek against his forearm, and if Jesse had his way, they would've stayed there like that all day. "That doesn't happen very often in our community. We don't believe in divorce. But I guess my father only believed in certain things about the 'old country.' Like keeping his wife at home and having her ignorant of everything he did."

"So your mom was basically sandbagged by this.

And she's given him her whole life." Jesse had to admit he was ignorant of Dash's culture. "I hope she's going to make sure to get alimony."

"We don't have money for lawyers. And I think she's probably too proud to take money from him."

"Pride doesn't pay the rent. Harry—my stepfather—was a pretty well-known divorce lawyer. I can ask him to help."

Warm lips pressed against his arm. "You're a good friend. But I just said we can't afford lawyers."

"And Harry doesn't need the money. He'll do it because one, I'm going to ask him, and two, it's the right thing to do. Your mother deserves to be given back everything she gave to the marriage."

A heavy sigh escaped Dash, and he swiveled around in his seat to gaze up at Jesse. "I will guarantee my father will say he has no money, even though I know he flashes around wads of cash and recently bought a Rolex. Legal or not, his new lifestyle is paying off for him."

"We'll make sure she gets her due. I just want to help you and your family."

"Having you to talk to helps me." Dash reached up, grasped the nape of his neck, and threaded his fingers through Jesse's hair. Desire poured through Jesse, and he eagerly leaned into the kiss. Their tongues met and stroked, igniting the fire always simmering between them. Dash licked at his mouth, and Jesse slid his arms around Dash's neck, slanting his mouth across Dash's to plunge his tongue in deeper. Dash stood and wound his arms around Jesse's waist, sliding a thickly muscled thigh in between his legs.

"Oh, God." Jesse flung his head back and rode Dash, rubbing his aching, stiff cock against Dash's leg. The buzz of excitement from being so close to Dash brought him to the brink of orgasm embarrassingly quickly. "Oh God, gonna come if you don't stop."

"Do it." Dash palmed his ass, thrusting Jesse even harder against him. "Wanna feel you against me. Smell you on me for the rest of the day. Come on." He sucked Jesse's earlobe, and Jesse shivered.

Thinking of his scent on Dash's clothes, coupled with the man's wicked fingers sliding up and down the crack of his ass, sent a rush of toe-curling lust through Jesse. His dick swelled and throbbed, the ache of his desire washing over him in slow waves. His eyes widened, and Dash pulled him against his chest, their mouths tantalizingly close.

"You're amazing." His leg pressed hard against Jesse's balls, creating a pleasurable zing of pain in his groin.

"Dash," Jesse gasped and came, his dick pumping hard against Dash's thigh. A sticky wetness spread through his boxers, but he continued to rub and thrust against Dash as his head buzzed.

"Ahh, babe, look at you." Dash covered his mouth in a heated kiss, and his strong hands kneaded his ass while his tongue invaded his mouth, leaving Jesse breathless and his world reeling. "Jesus, you're too much."

"What about you?" Jesse murmured, running his fingers down the thick bulge in Dash's pants. "Let me take care of you."

"Not enough time…*oh*…"

Paying no heed to Dash's protest, Jesse undid his zipper and reached inside Dash's trousers to cup his cock through his damp briefs. "You're so hot and ready. I want my mouth on you. Lift up a little."

Dash lay back against the barstool, and Jesse pulled down his briefs and pants to midthigh, exposing his erect cock. It thrust out, ruddy and stiff, and Jesse's mouth watered. There wasn't anything he wanted more than Dash. His scent rose up between them, thick and strong, and he nuzzled into Dash's groin. The heat pouring from Dash enveloped him, and Jesse couldn't get enough of his taste as he licked the wiry, dark hair.

"Jess, we shouldn't…" But Jesse ignored Dash and ran his tongue over the gleaming tip of Dash's cock, loving the sharp taste of his skin and precome against his tongue. He took as much of Dash as he could in his mouth, and cupping his balls gently, began to suck, his tongue flirting and swirling around Dash's shaft.

"Fuck, not gonna be able to hold it. Oh, *God*." Dash's hands came to rest on Jesse's head and gripped his hair. Jesse moved faster, his saliva mixing with the precome leaking from Dash's cock.

"Jess. *Jesse*." Dash breathed out his name in an agonized whisper as he came, and it was the sexiest thing Jesse ever heard. He swallowed every drop, licking Dash dry.

Happy to see Dash relaxed, his face cleared of the tense worry lines, Jesse kissed his lips. They spent the next few minutes exploring each other's mouths until

Dash broke away with a heavy sigh. Jesse wished they could go for round two, but he knew Dash had responsibilities, and the last thing Jesse wanted was for Dash to get in trouble because of him.

"I gotta go. You know I wish I didn't, but…" He tucked himself into his briefs and hitched his pants up.

"I wish you didn't either, but I really do understand. So if you want to come on Sunday like you said, I think that could be a great alternative. And the overnight still stands. What's your shift Monday morning?"

A grimace pulled Dash's lips downward. "Seven a.m. But it's good 'cause I get out at three. That gives me plenty of time to study for classes."

"Beauty and brains." Jesse ran a hand over the heavy curves of Dash's biceps, thinking how much he wanted to be held in those strong arms. "How did I get so lucky?"

"Funny," Dash said, tangling fingers in his hair, bringing their mouths close. "I was thinking the same thing. Look at you. I could spend all day kissing that mouth of yours."

Reckless, Jesse brushed their lips together. "Guess we'll have to wait for Sunday then, right?"

A twinkle lit Dash's eyes. "Why do I feel like we're gonna need to DVR this game?" He caught Jesse's lips in one final kiss, and Jesse held on to him, merging their breaths, capturing his sweetness, their chests pressed tightly together, their hearts beat in a matching galloping rhythm, and Jesse felt himself falling…tumbling over and into Dash.

"Jess, I gotta go now, or else I'm not gonna be able to leave."

Sounded like a perfect way to spend the afternoon, but Jesse gathered his wits and let Dash compose himself. "I'm sorry."

"Don't be sorry for being on my mind. I can't wait for Sunday now. I feel like a high-school kid again."

Laughter brightened Dash's face, and Jesse loved that the earlier sadness and worry had been erased. "I'm glad we could make it work out. And I hope your mom will be okay. Please give her my best, and you guys should seriously consider using Harry."

"I will."

They walked out of the kitchen and found Miranda sitting in the living room, immersed in her laptop.

"Oh, hey. I didn't hear you come in."

Her cheeks flushed pink, and she remained glued to the screen. "Yeah, I came back a little while ago. I'm busy getting your calendar set up for next week. You have several requests to write articles, some from publishers requesting you to blurb books, and a few new authors asking you for critiques and reviews."

"Okay, let me just say good-bye to Dash, and I'll be right back."

"Okay. Hi, Dash. Bye, Dash."

"Bye, see you."

The two of them walked to the front door, and Jesse put his hand on Dash's shoulder. "I think she heard something."

Dash paled, then flushed a deep red. "Shit, really? Damn." He rubbed his face. "I'd better get out of here.

I-I'll see you Sunday."

Without a good-bye kiss, he pulled open the door and left. Jesse stood by the door, gathering his wits. It was his apartment and he shouldn't feel embarrassed, but it wasn't fair to Miranda, for her to walk into her workspace and find him in the throes of sex.

Time to face the music. Jesse walked back into the living room and found Miranda still staring at the laptop, but he had the feeling she wasn't seeing what was on the screen.

"Hey." He sat across from her.

"Hi. Did Dash leave?" Her eyes focused everywhere but on him.

"Yeah." When she remained silent, Jesse drew in a deep breath. "You heard us."

Without responding, Miranda turned bright red and ducked her head so her hair fell in front of her face.

"I'm sorry. I didn't think. It just kind of happened."

"It's your home. You don't have to explain or say sorry to me."

"And yet you can't look at me. It wasn't fair to you that we got carried away when you were working."

She peeked at him from beneath the fringe of her bangs. "You really like him. I'm happy for you."

Now it was his turn to grow warm. "Well…yeah. He's really nice."

"It's okay. I get it. When you really like someone, you don't want to share all the details 'cause you don't think it's real."

"Yeah." They sat silent for a minute. "Are we

good?"

"Yeah." She grinned at him. "You sure are, from what I heard."

"Miranda." He threw a pillow at her, and she cackled with laughter.

"Do you realize ever since you met Dash, you've been coming out of your shell more and more? You're like the miracle of a caterpillar turning into a beautiful butterfly."

"I don't know how I feel about you comparing me to a fuzzy, wriggling bug." Emotional now, Jesse left his chair to sit next to her on the sofa. "But I get it. And it's not even all about Dash. Maybe it had to do with me taking stock of my life. My father being gone so long, and then my mother marrying Harry and leaving...I don't know, but every morning, I look out the window and see life passing me by. I'm losing my will to live, being in this apartment, but it isn't as easy as simply walking out the door."

"I know. And it was killing me to see it happen, but I couldn't push you. Now you want it. Last year, you were sleepwalking. Not this year. This year you woke up."

Jesse agreed. He could feel life humming in his veins, beating in his heart, warming him from the inside out. "I think you may be right."

Chapter Fourteen

T HAT NIGHT, DASH sat with his mother and sister,
eating dinner, but his mind was miles away—on
West 72nd Street, to be exact. He chewed his food but
didn't taste it, answered questions automatically but
without really hearing them. Much as he loved his
mother and wanted to support her, he couldn't help
but wish he were in Jesse's apartment, snuggled on the
big sofa, watching the game. And maybe kissing him.

Damn, Jesse was a fine kisser. Dash's lips still tingled from their session in the kitchen.

"Dash, don't you think so?" Drita's dark eyes narrowed. "You aren't even paying attention."

"I'm sorry. What did I miss?"

"I *said* Mama needs a good lawyer. And quick. We
can't let that man get away with dumping her."

That brought his attention back to the present
company. "I have someone for you." The words came
out before Dash even thought about it. Before tonight,
he hadn't made up his mind to accept Jesse's offer to
speak to Harry, but he knew now he would.

"You do? Who?"

"This guy I'm friendly with at work—Jesse—his

stepfather was a big divorce lawyer. When I told him what happened, he offered to speak to him for us."

"Oh, really?" Hope kindled in his mother's eyes, then faded. "I don't have money for a big lawyer."

"I think we should hear what he has to say. Maybe he can refer someone to us who won't be so expensive."

"Who's this Jesse person?" Drita asked, giving him a thorough once-over.

"That's the man who gave me the beautiful present for making lunch, right?" At his nod, his mother's eyes warmed. "Now will you admit he's more than just a friend? Am I right?"

"Who is this? Are you dating him?" Drita knocked his elbow. "Why're you being so secretive?"

Because they were so close in age—less than two years apart—Dash had naturally gravitated toward his sister for personal advice when he was younger. Unfortunately, she didn't understand boundaries too well—or chose to ignore them, as he suspected—and was constantly pestering him to talk about the men he dated.

"I'm not. Stop. We're just friends. And yes, Jesse is that man, *Nënë*."

"It's very nice of him to offer. Why don't you bring him for dinner sometime? I'd love to meet him."

This was what Dash feared. He couldn't tell his family about Jesse's issues. It would betray the trust building between the two of them.

"I will, but he's been very busy lately." That excuse would work. It would have to.

"Well, I'll need to thank him if I end up hiring his

lawyer. And I still want to meet him soon. He seems to have become very important to you. Which makes him important to me."

"To both of us," Drita added.

Later that evening at home, he turned on the Yankee game. They were winning, and he texted Jesse.

Good game? I just got home.

Yeah. How was dinner?

Good.

He hesitated a moment before sending the next text, but he knew his mother wouldn't stop asking.

My mother wants to meet you. She's interested in talking to your stepfather.

The Yankees scored again while Dash waited for an answer.

Would she come to me? I can ask Harry to come over.

I can ask.

It had been a very long time since his mother left the Bronx, but he'd make sure to go with her.

Okay. BTW, I talked to Miranda. She heard us.

I guessed. Embarrassment and shame washed over Dash, turning him first hot, then cold. *Shit.*

It's ok. We talked and it's all good.

Maybe for you. I can't look her in the face now.

Recalling the sounds he made from the feel of Jesse's mouth on his dick, Dash wanted to die.

Seriously, it's fine. So I'll see you Sunday?

Yeah. Gonna do some homework tonight so I can be free for the rest of the weekend.

K. See you Sunday. Come anytime. Game starts at 4:30.

See you then.

He clicked off and lowered the volume on the game, then pulled out his computer and spent the next two hours working on homework for his auditing and management classes. The last thing he wanted on Sunday was to have assignments hanging over his head. Sunday night would be all about being with Jesse.

And the game, of course.

✧ ✧ ✧ ✧

"COME ON IN."

Jesse held the door open wide, and Dash passed by him, catching a whiff of his fresh, soapy-clean scent, as if he'd stepped out of a shower only moments before. It was hard enough to keep a lid on his self-control during the day when he could only see Jesse for a limited time. Having the entire evening, and if he chose, the whole night to spend with him, put Dash into a bit of a tailspin.

Everything about Jesse pushed his buttons. His flushed, pale skin, the gleam in his wide eyes, the curve of his full mouth, all turned Dash on. Normally when he met a guy at a club, he was the passive one. He never got down on his knees for anyone, yet with Jesse, he wanted to give rather than take.

They stood in the foyer, both a bit self-conscious, as if they realized the world of possibilities that lay ahead for the evening.

Dash had gotten odd looks from the staff when he came in, but when asked why he was at the Dakota off-shift, he'd only mentioned having some things to take care of. Hopefully they would assume it was to do off-the-books work for residents. If they wanted to talk among themselves, they would, and most likely did.

"Are you hungry?" Jesse bounced on the balls of his feet. "This time I ordered food in, so we won't have to be interrupted to heat things up."

"Good thinking." Dash planned on heating things up outside of the kitchen. "What did you get?"

"Oh, besides wings, I got hero sandwiches. I got roast beef, turkey, this thing they call The Monster, which is like six different kinds of meats and cheeses with all these toppings. Plus coleslaw and fries."

"Sounds great." He rubbed his stomach and saw Jesse's eyes follow his hand.

"I have the drinks set up, and the pregame is about to start."

Both of them were so wound up and tense, if they did have sex, they might burn the place to ashes. Jesse's pink-tinged cheeks and breathless voice weren't a surprise. He'd let Jesse decide how far they'd go. There'd be no regrets in the morning from either one.

"Sounds good. Lead the way."

He trailed behind Jesse, and they made themselves comfortable on the sofa, cracking open beers and munching on chips. The commentators were spouting off some nonsense, and Jesse set his beer down.

"So, your mom wants to meet Harry? That's great."

"Yeah, but I still don't know how I feel about taking charity."

Bristling, Jesse folded his arms. "It's not charity. Harry is retired and doesn't need the money. Trust me. He'll do it because he's always been involved in pro-bono work."

"What's that? Pro bono?"

"It means doing work for people who can't afford to pay."

Dash's mouth stretched thin. "So like I said. Charity."

"Our country was formed on the foundation that all people are created equal, and they should all have equal opportunity and access."

"But you know it doesn't work like that. You may not have been outside the walls of this building for some time, but you've seen what's happened over the past years, am I right?"

"Yeah, of course I have. And I know that for every step we take, there's two or three or ten backward. That's why it's more important than ever to give everybody equal footing. Your mother deserves to be taken care of for all the years she put her own life aside to take care of her children and husband. So if someone is offering her help, why shouldn't she take it? Pride should never stand in the way of common sense."

Jesse's chest heaved, and fire sparked in his eyes. *Damn.* The more he spoke, the sexier he got, and the more turned on Dash became. His dick swelled, and his breathing grew short. Forcing himself to think of something, *anything*, other than stripping Jesse naked and sliding inside him, Dash grabbed a sandwich and shoved it in his mouth, taking a huge bite.

"Good," he said in a garbled voice around the food. He chewed and swallowed. "Maybe you're right."

"I know I am. We can call him later, and you can talk to him if that would make you feel better." Taking his own sandwich, Jesse placed it on a plate, then took a few wings as well. From beneath lowered lids, Dash watched him nibble the sticky flesh off the bone, then lick his fingers. Like a voyeur, he was incapable of looking away. Everything the man did was sexy, from the way he bit the meat off the bone to how his tongue, so soft and pink, swept over his lips.

"Um, yeah." He took another bite of the sandwich. Damn, it was going to be a long night. "Sure. Sounds good."

"Oh, and before the game starts, I have something for you." Jesse bounced off the sofa. "Be right back." Bemused, Dash waited, his brows raised when Jesse showed up with a big box in his arms. "Here. I got this for you."

"Okay…" He took the box from Jesse and opened it, his eyes growing wide when he saw what was inside. "What? Why did you get this?" He pulled out a leather jacket, so soft and supple, it felt like silk. He saw the label and almost dropped it, afraid to damage it.

"Don't you like it?"

Annoyance bubbled up inside Dash. "I can't accept this. It's too expensive."

"It would look great on you. And think of it as an investment. You'd never have to buy another leather jacket again."

Keeping his patience under control, Dash folded the jacket up and put it back in the box on his lap. "A house is an investment. Not a leather jacket that probably cost more than I pay in rent each month. Thanks, but I've never had a leather jacket, so I don't need one now, especially a Fendi one."

"It's not a big deal."

Incredible that Jesse didn't understand. "Babe. It is to me. I can't."

"I just wanted to show you how much I care. Understand me. It's not like I'm trying to buy you or shove my money in your face. This is how I've always been. I don't know any other way, so don't think badly of me. I'm doing it because I like you and you'd look great in it." His big eyes pleaded, and Dash, despite himself, couldn't help but run his hands over the leather.

"You don't have to buy me things to show me you care."

"I can't take you out to dinner or the movies. Let me give you this, at least." The game started. "How about we leave it? You don't decide until you have to go?"

"Okay." Dash put the box aside, and they got caught up in the action as the Twins immediately hit two home runs, putting the Yankees in the hole. After the second inning, it was tied, and it stayed that way until the top of the ninth. Minnesota was threatening. Jesse handed him another beer, never taking his eyes off the screen. The bases were loaded, and it was two outs. If the Yankees won this game, they'd move into first place in the American League East. At this point in the season, every game was crucial.

"Don't walk him, don't walk him." Jesse moved to the edge of the sofa.

The count was three and two. Dash set his can

down and balled his hands into fists, shifting closer to Jesse. "Come on, over the plate. Strike him out." He leaned forward as the pitcher wound up and threw the ball.

The player at bat swung and missed, and the crowd erupted in cheers.

"Yeah! Yeah! That's what I'm talking about."

"All right!" Jesse whooped and fist-pumped.

They exchanged high fives that somehow ended up with their arms around each other, lips locked together in a frantic, desperate kiss as they rolled on the sofa.

"Jesseeee," Dash moaned, his hands diving into the waistband of Jesse's sweats, brushing the satin-smooth, heated skin.

"Yeah, oh God, please."

Dash drank in the sight of Jesse over him, still disbelieving he was here, free to kiss and touch. Jesse's breath came in hot, heavy pants, his hair lay in messy waves over his brow, and his swollen lips gleamed red.

"Are you sure?" His dick swelled at the jerk of the thick bulge in Jesse's sweats.

At Jesse's nod, Dash grabbed him by the neck and pulled him down. His tongue swept inside Jesse's mouth, tasting, probing, *claiming* him. He dug his fingers hard into Jesse's shoulder, and the thought of marks on that pale skin, marks that he might feel and think of for days, sent a shiver of pleasure through him. Jesse moaned into his mouth, his body vibrating and writhing, and Dash had never felt so desired. Blood rushed to his groin as he thought of being inside Jesse's beautiful body.

"Jesse...I want you so much. I dream about you, can barely eat. I can't think about anything else." As he spoke, he cupped Jesse's crotch, trailing his fingers down the thick ridge of his cock. God, the man was on fire. Dash wanted Jesse's hot skin on his, and it took all his willpower not to take what he wanted right then. But he needed that signal from Jesse, so he waited, his hand slowly rubbing Jesse's erection through his increasingly damp sweats.

"Me too. I need you, Dash." A bit hesitant, Jesse pressed against the zipper of his jeans, and his fingers circled around the button of the fly. "Let's go to the bedroom." He turned off the game and stood, swaying.

Drunk on the passion coursing through his blood, Dash let himself be led through the spacious apartment to Jesse's hushed bedroom. The king-sized bed looked cool and inviting with its dark-red comforter and white, white sheets. When Jesse began to undress, Dash awoke from his stupor and pulled Jesse to him.

"Let me." Dash slipped the T-shirt over Jesse's head, then kissed down the madly pulsing vein along the side of his neck. "So perfect." They tumbled to the bed, holding fast to each other. The curve of Jesse's shoulder begged for his mouth, and Dash couldn't stop nibbling and sucking at the tender skin. He moved down to the flat, brown nipples of Jesse's smooth chest and sucked at the tight points, first the left, then the right, flicking and mouthing each one, back and forth, until Jesse lay squirming and thrashing beneath him.

"Dash, *Dash*."

A thrill of pride swept through him. None of his

previous lovers had ever called out for him. They'd get down to business, and while the sex was good, he'd never had this hunger, this desperate need to be with anyone.

He hooked his fingers in Jesse's sweats, catching his boxers, and pulled both down in one swift move. Jesse's erection bobbed before him, rising up against his sleek abdomen. Dash's fingers shook with unexpected nerves as he undid his own jeans, and in a minute he was as naked as Jesse. He joined him on the bed, and the wonderful friction of their cocks sliding together nearly made him lose the tenuous grip he held on his desire.

"Please tell me you have lube and condoms."

Jesse smiled. "I have lube and condoms. In the drawer next to the bed. I got them yesterday…hoping." His already pink face flushed even brighter.

"You went out?" A thought hit Dash after he got the bottle and tore off a condom from the strip, and he turned hot, then cold. "Don't say Miranda got them, please God, no."

Shaking with laughter, Jesse slid his hands over Dash's shoulders. "No. That's the beauty of the Internet. You can get anything delivered." His eyes crinkled with amusement. "But you should see the ads I'm getting now on my feed for sex toys and all sorts of other things I've never heard of."

Reassured, Dash resumed his exploration of Jesse's body, his lips tracing every freckle dotting the quivering skin of his stomach. "I'm happy to explore those with you if you want." Dash licked at the springy dark-blond hair of Jesse's groin, learning his taste, immersing himself in the scent of everything Jesse Grace-Martin.

"I want you. I don't need anything else to make me feel good."

The sweet sincerity in Jesse's words caught him off guard. He wasn't used to this closeness. This sharing. He liked it.

"How long has it been?" he asked, slipping his finger between the cheeks of Jesse's ass. He teased at Jesse's opening, and without even looking, Dash knew he'd be tight. His cock swelled at the thought of all that heat clenching his dick, and he grew impossibly harder.

Avoiding his eyes, Jesse answered, "Five years. And Sean was the only guy I've ever been with, so..." The red stain of embarrassment crawled up his neck.

"Hey, I'm not judging you. I need to make you ready for me." He kissed the silky head of Jesse's cock, licking at the sharp, salty taste of his precome. "I don't want to hurt you."

Sighing with obvious pleasure, Jesse's hungry gaze devoured him. "Yeah. You're big. Much bigger than Sean."

Inordinately pleased by that, Dash slicked his fingers with lube and pushed Jesse's legs apart. As predicted, his pink hole was small, but so damn pretty, Dash couldn't help but sigh. He circled the rim with one finger, and Jesse whimpered and shifted beneath him.

"Oh..."

Encouraged, Dash slid inside, the simmering heat even better than anticipated, and he struggled to hold himself in check. All he wanted was to fling Jesse's legs over his shoulders and plow into him. Instead, he set his jaw and worked his finger all the way inside until he brushed the spot he was looking for. He rubbed his finger against it, and Jesse almost flew off the bed.

"Fuck, oh my God…"

"Feels good, huh?" Dash chuckled and tried to add a second finger, but it was tight going. His patience was soon rewarded as Jesse worked himself on Dash's hand while he fisted the bedsheets and panted out his pleasure.

"More. Not enough. I need…oh, God. Need you. Please."

Dash withdrew his fingers and rolled the condom on. "I gotta go slow. Don't want to hurt you."

Jesse licked his lips, his gaze disarmingly clear, and said, "I don't think you could ever hurt me."

Those words of trust etched themselves on Dash's heart. "I'm trying not to." He kissed the jut of Jesse's hip bone. "I want to make you feel good."

Dash pushed inside Jesse, and as expected, Jesse was so snug, it took a while to breach past his entrance. Dash held on to Jesse's hip, and inch by inch buried himself deep, feeling Jesse's body opening to accept him, then grasping him so tight, he became a part of Jesse. Their flesh bonded, Jesse's passage clenched around his cock, and Dash lost sight of who he was. In Jesse's eyes, Dash saw the reflection of his own confusion and wonder, and he touched Jesse's face to prove this was real and not a dream.

Dash rocked in shallow thrusts so as not to hurt Jesse, but his lover surprised him by tilting his hips and encouraging him. "More." Jesse rose up to meet him. "Dash, please. Want to feel you. Need it."

Seeing the unfocused expression of lust in Jesse's eyes, Dash let go, slamming into Jesse hard, his pumping hips unrelenting. Mystified that this special man trusted him, Dash needed the reassurance that he wasn't wrong about this strange yet beautiful connection between them. He'd never had much faith in the heart. It was why he preferred the cold truth of numbers, but there was nothing cold about Jesse. He was all sunlight and warmth, and his sweetness poured over Dash like a summer shower.

"You want me?"

Sex had become so much a mere physical release for him that Dash was caught by surprise when Jesse arched up against him, seeking a kiss, his breathless whispers sparking tingles down Dash's spine.

"Yeah. So much."

They met in a wet, hungry kiss, all sliding lips and tongues and teeth. Jesse's cock thrust up between them, and with his hand over Jesse's, they both stroked him to orgasm. Jesse came on a choked cry, spilling over their hands, shuddering hard, clasping Dash's cock so firmly inside his body, it caught Dash by surprise, his orgasm sweeping through him like a wildfire to dry brush, uncontainable and out of control.

Too choked up to speak, Dash held on to Jesse as he came in bursts of hot, hard pleasure, and when he relaxed and awoke from his drowsy stupor, they remained plastered together by sweat, Jesse's arms still holding him tight.

"You're amazing," Dash whispered, out of strength to do anything but move his lips.

Jesse held him closer. "You're more than I'd ever imagined."

With reluctance, he slipped out of Jesse and took off the condom, tied it, and tossed it into the wastebasket. Through dreamy eyes, Jesse gazed up at him. "Are you staying?"

Dash studied him. What was he really doing here? He remembered watching movies about the rich guy sleeping with the housekeeper, or the wealthy woman having an affair with the young pool guy, and snorted at the obvious stupidity of the situation. And yet here he stood, the porter sleeping with the trust-fund baby. And then he remembered the leather jacket. He hated disappointing Jesse—he meant well, after all—but if he accepted it, wasn't that giving in to everything he refused to be? On the other hand, if he didn't, he'd hurt Jesse's feelings, and he didn't want to do that. He could take it and only wear it on special occasions. It wasn't an ideal situation for sure...

But, he reasoned as he slid back into the warmth of Jesse's arms, he was smart. He knew the score. He wasn't going to fall in love. They'd have their fun until it ended, like it always did, and then he'd walk away. Half in the throes of sleep, Jesse nestled against him, his breath soft against Dash's cheek, and Dash pulled him closer, wrapping his arms around him.

"Yeah. I'm staying."

Chapter Fifteen

L IGHT FILTERED IN beneath his closed eyes, and Jesse groaned, then stretched. An unfamiliar soreness in his ass had him wincing, but he couldn't help smiling.

Dash.

He rolled over to give him a proper good-morning but found instead an empty bed, the sheets cool to his touch when he smoothed his hand over the space. A note lay on the pillow: *Had to get up for my shift. Talk to you later, I hope.*

Well, there went his plans. Frustrated that he'd slept so deeply, he hadn't woken to say good-bye to Dash, Jesse rolled over, hugging Dash's pillow to him like a lovesick teenager. The illuminated dial read 8:10, which meant he needed to get up, shower, and dress before Miranda arrived. Today was a business day, when they'd go over all his accounts and paperwork, file his estimated taxes, and all the other distasteful things he hated.

One last sniff of the sheets to take in Dash's scent and then Jesse jumped out of bed, ignoring the ache rolling through his extremities. He lingered in the shower, running his hands over the sore spots on his body, touching the finger marks that had blossomed on his hips overnight. He recalled Dash's intensity as he pounded into him, and his breath grew short.

God, I want him.

Not only for sex, Jesse contemplated as he dried off and dressed, forgoing shaving for the day. He enjoyed Dash's dry wit and laughter too.

He walked into the living room and peered out the window, and seeing as it was another bright sunny day, he thought he might once again go out to the courtyard for a walk. Yes. He would. It had to become part of a natural routine, one that would lead him to the outside. His heart kicked up at the thought, but he wouldn't let it suffocate him. Not anymore.

The coffee had dripped its last into the pot when Miranda opened the front door. "Jess?"

"In the kitchen. Coffee's ready."

Her heels tapped on the wooden floors, and he smiled when she came in with a bag in hand.

"Bagels, I hope?"

"Of course. We'll need fortification for all the dull paperwork today."

He made a sound of disgust around the rim of his cup. "I know. But I want to make time to go outside today, do another stint around the courtyard. It's important for my recovery to keep it up."

She dropped the bag on the island and gave him a hug. "You don't know how long I've waited to hear you say that word. Recovery. It means you're moving forward."

"I don't want to go back to being that scared man anymore."

"You won't."

He let her go and turned around to surreptitiously wipe the wetness from his lashes. "I can't say for sure. But I do know I'm so much better now. The nightmares of being chased and attacked have petered out to only once a month or six weeks rather than every other day." It was rude to stand with his back to her, so he faced Miranda again and picked up his coffee. The smell of the everything bagels she'd brought hit him, and his stomach growled.

Miranda gazed at him with fondness. "I don't care what you say. I see the difference." She poured herself a cup. "Would it have anything to do with a good looking handyman I saw this morning?"

His cheeks heated at her casual question, but he faced her squarely. "No and yes. I was anxious to do this before I even knew Dash. Remember, the first time I met him I was already outside in the courtyard. I'd made the decision to move forward before knowing him. But I won't deny I might be pushing myself a little harder because of the time I've spent with him."

Nodding with approval, Miranda nudged his shoulder. "I can't say I blame you. He's pretty hot. He's got that big, dark, and muscled look."

Shocked, Jesse stared at her. "Miranda."

"What? You think because I'm over fifty, I'm dead?" She snorted. "I'm not blind. I know a hottie when I see one."

"Who are you, and where is the Miranda I've

known for the past five years?"

"Oh, honey, it's always been me." She pushed a plate with a bagel in front of him. "It's just that you haven't been you. Until now." She winked. "Until Dash."

To hide his embarrassment, Jesse shoved half a bagel in his mouth and chewed. "Let's get this stuff started," he mumbled, but he couldn't deny the sizzle in his blood at the thought of seeing Dash this morning. Everything had changed, at least for him. He had no idea about Dash.

✧　✧　✧　✧

"OH, IT'S EVEN nicer today than yesterday. You didn't go outside at all, did you?"

They sat on a bench in the courtyard, watching the cars and taxis pull in and out. The Dakota was strict about enforcing the rule that cars could only stand for a maximum of ten minutes inside. After that, the doormen would tell them to move along, and if they refused, they called the police. People rarely violated the rules.

"No." Ashamed, he faced away from Miranda. "I should be at the point where I could, but..." He shrugged and peered closer at a group of men walking toward them, carrying hoses and cleaning material. Dash was in the center, talking with the person next to him and laughing. He looked impossibly handsome, and with his sleek, dark looks and rippling muscles, he could've been a model.

"It'll happen." Miranda gave him a quick hug. "I'm not worried."

Jesse sneaked occasional glances over to where Dash and another worker were cleaning the mess pigeons had left on the walkway. The muscles in his powerful arms flexed as he scrubbed, and Jesse shivered, recalling how hard Dash fucked him last night and how much he loved it. Dash glanced over his shoulder, and Jesse caught his breath, the dark intensity of Dash's gaze sucking him in.

For a moment, the world slipped away to when Dash had pushed inside him, rocking Jesse to his deepest. Peace, the kind he hadn't known since before his father died, had descended on him, and Jesse wished they could've stayed like that forever, with Dash holding him as if he was something precious instead of the mess of a man he truly was.

"Let's finish up this part. I'm glad you suggested coming out here to run these numbers. It's gorgeous." Jesse tapped on his iPad to wake the screen, and his expenses popped up. "I have all my receipts here."

Acting as if she hadn't heard him, Miranda set her iPad aside. "What was that about?"

"What?" His brow wrinkled.

"Are you kidding? The way Dash looked at you would've set a house on fire. I almost needed him to turn that hose on me to cool down."

Face burning, Jesse ducked his head. "I am so not talking about this with you."

"So there is something going on. I thought so when I went into the television room and saw food and stuff left over. Did you have a visitor last night?"

Damn. They'd gotten so caught up, he totally forgot about the food. "Uh, yeah. Dash came to watch the game." Unable to concentrate on the screen, Jesse set the iPad aside on the bench.

"That's good."

When she didn't elaborate, Jesse gave her a wry smile. "You have other questions, I presume?"

"A million," she said cheerfully. "But I don't plan on pushing. You're an over thirty-year-old independent man, Jesse. You don't need to answer to me or anyone for your personal life."

"I don't feel very independent, that's for sure." He propped his hands under his chin, scanning the area. As much as his apartment had become his prison for the past five years, he'd now simply replaced it with this courtyard. The sounds of the city filtered in, and he looked up at the birds flying in the endless blue sky, wishing he were one of them. Able to pick up and soar.

"You'll do it when it feels right."

"I think," he said and stood, causing Miranda to gape at him, "that time may be now. Stay here, please. I have to try on my own." With a long, confident stride to hide his terror, Jesse walked to the front of the courtyard and stood by the glassed-in security booth under the arch. The Dakota was so sensitive and concerned about its residents' privacy, they had a second security booth installed inside the courtyard. The guard side-eyed him with raised brows for a moment, then gave a genuine smile.

"Jesse...uh, I mean, Mr. Grace-Martin. Good to

see you."

Heart pounding and palms sweating, Jesse leaned against the booth to catch his breath. "Hi, Sergio. Please. No one calls me that. I'm Jesse."

Mr. Grace-Martin would always be his father, and Jesse hadn't yet reached the point in his life where he felt comfortable enough to be addressed as such.

"Okay, well, it's good to see you."

Sergio had aged quite a bit since he'd seen him. Jesse recalled his son, Sergio Junior, had been sick last year, and the building had taken up a collection to help with his medical care. "How're you doing? How's S.J.?"

Sergio raised his eyes to the sky. "Thank God. We're okay. Doing better."

"I'm glad."

"You doing better? I can't tell you how good it is to see you out here again. You were always so friendly and nice to all of us."

Touched, Jesse hadn't realized anyone noticed. "That means a lot to me."

A burly man in a uniform approached, and Jesse stepped back, his heart racing. He wasn't used to having a stranger this close to him, and he was happy to have the sturdiness of the security booth to keep him upright.

Perhaps sensing his unease—though more likely it was the fact that Jesse looked like a frightened deer—Sergio stepped out from the booth.

"That's Ricardo, my replacement. It's time for my break."

Feeling a bit foolish, Jesse mustered a faint smile.

"Oh. Thanks."

Sergio nodded to Ricardo as he came within range. "Hey, Ricky. This is Jesse Grace-Martin. He lives in apartment 70."

"Hello, sir."

"H-hi."

Every instinct in him was screaming: *Run, hide, you're going to get hurt*, but he struggled hard to maintain his upright position, ignoring the sweat running down his back.

"Can I help?"

Jesse sensed Dash before he saw him, and as if his body recognized a friend, the air seemed clearer and it was easier for him to breathe.

"Hi." He swayed toward Dash, who stood at his shoulder so Jesse could lean on him. He licked his dry lips, and the words burst free. "I, um, was talking to Sergio and...I thought I'd walk to the street. Maybe not to walk, but just to stand by the entrance and..." He broke off, ashamed at his babbling.

"And I think that's great. Lucky for me, it's my break time. Would you want some company?"

More welcome words had never been heard. But Jesse didn't want a babysitter. He needed a friend. "I'm okay," he said, tipping his chin up, hoping to convey to Dash that he was fine but still wanted his support. "I mean, yes, some company would be great."

"I'm sure the guys in the front will love you hanging around out there," Dash said with a snicker, and then his eyes softened and he lowered his voice. "Are you really ready to do this?"

No. I'm scared. But I'm all out of options.

With a sickly smile, he nodded. "I need to."

He found it difficult to convey his emotions even without his precarious mental state. He doubted he'd ever get over the devastating loss of his father, but the joy he remembered them sharing—sledding in the park, ice-cream cones in the summer, and best of all, their Yankee games—weighed heavily on him now. He'd lost so many years to fear. Time to start learning how to live again.

"Then let's do it."

Standing close enough that their shoulders overlapped and Jesse could lean on Dash if he so chose, they walked together through the high-arched entranceway of the Dakota. Jesse appreciated the silence, and that even though 72nd Street and all its crowds were only steps away, it was as if he and Dash were the only two people around.

"I'm sorry I left without waking you," Dash murmured. "You were sleeping so soundly, I didn't have the heart."

"It's okay. I-I had a great time last night."

"Me too. It was a great game."

Darting a quick glance at Dash's profile, Jesse saw his dark eyes alive with laughter.

Okay, buddy. Two can play that game.

"Yeah. It was definitely the highlight of my night." He smirked at Dash, who stopped walking.

"Not mine. Not by a long shot. Wanna know what was?"

The laughter had been replaced with heat, Dash's

eyes catching Jesse in their smoldering depths. Breathless and turned on, Jesse nodded.

"Being inside you. Hearing you call my name when you wrapped those long legs around me and I fucked you so hard, I saw stars."

Jesse panted, his gaze focused on Dash's mouth as he spoke.

As if he could read Jesse's mind, Dash licked his lips. "I wish I could kiss you, or at least touch you, but instead I'm gonna settle for walking with you and standing by the gate."

"Thanks," Jesse said, a bit shaky. "I need you there. I know it makes me weak, but…"

"No." Dash shook his head emphatically. "Don't even think that. Ever. You're so damn strong for doing this. I feel lucky that you trust me to be here for you."

"Of course I trust you. Especially after last night." Jesse wondered if Dash understood the double meaning behind his words. Not only had they had sex, but Dash had gotten inside his heart. "Okay, I'm ready now." He clenched his teeth so hard, he hoped they wouldn't break.

With Dash solid and comforting beside him, the looming presence of the outside seemed less threatening, and Jesse straightened his shoulders and pushed forward. Dash stood close enough that Jesse could feel his heat and smell the scent of his shampoo, which he realized was his own, and a flood of warmth rushed through him.

Three more steps and they were at the front, and for the first time in half a decade, Jesse stepped onto the sidewalk of 72nd Street. His eyes widened at the crowds, but then he remembered how the gates themselves had become a tourist attraction since the day John Lennon was killed right where he stood.

Too many people. So much empty space. Fear crawled up his arms, and he hugged himself. Strangers rushing by stared at him. Did he look as sick as he felt inside? As pathetic and helpless? All his hopes for an easy transition to normalcy faded, and he struggled to draw a breath. The edges of his vision darkened.

"It's lunchtime," Dash said in his ear. "Tons of people are out. Let's go stand over here by the security booth."

Jesse allowed himself to be led to the side, past the security guard, who didn't blink an eye, as if it was an everyday occurrence for a pale, sweating man to emerge from the Dakota and need help to walk four steps. All the self-confidence he'd built inside began to crumble as his legs shook.

"Here," Dash said gently. "Let's lean against the wall. You can hold on to the booth if it helps."

The Dakota's security booth had been a dingy rectangular compartment the last time Jesse had been outside. From his apartment, he'd watched the scaffolding go up and then come down around the building, but it hadn't meant anything to him. He hadn't figured on ever seeing the outside again.

Now, though, he saw how the booth's original bronze shone bright in the sunlight. Its surface, warmed from the sun's rays, was smooth to the touch as he placed his hand on it to steady himself. Sweat trickled down his back, but it wasn't from the balmy temperature of a perfect fall day. It was the sheer terror of exposure.

He reached the wall, and though he trembled and knew people slanted those questioning, pitying glances at him as they raced by—*What's wrong with him, do you think? I wonder if he's on drugs?*—he was seized with an overwhelming sense of accomplishment.

He'd done it. It had taken five years, from the time he was attacked and brought home from the hospital to this moment, but he'd done it. He made it outside. Walked through the black wrought-iron gates, past the blue-uniformed guards, to stand with his feet on the sidewalk and his face to the sun.

"Jesse."

He watched Miranda hurry toward him, conflicting emotions of worry and pride evident on her face, and braced himself for the inevitable third, fourth, and fifth degree.

"Hi." The rough stone of the wall dug into his back, but he didn't mind. He didn't mind anything today. Hell, as hot as it was, he wouldn't even have minded a smelly garbage truck rolling on by to catch a whiff of its long-forgotten odor.

"Are you okay? I couldn't believe it when I saw you walk outside. I thought you only meant to speak to the security guards, not go outside the gates. Is it too much for you?"

Dash hovered by his side, silent but protective.

"I-I don't think so." Jesse cleared his throat, hating how choked up and weak he sounded. Didn't this mean he should be stronger now?

"You should've told me you were going to do this. I know you want to prove something to yourself, but what if you had a panic attack?"

"Then I'd be there for him."

A fluttery thrill ran through Jesse at Dash's words. "Miranda, I know you're worried, and I love that you're concerned for me. But I had to try. To see if I could do it. And I did."

Their little crowd stood only a few feet from the guards at the gate, and Jesse could only imagine what they were thinking behind their stoic expressions. But the longer he remained outside the gates, focused and aware, the wind in his face and Miranda and Dash beside him, the more Jesse believed the world was his.

"I know." Tears welled in her eyes. "I'm happy and scared for you. It's what we've been waiting for all these years, and yet now that it's here, I'm terrified for you."

"I'm here, out on 72nd Street, and I'm okay. Not great. Shaky and kind of nauseated, but standing." He squared his shoulders. "And yeah, I might be scared shitless, and my nerves are all twitchy. I'm on a tightrope, waiting to fall, unsure if that safety net will hold me or if I'll go crashing through. But knowing I have good friends and people in my life means my safety net is secure. And I think it also means it's time for me to push myself to try harder. Test my limits."

Dash brushed against him, the strength of his presence a force for him to cling to. It wasn't that he needed Dash to make the change in his life, but knowing he had someone besides Miranda to be there for him gave him fresh hope.

Warm, rough fingers laced with his and gave a squeeze. "You got this, Jesse. You're strong, man. You're one of the strongest people I know."

Funny. He didn't feel so strong. "How so? I'm standing here in a pool of sweat, and my heart's about to pound through my chest. I want to walk, but my legs feel like lead."

And yet...the sound of a bird chirping from one of the overhead porticos, the traffic noise, and even the smell of grease from the hot-dog stands on the corner were as new to him as if he were a baby taking his first steps. The sight of Central Park across the street, so fresh and alive, set off a yearning inside him for those days when he could simply wander over its green expanse, finding beauty in the flutter of a butterfly's wings.

"Because you're doing this on your own. You know yourself, and you're breaking free. You're making the choice now, not letting your mind lock you up tight anymore."

"You have a lot of faith in me."

"We both do," Dash said with a nod to Miranda. "I may not have known you that long, but we're close enough that I think I know you pretty well."

A faint blush tinted Dash's cheeks, and Jesse's face warmed as well, knowing they were both thinking of their incredible night together.

"Yeah, you do," he said softly.

"So take it slow, but don't give up. You've got me and Miranda here to help."

"Dash is right. There's no timeline you need to follow."

"I...I just want to be happy again. And that means one step at a time, but I think I'm on the right track. As I see it, I can allow this to continue to hijack my life...or I can fight it. For five years it's stolen my freedom, but I won't let it steal my heart...my breath...my soul. I can't allow it to take that away from me. If that happens, I might as well give it all up."

"Don't say that, please, Jesse." Tears streaked down Miranda's cheeks.

"I told you," Dash said with another squeeze to his hand. "You're the strongest person I know."

Without a doubt, Jesse knew that this man, whether as friend or lover, was part of his recovery. When you've lived only in darkness, you could choose to either fear the light or embrace it. Jesse was finally ready to accept his light.

Chapter Sixteen

GROANING, DASH FLOPPED down on his bed. With his classwork done for the night, he glanced at the clock and winced at the glowing numbers. After midnight. He should've been asleep an hour ago, but that last coffee at eight p.m. now raced through his bloodstream. The seven a.m. shift he'd chosen was going to be damn hard to get up for, but it was his fault. He wanted it so he could spend the evening with Jesse, but more importantly, tonight was the big meeting with Harry, so after his shift ended, Dash had to go back uptown and bring his mother over to the Dakota, to Jesse's apartment.

Jesse.

The thought of him brought a smile to Dash's face, and he rolled over, hugging his pillow close. Like he was a high-school kid again with a crush on someone, he wondered what Jesse was doing now, and even though it was late, Dash messaged him.

Hey.

Immediately, Jesse responded: *Hey. What's up? Looking forward to meeting your mom.*

Tomorrow—actually, today—Jesse would be meeting his mom, and Harry would listen to her story. A battalion of nerves marched through him.

Yeah. Um, is your mom going to be there too?

No. It's...complicated. As much as I can't leave the apartment, she finds it hard to be here.

Dash could understand. Jesse had mentioned his parents had lived there from when they first married. Her whole life with Jesse's father was within that apartment. The memories could be overwhelming.

Okay. I'd better get some sleep. See you later.

K. Nite. It was nice to talk to you.

Warmth settled low in his stomach, and he wondered what it would be like to lie next to Jesse every night. He sighed and punched in the thumbs-up emoji, then tossed the phone aside. Now more than ever, he needed to do well in school and not become sidetracked by anything else. If he could land a good job, one that would let him give up the job as a porter and pay him well enough to take Jesse out to nice places, Dash would feel more comfortable to even think about a relationship. The way things stood now, Jesse had spent all the money whenever Dash had come over, and it made him uneasy. Every time he pointed it out, Jesse blew him off, saying it didn't matter, but Dash knew the gulf between them yawned wide and endless. He needed to close the gap. For his own pride.

He turned over and closed his eyes.

DASH HAD TO temper his annoyance as he and his mother entered the car Jesse had sent for them. He shot Jesse a text that he could've taken a Lyft. It bugged him that Jesse simply made the arrangements without asking.

Next time let me call the car, please?

I'm sorry. The car is from Harry's firm, so I didn't think anything of it.

That was the problem. Jesse didn't think it meant anything. Dash concentrated on his mother, who asked him for the tenth time, "Are you sure I look okay?"

"Mom, you're beautiful. And Jesse's stepfather isn't interested in what you look like anyway. You're there to talk to him about the divorce."

The dark fringes of her lashes swept against her cheeks. "Never in a million years would I think your father would do this to me."

The last thing Dash wanted to do was argue with his mother, so out of respect he remained silent, even though he wanted to call bullshit on what she said. From his earliest memory, Dash had never connected with his father. There had always been something cold and distant about him. Even at birthday parties he remained on the sidelines, only posing for family pictures when pushed.

"When did he change?"

Hard as it must've been to admit, his mother faced him squarely. "He never did. He was always a bit distant. But I was taught growing up not to think about such things. Have my children and accept that he was the man, and as long as he provided, I should be grateful."

Infuriated, Dash let his temper show. "That's garbage. You deserve more than that. You should've left him a long time ago."

A gentle smile touched her lips as she regarded him with love. "Where would I go, Dashamir? I had two small children and no education. When we got married, I believed in his stories. He'd tell me how he'd make enough money to buy a big house and we'd have anything we wanted. He was so handsome, so forceful. I loved listening to him, and I believed him. At that time I believed anything. Then we left Albania and came here. I had you and Drita and never saw him. He worked such long hours. We grew distant."

"He never bothered. It was always about money. Or being with his friends. He never put us first."

"Maybe I should've done more. But this? Leaving me for a woman younger than his daughter and having a child with her?" Her laced fingers tightened until they turned white. "I don't know what to say."

"I do," Dash said, visions of beating his father to a pulp playing in his head. "But I'll keep it to myself."

"Dashamir, please." She shot him a reproachful look. "Tell me more about Jesse. You're good friends? Yes?"

Good friends? That was one way to describe it. They might not have had sex since that first time after the game when he'd stayed the night, but in the weeks that followed, there had been some heavy make-out sessions when he'd managed to schedule his lunch break to coincide with Jesse's. During those times, Miranda had tactfully left them alone. Sometimes Jesse would greet him at the door, pull him inside with an eager kiss, then sink to the ground to take Dash in his mouth, bringing him to a quick and dirty release that left him reeling. Sometimes it would be Dash taking control, slipping his hand into Jesse's pants while Jesse did the same to him and they rubbed and humped against each other right up against the wall until their mutual orgasms exploded in their hands, leaving them sticky and breathless.

Earlier that afternoon, he'd ordered Jesse to the sofa, where he stripped and spread him out, then tongued his hole while jerking him off. Watching Jesse come alive under his mouth and hands was always a beautiful sight to behold, but that day his cries and groans, coupled with his smell and taste, stayed with Dash for hours. Their somewhat illicit afternoon getaways were quickly becoming addictive.

"Yes, we're friends. He's a very nice person."

She pursed her lips, and he could see her figuring out what to say. His stomach clenched. They might be close, but he kept his personal life to himself.

"You know, all I ever wanted was for my children to be happy. That was why I wanted to move here. So much opportunity for children. To see you as a college graduate when I came from nothing is something I dreamed about for you."

"And Drita. You know she plans to go back to school once Arian is old enough."

"I know. It's good. Children should see their parents striving to be better. Not like me, sitting home all day, doing laundry and cooking. What did I do with my life? I can't blame it all on your father."

The car stopped at a red light on Columbus Avenue and 72nd Street, and Dash shifted in his seat to face his mother. "You did your best with what you knew. I won't let you put yourself down. That's what he did all these years, and now you're spouting off his words back to me."

They sat in silence until the car pulled into the front gate of the Dakota.

"Dash?" Spencer, the front-gate guard, peered into the car.

"Hey, Spence. I'm taking my mother up to Jesse Grace-Martin's apartment."

"Lemme check the list."

While Spencer looked over the log, Dash could see his mother taking it all in. It was pretty intimidating the first time. No one was allowed past the gates—hell, no one was allowed near the gates. The guards stationed there had some minor celebrity status. This was as close to a royal residence and the guards at Buckingham Palace as a New Yorker was going to get. Tourists from all over the world asked to have their picture taken with whoever was on duty, and Spencer had told him of the multiple offers he'd had from men and women promising money, theater tickets, and even sexual favors if they could only go through the archway.

His mother's hand crept into his, and he leaned over to whisper in her ear. "What?"

"What is this place you work in? Why are there guards?"

Realizing he'd never given his mother the background of the Dakota, Dash quickly filled her in on its celebrity status and watched her eyes grow wide with wonder.

"Have you ever seen movie stars?"

"Yeah. There are quite a few who live here." Standard protocol in apartment buildings that housed celebrities was to have the staff sign nondisclosure agreements, so Dash couldn't give names.

"You're good to go, Dash." Spencer waved the car in.

The sedan rolled in through the iron gates and passed the second security booth, then swung around the paved road of the inner courtyard. There were four separate entrances to the apartments, and Jesse's apartment was at the opposite end of the main gate. The car halted, and he and his mother got out.

"Wow," the driver said, lifting his cell phone. "I ain't never been inside here. Gotta get me a pic."

"No pictures." Eddie the doorman stepped in front. "You can't stop the car here. You dropped off, now you gotta go."

Grumbling under his breath, the driver pulled out slowly, and Dash knew the man was most likely filming on his cell phone. That wasn't his concern. Holding his mother's arm, Dash walked behind Eddie as he returned to the concierge desk.

"We're going to Jesse Grace-Martin's apartment."

"Yeah, I see." Curiosity filled Eddie's eyes.

"Oh, uh, Mom, this is Eddie. I work with him."

"Nice to meet you."

"The same. Jesse's stepfather went up about fifteen minutes ago."

"Thanks, Eddie." They walked inside and took the elevator to the seventh floor. Dash could feel his mother trembling, and he gave her arm a squeeze. "It's okay. Don't worry. Jesse is great, and I'm sure his stepfather is a nice guy. He's offered to come, so he must think he can help you."

"Okay. I know. You've said it. I just can't believe it's come to this."

There was nothing more to say. The elevator opened, and he stepped out with his mother. "This way." He walked down the now-familiar hallway and self-consciously ran a hand through his hair. He'd dressed up, putting on a nice pair of pants and a button-down shirt. He might live uptown, but Jesse's family didn't need to think he wasn't good enough.

The door opened before he had a chance to knock, and Jesse greeted him. "Hey." His gaze swept over Dash with frank approval, and Dash felt that inexplicable tug toward him that was becoming so familiar.

"Hi."

The door swung open wide. "Come on in."

Dash stepped aside to let his mother into the apartment first. She stopped in the foyer and waited for Jesse to shut the door.

"Mrs. Sadiko. Nice to meet you."

"Thank you so much for having me in your home. It's very beautiful."

"You're welcome. Please come inside. I can give you a little tour."

The three of them walked past the kitchen and into the dining room, his mother murmuring words of astonishment.

"I'm sorry if I'm staring, but I've only seen places

like this in the movies or on television." She wandered through the large and airy room, gazing up, down, and all around, lost in thought.

While she admired the apartment, Jesse shot Dash a small smile, which Dash returned. Jesse leaned close. "You look really good."

Dash gave his hand a squeeze. "Thanks," he whispered. "Harry's here already, right?"

"Yeah. He's waiting in the living room. I told him briefly what you told me, but he's waiting to hear it straight from your mother."

"Okay. Mom?" Dash called out to get his mother's attention. "Ready to meet Harry?"

Her face shuttered, her smile fading. "Yes, of course." She seemed to fold into herself, and Dash felt both angry and hurt for her.

The three of them exited the dining room and walked down the hall to the spacious living room where Harry sat. Self-conscious, Dash stood a bit taller and set his shoulders back, but seeing Harry's broad smile, Dash relaxed. Harry possessed that ruddy complexion of a man used to the outdoors, probably from playing too much golf, but more importantly to Dash, his brown eyes were kind and smiling.

Jesse introduced them. "This is my stepfather, Harry Spears. Harry, this is Mrs. Sadiko and Dash Sadiko."

"Dash." Harry took his hand in a strong grip. "Good to meet you. Jesse's told us you've become a good friend, and those words don't come lightly to him. So any good friend of Jesse's is mine as well."

"Thank you, Harry. This is my mother, Elira Sadiko."

After a second's hesitancy, his mother stretched her hand out. It might be modern times, but Dash knew his mother had been raised very strictly, which meant she didn't normally shake strange men's hands. But times and people changed, and so there they sat in his lover's multimillion-dollar apartment while his mother was about to give details of her personal life to a stranger.

"So, Dash," Harry said once they'd all become comfortable.

A pitcher of iced water sat on the coffee table with glasses and a cheese plate Dash imagined Jesse had ordered specifically for his mother and him. Everything this man did was thoughtful and touched Dash. He sat by his mother on the sofa, and Jesse and Harry took the two large leather club chairs on the opposite side of the low coffee table.

"Jesse told me a little, but I'd like to hear the background." He turned to his mother. "Mrs. Sadiko, would you mind starting from the beginning with how you met your husband and when you got married? Is that going to be okay with you?"

His mother nodded, and Dash caught Jesse's eye and gave him a slight smile. He could never repay Jesse for this. He listened to his mother tell her story of meeting his father when she was fifteen and their parents agreeing, after only one month, that they could marry. How his father told her she needn't ever worry, that he'd always take care of her. How in America, you can be and do anything you want.

"But," she said after wiping her eyes with a tissue from her handbag, "it wasn't enough. He always wanted more. It didn't matter that I never asked him for anything, he was the one who said we needed more money and he needed to work two jobs. I never saw him, except for a few hours when he'd come home to eat and change his clothes. His children grew up barely knowing him."

Harry frowned. "He didn't help you? Or get you help?" As he spoke, he jotted down notes on a pad with a silver pen.

Color flooded her cheeks. "I feel so foolish. Stupid even. I accepted everything he told me. If I needed money for groceries or to buy the children things, I asked him. I never questioned him. I wouldn't think of it. But that's how I was raised. To be obedient to my husband. Keep the house and the family. That he would do right by me and my children. I kept my promise."

"I know it's difficult to recount." Harry stopped writing and focused on his mother. "But can you tell me when you found out he was seeing another woman?"

Her hands gripped together so tightly, her knuckles turned white, and Dash whispered to her, "Do you want a break? Are you okay?"

She shook her head and lifted her chin. "I have nothing to be ashamed of. I kept my sacred vows. And if I was foolish enough to believe everything he said to me, well, then it's my fault. But to answer your question, I found out when he came to me and said he wanted a divorce. That he had met someone. A girl younger than his own children." For a second her voice caught, and Dash put his arm around her shoulder.

"It's going to be fine, Mom."

She nodded, her damp eyes turning hard. "I know." She straightened, and Dash's heart swelled with pride at her strength. "He's having a baby with her, so he wants to divorce me, who he's been married to for over thirty years, and be with her." Her voice quavered for a moment, then grew hard. "And I'm fine with that. Good riddance."

"My mother has no means of support other than what my father provided for the family. My sister and I help out, but it isn't much. Hopefully, that will change when I graduate and find a good job, but for now, he needs to pay her."

"Just give me one second while I finish." Harry continued writing, and Dash found Jesse's gaze on him, an encouraging smile resting on his lips, but Dash's nerves had taken control, and he found himself unable to return it.

"Okay," Harry said and set the pad beside him. "Unfortunately, we see this quite often, and the man has this warped belief that he doesn't need to provide for the wife he left behind. Obviously, you won't get child support since both your children are well above the age of majority and are living outside the home. What I need from you, when you have the time, is an itemized list of your monthly expenses—rent, utilities, and food."

Having anticipated this, and because numbers were

the one thing he could contribute to this conversation, Dash spoke up before his mother could utter a word.

"I created a spreadsheet for you with everything I think you'll need, covering the past two years. If you give me your email, I can send it to you tonight."

"Perfect," Harry said, nodding with approval. "Mrs. Sadiko. If I can accomplish anything tonight, it's to put your mind at rest. I promise you, and I don't say that often but I'll stand by my words. I promise I'll make sure you come out of your divorce with enough income so you don't have to change your lifestyle at all."

"How can you be so sure?" His mother fidgeted with the strap of her purse. "My husband...he's very strong. Very persuasive."

"What my mother means," Dash interrupted, "is that he's a bully who's used to pushing people around to get his way."

"Well, we'll have to see about that now, won't we? I'm not a fan of bullies. They make me angry. And when I get angry, I win bigger settlements for my clients." Harry's smile gave Dash all the reassurance he needed.

"How about I make some coffee or tea? Which would you prefer, Mrs. Sadiko?" Jesse stood.

Dash wished...what did he wish? The fantasies of having a relationship with Jesse grew stronger each time they were together, but the socioeconomic gap made him hesitant to push for more.

"Oh, you don't have to bother."

"It's not. Besides, I was going to ask Dash to help me."

"Well…if you're sure, I'd love some tea."

"Coming right up. Dash?" Jesse passed by him on his way to the kitchen.

"Yeah, sure. I'll be right back," he said to his mother, hoping she'd be okay alone in the room with Harry. He really wanted to see Jesse alone, though, even if only for a few minutes.

Harry's eyes twinkled as he said, "Don't worry. I'm just going to get a little more information from your mom while you guys make the coffee. It's no different than if we were at my office and sitting with a desk between us. Except the coffee and company are much better."

Dash squeezed his mother's shoulder, then followed Jesse into the kitchen.

Jesse stopped so suddenly, Dash ran right into him. "Ooof. Sorry."

"I'm not." With a smile, Jesse put his hand on Dash's arm, and Dash swore his skin burned under the touch. "It was killing me to sit across from you when all I wanted was to kiss you."

Damn. How had he ever thought Jesse shy?

"We shouldn't," Dash whispered even as he swayed toward Jesse and sought his mouth. Jesse wrapped his arms around Dash's shoulders, and their lips molded together. He tasted Jesse's hungry need on his tongue, and the small, desperate sounds escaping him spurred Dash on to pull him closer. If he could bury himself under Jesse's skin, crawl inside and hold him tighter, he would. A fever rose inside him, burning through his blood. Jesse's long, pliant body surged against his while his hips moved in a sensual rocking motion.

Dazed and breathing heavily, Dash let go and moved out of Jesse's reach. Jesse was gazing back at him, dreamy-eyed, a red flush staining his cheeks.

"We gotta stop."

With a rueful expression, Jesse scrubbed his hands over his face. "I know you're right, but dammit, Dash. I can't help it." His gaze raked over Dash from head to toe, and Dash's cock swelled at his lust-drunk expression. "I want you. I haven't felt this way since…I don't know when." Jesse shook his head as if he was as confused about his feelings as Dash.

"Same. But it's not the time, although I gotta say I've had too many dreams to mention about you lately." Watching Jesse's eyes blur and grow heavy with need, Dash itched to rip Jesse's clothes off and bare all that soft skin he knew lay underneath, but it was more than sex. Dash loved Jesse's sensitivity, his kindness to others, his sharp intelligence and humor. He wanted to be there for Jesse to help him vanquish his demons and battle through the rough times he knew lay ahead. One night together wasn't nearly enough for Dash, but where was it all going between them? Could he have a relationship with someone in Jesse's social class? It was neither the time nor the place to start questioning, but Dash knew that talk waited in the near future.

"What's wrong? You're staring at me funny." Recovered, Jesse filled the teakettle with water and placed it on the stovetop, then set about making a pot of coffee.

"Nothing. I'm not sure how to say thank you for

tonight. Or if merely saying it is enough."

A somber expression darkened the light in Jesse's eyes. "Don't thank me. I hate seeing what your father's done—not only to your mom but to you and your family. Whatever I can do to help, I will."

Watching Jesse pull out cups and take out a tea bag for his mom, Dash imagined what it would be like to belong here. Sitting around the island having breakfast, then going to work. Taking walks in Central Park and stopping at one of the cafés on Columbus Avenue to have a drink before coming home for dinner. His chest ached, knowing his dreams of making it big would never bring him to the same level as Jesse. Was he wishing on a star that could only burn out eventually, leaving nothing but ashes behind?

He'd come to one decision tonight. "I want to pay Harry for his time."

Dash watched the set of Jesse's shoulders stiffen, and then he placed the cup down on the countertop before facing Dash.

"It's not necessary. I told you already."

"And I told you we don't accept charity." He lifted his chin, jaw set tight. "I have money saved and so does my sister."

Deep lines tightened along Jesse's mouth, but he didn't respond. The teakettle played its cheery whistle, and they remained silent while he made the tea. He put the mug on a tray, along with other cups. Finally he broke the quiet.

"Can you bring in the coffeepot and the milk? My hands are full."

"Sure," Dash said, hating the tension between them but knowing this wasn't a matter up for debate. He'd pay Harry like anyone else, and if he had to eat ramen for six months, then so be it.

When they entered the room, his mother and Harry were speaking quietly, and Dash could see from her body language that she felt more comfortable with him. It didn't matter if Harry was a part of Jesse's life. If his mother didn't want Harry to be her lawyer, they'd thank him and find someone else. But still, the matter of payment loomed large in the room, and Dash couldn't let it go further until it was settled.

He waited until everyone was seated and had taken their coffee and his mother her tea before bringing it up.

"I really appreciate your taking time to come into the city to meet with us, but before this goes any further, I think we need to talk about payment." He didn't miss the glance Harry and Jesse exchanged, which made him even more determined to stand on his own. He folded his arms.

"Dash, you know you don't have to—"

"Don't say it." Dash cut him off, knowing he sounded harsh, but he needed to get it out now, or he might never get another chance. He regretted his tone but not his words. "We appreciate your offer, but if you let me know what your rate is, we can give you a down payment by the end of the week."

Jesse opened his mouth, but at Dash's glare, pressed his lips together and said nothing.

Harry's thoughtful gaze settled on him. "Okay.

Well, I'm retired, as you know, so there is no fee per se. But if you want to pay the going rate, my firm charges between two hundred fifty and four hundred dollars an hour, depending on the skill of the attorney."

Dash's mouth dried, and his head spun. Jesus, that was a lot of fucking money. "Um, okay." A rapid calculation of his finances depressed and angered him. At fifteen dollars an hour, even with the cash tips, he had a hard time saving anything after taxes and living expenses. He knew Drita didn't have much either, but maybe if he took on extra shifts...

"It was very kind of you to give me this time. I'm sure I'll be fine now," his mother jumped in to save him, and he burned with humiliation that he couldn't take care of his family. At his age he should have more, but it had taken him a long time to save up for school. Even online classes weren't cheap.

"No, Mom, I'll think of something."

Dash shifted under Harry's continued, probing gaze. "I have an idea. Why don't you work it off by working for me? We can figure out what the bill is on a weekly basis."

It took Dash a moment to understand what Harry meant, and he squared his shoulders, his cheeks burning. Harry knew what he did at the Dakota. "You want me to come to Connecticut and do odd jobs around your house? Like rake the leaves and fix stuff?" That gap between him and Jesse widened to a fucking ocean.

"No." Harry's quiet yet forceful voice checked Dash from getting up and leaving the room altogether to hide his humiliation. "You're studying to be an accountant, Jesse told me. Is that right?" At his nod, Harry continued. "I may be retired, but I'm still a partner, and we always need accountants. I'm offering you an internship at the firm now, and then if things work out as I expect, a job there when you graduate."

Stunned, Dash couldn't speak and sat frozen, his gaze bouncing from Harry to Jesse, who gave him a nod and a thumbs-up.

Harry added, "We're always so willing to accept the bad that gets dumped on us, we forget that sometimes good things happen to good people."

Pulling himself together, Dash gathered his thoughts a moment before answering. "It's nice of you to offer. I mean, beyond nice. It's an incredibly generous offer, but why? I don't want a job because you feel sorry for me."

"Listen, son, I'm going to tell you something I don't speak about often. I didn't come from money. I've been working since I was fourteen years old. While other kids were out partying, I was studying. I needed a scholarship to go to City University, and I went to law school on a merit scholarship. I had no social life in school. Everything was based on me working to be the best. I made *Law Review* and graduated *magna cum laude*. So trust me when I say I recognize a person who has that fire in their belly to want to succeed. I see that in you. I'm not giving you a handout. I'm offering you a chance. I'm paying it forward. That's what it should be. You're not a charity case. I expect you to work and work damn hard."

Perception could often hurt as much as help, and in this instance, Dash had to eat a little bit of crow. "I, uh, I don't know what to say."

"I think, *Yes, Harry I'll take the job, thanks* would be a great first step," Jesse said. They all laughed but him.

"I'm still a student, though. I don't know enough yet to work full-time." Plus, he wanted to say, if he gave up this job, he'd never see Jesse, and that thought, more than anything else, held him back from accepting.

"So you start part-time. See about moving your shifts around here, if you want to keep working for whatever reason you might have to stay." Harry's gaze shifted to Jesse, then back to him. "I'm sure they'd let you work nights or weekends, and then you can do part-time at the firm....Say, twenty hours?"

"Yes. That would be good."

Harry continued. "Jesse said you graduate this year, so once you get your degree, you can study for the CPA exam and then come to work full-time at the firm."

His mother put her hand on his leg. "Dashamir. I don't see how you could turn down such a generous and wonderful offer."

"If you're sure...then yes. I'd be thrilled to come work for your firm. Thank you. But only once we work out the repayment of your fee."

"You got it."

They shook hands, and then he accepted a hug and kiss from his mother. When he faced Jesse, they stood grinning stupidly at each other for a few seconds until Jesse spoke.

"I'm really happy for you, Dash. I think it's going

to be the start of something great."

For the first time, Dash could agree. "All thanks to you." He dropped his voice. "I hope we still get a chance to see each other after I change my shift."

Jesse's stare grew heated. "I'm counting on it. When you finish work, you'll probably want a quiet place to sleep. Why not come here, instead of going all the way back home? You could take a shower and bring a change of clothes. Remember," Jesse said as he walked by to join Harry, who was talking to Dash's mother, "Miranda doesn't work evenings. We'll have the whole place to ourselves once you wake up."

An image from their one night together flashed through Dash's mind, and he grinned to himself as he followed Jesse, knowing there might not be a whole lot of resting going on. Not if he could help it.

Chapter Seventeen

"**D**ASH, TIME TO get up. You have to get back in fifteen minutes." Jesse pressed a kiss to Dash's neck and couldn't resist licking his salty, warm skin. Dash had been working the overnight shift for a week now. It hadn't been too hard to find people willing to give up working those graveyard hours and doing all the grimy work that came along with it. He took Friday nights through Tuesday, midnight to eight a.m., and though Jesse missed seeing him during the day for lunch, Dash had been able to come by in the early mornings to spend his breaks in Jesse's apartment.

The fatigue showed in how deeply he slept when he came upstairs. The nighttime work consisted mostly of hauling the day's garbage from the different apartments to the pickup area, and Dash would spend the first ten to fifteen minutes washing up to be clean enough to allow himself to get in Jesse's bed.

After shedding his clothes and exchanging a few kisses, Dash would fall into an exhausted sleep almost as soon as he lay down. The job with Harry wouldn't start until the beginning of November, so Dash had time to acclimate himself to his new schedule at the

Dakota.

"Mmm, lemme stay here." He threw an arm over Jesse and pulled him close to bury his lips in Jesse's hair. "You smell so good. So clean." A stiff erection pressed up against Jesse's thigh, and he reached into Dash's boxers to run his hand down its smooth length.

"You're so hot. And hard."

"God, babe, please." Dash moaned and thrust into Jesse's hand. The sticky precome gave Jesse enough lubrication to grip Dash and slide up and down. "Missed being with you this week."

Thrilled at Dash's words, Jesse rubbed his cheek against Dash's, reveling in the roughness against his flesh. "You're so perfect," Jesse whispered, licking and kissing Dash's neck as his hand moved faster. "Hard as a diamond yet soft like velvet." His own desire became irrelevant at that point. Giving Dash pleasure was enough to satisfy him. Abandoning Dash's cock for a moment, Jesse hooked his fingers over the elastic waistband of Dash's boxers and shimmied them over his hips, granting himself unfettered access to his beautiful, thick cock.

"Too good to waste," he murmured and licked the pulsing vein from root to sticky tip, then engulfed the entire rigid length, taking Dash to the back of his throat.

"Holy fuck," Dash moaned, and Jesse began to bob and suck, taking every thrust Dash gave him, while simultaneously running his hands over the wiry hair of his strong thighs. His entire world centered around the thick shaft in his mouth, the warm scent of his skin, and the sharp taste on his tongue. Dash began to tremble beneath him and bucked his hips.

"Oh God, oh God."

Jesse trailed his fingers beneath Dash's tight balls, past his taint, to tease at his puckered hole. Dash had one hand buried in Jesse's hair and the other fisted into the sheet while he rolled his hips, forcing his cock farther down Jesse's throat. Jesse didn't mind. He loved being filled by Dash, in any and every way possible. He loved everything about Dash.

Oh, God. He *loved* Dash.

With that revelation running through his head, Jesse sucked hard and strong on the slick, hard cock while Dash twitched and moaned beneath him. With a harsh cry Dash came, the hot, salty taste of him filling Jesse's mouth. Jesse drank him down as if he were parched.

When he finished licking every drop, he sat back on his knees and regarded Dash, whose ragged breath and heaving chest didn't stop him from opening his eyes and giving Jesse a smile. He reached out a hand, and Jesse leaned down to kiss his palm.

"What was that?" Dash asked, a touch of wonder in his voice.

"That was us," Jesse whispered, rubbing his cheek against Dash's hand like a cat seeking to be petted. "I like us. You and me together." It took all his courage to say things like this, knowing Dash wasn't the demonstrative type.

That was why it shocked him when Dash pulled him in for a heady, heart-pounding kiss that nearly had him melting into a puddle. "I like you too. You're the most amazing thing to ever happen to me, and sometimes I still don't believe you're real."

"Oh, I'm real, all right. Feel." With Dash's hand in his, Jesse pressed their palms to his own painfully hard cock.

Dash's heated gaze seared through him as he fondled him through his sweatpants. "I feel you. I…" He shook his head with what Jesse knew was frustration. It wasn't hard to see Dash still struggled, and not knowing why stung Jesse. Was it doubt in himself or about the two of them? He'd hoped Dash would know by now that Jesse didn't care what he did for a living or how much money he had. All he wanted was Dash.

"Why don't you come back here when you're finished? I have some work to catch up on, but you can get some sleep and then use my computer if you need to study."

"Miranda will be here, right?" He swung his legs off the bed.

"Yeah, so what? She knows we're seeing each other. It doesn't make sense for you to go all the way back home. Does it still bother you that Miranda knows?"

"Nope." Dash stood and stretched, and Jesse drank in his fill of the man's beautiful physique. He caught Dash's eye. "Like what you see?" He circled the bed with surprising speed and slid his arms around Jesse's waist. His breath caught in his throat at the feral, hungry look in Dash's eyes. "I was hoping we could be together again. That one time wasn't enough." His hands grew busy, sliding under the waistband of Jesse's sweats to cup his ass, and Jesse moaned. "Maybe I can do more than study."

Jesse had never been so swept up in physical need for someone. Sex with Sean had been comfortable— calm and sweet. But Dash filled him with an insatiable hunger to be taken.

"You're going to have to hold on to that thought until you come back in the morning." Dash groaned, and Jesse's smile grew wicked as he reached down to give him a squeeze. "I'd like to hold on to this, but I don't think that would go over too well."

"Stupid." Dash snorted, but his kiss tasted sweet before he let Jesse go and went to the bathroom to get dressed. Jesse yawned and sat on the bed, waiting for Dash to finish, already missing him.

"Okay, I'm ready." Dash emerged from the master bathroom, dressed in fresh work clothes. "I still have five minutes. Can a guy get a cup of coffee around here?"

They walked side by side to the kitchen, where Jesse made him a cup and Dash downed it as fast as he could. "Another one? Something to eat to take along? I can throw a sandwich together."

"I'm good. I'll be back around eight thirty, okay?"

"Yeah. I've got an article to write and you can sleep, then do your schoolwork. Then maybe we could…" He pressed his lips together, annoyed he'd let it slip, but Dash, who'd been about to leave, hesitated.

"What? What could we do?"

"I thought maybe we could take a walk. Outside, to the park. If you don't have too much work."

Dash sprinted back to his side and pulled him close, squeezing him tight. "I'll make all the time you need. Whatever you need from me, you got."

"All I need is you."

✦ ✦ ✦ ✦

JESSE HAD POURED his first cup of coffee when he heard Miranda's key in the lock. "Jess?"

"In the kitchen." He poured her coffee and added the milk.

"Oh, thank God. My first cup seems so far away." She set her purse and the brown paper bag with bagels on the island, and Jesse caught a whiff of the everything bagels she brought every morning.

"Mmm. I'm starving."

"I brought a few extra." She gazed at him over the thick white rim of her mug. "In case Dash might stop by and want one."

People might not think he was lucky, but Jesse knew otherwise. To have people like Miranda, who cared for him like family, almost like a mother, and now to have Dash in his life, Jesse knew how lucky he was.

"Thank you. I told him to come back when his shift's over to sleep. He should be here in a little while."

"I'm glad," she said. "You really care for him, don't you?"

Face warm and heart racing, Jesse nodded.

"I could tell. Can I ask you something? Have you spoken to your mother lately? I think she'd like to know."

"Maybe."

She set her cup down. "No maybes. You and she have had some good talks, right?" At his nod, she continued. "Keep it up, then. She's your mother, and despite the fact that you haven't been close, you know she loves you. Give it a chance. Maybe this can bring you together."

He fished a bagel out of the bag, then poured another cup of coffee. "You're right. I guess I'm out of practice in keeping her up-to-date on my life."

At the knock on the door, Miranda slid off the stool and placed her cup in the sink. "I'm guessing that's Dash. I'll just go in the living room and start going through your emails."

Without waiting for his answer, she left, and he went to open the door. Dash waited on the other side, looking weary. He also didn't smell too good.

"I know. I'm going to take a shower." He heaved his backpack over his shoulder, and with Jesse on his heels, went directly to the master bathroom. Jesse said nothing, just straightened out the bed, pulled the sheet and comforter down, and fluffed up the pillows.

He heard the shower stop, and then Dash came out, water droplets gleaming on his naked shoulders, and sat down on the bed with a towel slung around his waist.

"Tonight I had to dig through the dumpsters because a resident thought she lost her keys. For an hour I crawled and pawed through those disgusting, filthy bags because she insisted her two-year-old threw them in the garbage. Then she remembered she left them in her new handbag she wore to some fancy event the night before."

That Jesse could believe, knowing some of the people in the building. "First-world problems for her, I guess."

"She didn't even apologize. Just tried to hand me a fifty-dollar tip, which I refused."

"Why?" Jesse asked, more curious than anything else. "That's the least she could've done."

"Normally, I would." He gave a huge yawn, his eyes growing heavy. "But it bugged me that she didn't even say sorry and she thought she could make up for the fact that I had to dig through all that crap by throwing money my way. She didn't even look at me. I bet she couldn't pick me out of any of the other guys."

"That's pretty judgmental," Jesse said mildly. "I mean, yeah, she should've said thank you, of course. But I'm also sure she was trying to be nice, and that was the way she thought could help. Maybe she was embarrassed."

"I don't know." Dash yawned again and slid into bed, under the covers, and snuggled against the pillows. "Why do you have to be so sensible about things?"

Jesse laughed at Dash's petulant frown and gave his cheek a kiss. His skin smelled warm and soapy-clean.

"Part of my charm. Now go to sleep, and I'll see you later."

He shut the door behind him, and on his way back to the kitchen, saw Miranda working in the living room, her head bent over her laptop, the early morning sun slanting bright across the polished wooden floor. A picture rose to his mind—his father sitting on the sofa every morning, drinking his coffee while he read the papers—but the pain no longer stabbed at him like a fresh, open wound. It was poignant and reflective of the happiness that once resided in the apartment: a bittersweet memory of something lost that could never be regained. He entered the kitchen to grab his coffee cup. On an impulse, he picked up his phone.

"Mom?" He hitched the stool closer to the countertop.

"Jesse, what's wrong?"

"Why does something have to be wrong? I thought we agreed to keep in touch better."

"We did," she said, cheerful now that he'd reassured her. "But neither of us kept up with that, did we?"

"No. But I'm calling you now." Jesse drew a breath to figure out what to say and how to say it.

"Something's going on. I can hear it."

He laughed. "I haven't said anything yet."

"That's the point. If this was simply a social call, you'd already be asking me how I feel, how Harry is, and what was new. Those obligation questions. But you're not. So I'll ask you. What's new? What's going on?"

He'd forgotten how enjoyable talking to his mother could be. "I wish you would come to the city."

"Oh, honey." Her voice caught. "I wish you could come to Connecticut. But I understand."

"Maybe I could. Soon."

"Wh-what? Did something happen?" Her voice rose, shrill in its concern. "Did you have a breakthrough? Are you going outside now? Jesse, tell me, please."

Her emotional response surprised him. "Mom. It's okay. I've…I'm better. I'm thinking about it. Tonight, in fact."

"Oh, my God. Thank you. Thank you for telling me. You have no idea how much this means to me, that you called to tell me this."

"I'm sorry, I'm really sorry. I was wrong not to talk to you sooner." He was full of genuine regret, his heart thundering loudly in his ears. "I've been going outside more. Walking in the courtyard, and I even went outside the front gate once."

"Oh, baby, that's wonderful. I knew it would happen." He listened to her sniffle. "Harry told me about your friend and how he's helping his mother. He said you two might be closer than friends?"

Holding back a grin, Jesse decided to tease her. "Maybe."

"Jesse…" she warned. "You're not too old for me to come over and spank."

"Dash is a great guy. He's helped me more than I ever imagined possible. I owe him so much."

"Then I need to meet this Dash and give him a hug."

"Until you can, I'll give him all the hugs for you." He sobered. "I care a lot about him. I think you'll really like him, and I know Dad would've."

"Of course he would. If he's important to you, he's

got to be wonderful."

"Thanks, Mom. I'll call you later."

With a smile on his face, he joined Miranda in the living room.

She glanced up at him. "I heard you speaking to your mother. Did you have a nice chat?"

"She was thrilled. And I told her about Dash. You were right. I should talk to her more."

"Oh," she smirked, "I know. Now let's get to work. You have an article due for *Travel in Style* by the end of the week. I submitted all your other articles to the National Geological Society and the Gemological Society."

"Thanks. I'm going to write about Larimar. The prettiest stone you've never heard of."

Miranda tapped on her iPad. "Ohhh. It is pretty. This is it, right?" She turned the screen around. "I've never seen such a gorgeous blue."

"Yeah. Pectolite is the natural mineral and is pretty common. But that blue? That brilliant blue? It's only found in the Caribbean, specifically the Dominican Republic. It ranges from a milky blue-white to that gorgeous blue-green like the sea."

"It's stunning. And such pretty jewelry. Look at those necklaces and bracelets."

An idea struck him. "Do me a favor? Order a necklace for Dash's mother and sister. And for yourself."

"Oh, please, you don't have to. Not for me."

"I know I don't have to. I want to. The blue will look pretty with your eyes." Jesse propped his chin on his hand and stared at the laptop screen, pulling up his research. "Okay, I'm on this."

They had a system worked out where he would focus on his articles and Miranda would answer his correspondence and run his errands. At lunchtime, Jesse ate the sushi Miranda brought him, but otherwise he was in the zone and didn't take a break. The sun moved around the room, and by the time he looked up, a series of puffy white clouds had spread over the formerly blue sky, dulling the light, so Miranda turned on the lamps on the side tables. Soon it would be getting darker earlier, and Jesse wondered if he'd be out in the cooler night air, walking side by side with Dash.

"Oh God, my back." He stood and stretched, moving his neck side to side. "Maybe I should start using the desk in the office."

"Like I always say to?" Miranda arched a brow, her eyes bright as she slipped on her jacket.

"Yes, like you always say to." Jesse kissed her cheek. "Thank you for everything. You were right as usual."

"It's not a matter of being right, but of doing what's right for you."

At the sound of movement in the bedroom, she gave him a friendly nudge. "Or having someone who's right for you."

"Good night, Miranda." He draped his arm over her shoulder and opened the door. "See you in the morning."

She waved good-bye, and he shut the door as her footsteps faded away down the hallway.

"Hey."

He spun around to face a sleep-rumpled Dash,

deliciously bare-chested, his jaw dark and scruffy with beard growth.

"Hey yourself. How'd you sleep?"

"Like a ton of bricks hit me. Guess all that garbage-picking tires a man out."

Jesse didn't smile. He knew how much that bothered Dash and that Dash mentioned it as a way to show how different they were. Jesse had to find a way to show Dash that when it was the two of them, they were more the same than different. The trouble was figuring out how.

Choosing to ignore Dash's response, Jesse instead gave him a kiss on his warm cheek. "I have sandwich stuff if you want. And Miranda got you a bagel. I'll make some coffee. Come on."

Once in the kitchen, Dash took his bagel and popped it in the toaster. While Jesse made the coffee, Dash took the cream cheese and milk out of the refrigerator, and for Jesse, it was so domestic, he wished it didn't have to end. He wanted Dash with him all the time. The toaster dinged, and after Dash made his food, they carried everything into the living room and sat together on the sofa.

"I have the laptop set up in the TV room, but I can bring it out here if you want." Jesse tucked his feet under him and watched Dash finish the last bite of his bagel. "Or you can use the dining table if it's easier for you. I have some stuff to do in the bedroom. But I was thinking…" He broke off, almost shy now with what he wanted to say.

"Thinking what? And yeah, the dining-room table

would be best 'cause I have to take notes and stuff." He licked his fingers and stood over Jesse, who remained seated.

"Um, that maybe after you're done…maybe we could go outside and take a walk. Down to the park? I know it's going to be dark, but I was hoping to do it with you first, and since you're on nights now…"

"Babe, really?" Dash jumped on him and gave him a tackle hug that almost knocked the breath from him. "You wanna go outside? I'm ready whenever you are. Everything else can wait—school, the job. We can go now."

"No," Jesse said firmly. "I want you to take your class and finish your assignment. I'm going into the bedroom."

"Okay." Dash kissed him, his tongue playing against Jesse's, and for a moment Jesse was tempted to say to hell with it and bring Dash into the bedroom. Then Dash pulled away, flushed and breathing hard. "You better get out of here, then. I only have one class and a short assignment. It shouldn't take too long."

"Okay, yeah. Let me give you the laptop, and I'll make myself scarce." He left Dash to bring him the computer along with a pad and pens. "Here. Use what you need."

"Thanks. I'll see you in a bit."

Jesse gave him a wave and retreated to the bedroom. He knew he had to leave Dash alone, and sitting there watching him work would be too much of a temptation. He puttered around for a little while, straightened out the bed, separated his clothing for laundry and dry-cleaning, and wrote in his journal like Dr. Mingione had asked him to do, then sat on the window seat and gazed out onto the street. Children walked with their babysitters, clutching their hands or holding on to the stroller handles. People streamed down 72nd Street, maybe on their way to the park or to the subway station at the corner.

He placed his fingers on the glass, as if to capture the memory that rose in his mind's eye so strong and bright, it felt alive before him. He and his father, coming back from an afternoon at the park. They'd stop to pet the horses lined up in hopes of getting someone to buy a carriage ride. He didn't mind the smell, and sometimes the driver would give him a carrot and Jesse would giggle as the horse's velvety lips nibbled at his fingers. Then his father would buy them big salty pretzels from the man on the corner, and they'd walk up the street, chewing, and his father would say, "*Don't tell Mommy. She'll get mad at me and say I've spoiled your dinner.*" Of course she knew but never said a word.

Jesse laid his hot forehead against the cool glass and spied a boy with his father on the corner. The boy held a pretzel almost as big as his face. The light changed, and as his own father had done with him, the man put his arm around the little boy as if to shield him from any possible harm. And Jesse couldn't stop the rush of tears.

All gone. In the blink of an eye. Gone forever.

He watched the boy and man walk down the street until he couldn't see them any longer.

"You're a fool. You're not better."

"Jess?" Dash stood in the doorway, his dark brows knotted together in confusion. "What's wrong?"

Ashamed at his weakness, Jesse turned away from him. "Me. I'm an idiot. I can't do this. I can't do anything. Go away, Dash. Find someone normal."

Chapter Eighteen

D ASH CLOSED THE laptop with a grunt of satisfaction. He'd finished the class and done the assignment with little trouble, and it had only taken an hour and a half. He smiled to himself as he rose from the table; as his reward, it was time to be with Jesse.

The apartment was so quiet—not a sound from outside filtered through the windows, unlike in his own apartment. This beautiful living space with its high ceilings, shining floors, and spacious rooms was as if from a different world. Even the air felt different. He thought he heard a voice and wondered if Jesse was on the phone.

The bedroom was dim in the early evening twilight, but Dash saw Jesse sitting on the window seat, face pressed to the glass.

"Jess? What's wrong?"

"Me. I'm an idiot. I can't do this. I can't do anything. Go away, Dash. Find someone normal."

"You're none of those things." Crossing the large space in long, hurried strides, Dash sat next to Jesse, and feeling helpless over the pain etched on Jesse's face, he did the only thing he thought might help and wrapped his arms around him. Jesse squirmed, but Dash held him tight until he relented and rested his cheek against Dash's shoulder.

"I'm such a fool. I've been sitting here watching all the people walk by and thinking about my father. Remembering. I don't know why I can't forget. It's so stupid. *I'm* stupid. All these years have already passed. I should be better. I should be stronger."

Not knowing what to say, Dash ran his fingers through Jesse's hair, hoping it would soothe him. "It doesn't mean you're not okay because you remember or still feel sad about the way things used to be."

"But it's been so long, and he's been gone so many years. Shouldn't I be better?" His plaintive voice pierced straight through Dash's heart. But he understood and rubbed Jesse's back, hoping the right words would come to help.

"Everyone reacts differently to tragedy. And you were just a kid when it happened. It's natural for you to feel this way. You lost your father, and—"

"No." Vehement, Jesse pushed away from him, his tearstained face flushed and his mouth a thin, trembling white line. "I didn't *lose* him. Don't say that. I knew where he was. In his office, where he was supposed to be. I didn't lose him," Jesse repeated, his voice rising as his hands clenched into tight fists at his side. "They took him from us. They *stole* my father from me. And I let them steal my life."

Powerless to do anything but watch Jesse fall apart in front of him, Dash gave in to his instinct to care for those he loved and slipped his arms around Jesse again, covering his trembling body while he wailed out his grief. Dash believed this breaking apart had been a long time coming for Jesse and that letting his emotions out might be more helpful than Jesse imagined.

"It's okay, babe. There's nothing wrong with still loving your father and missing him. I'm thinking how lucky he was to have had someone like you for his son. Because being loved by you must've been the best part of his life. Anyone would be lucky to be loved by you."

"I don't know. I loved my father, and he died. My mother can barely stand to see me because I look so much like him, and she hates coming to the city. I don't feel so lucky." A few moments passed before Jesse's shuddering breaths calmed, and Dash caught his quick, wary gaze. "I'm sorry. I didn't mean to cry like a baby. I've probably ruined it with you now too."

He tightened his arm around Jesse's shoulder. "It takes a lot more than a good cry to get rid of me."

"You said anyone would be lucky to be loved by me. Do you? Feel lucky, I mean?" Jesse turned and faced him. " 'Cause I love you, Dash."

Frozen with surprise and joy, Dash had to wait for his heart to return to its normal rhythm so he could find his voice.

"Me?"

A smile teased Jesse's lips. "Is there another Dash? I think one is all I can handle at the moment, honestly." He rubbed his cheek against Dash's shoulder in a gesture of trust that made up for all the wrongs in Dash's life. "But yeah. You. From the first day when you kept me from falling, somehow I knew you might be the one to always catch me."

"I never want to see you hurt."

"Hurt is inevitable, I've come to realize. Living with it and learning to put it behind me is where I've failed. Until now, maybe."

"You have?"

Jesse nodded. "I think so. Knowing I have you to help me and stand at my side makes it easier for sure."

"I like being at your side. But right now?" Dash took his chin between thumb and forefinger and covered his lips with his mouth, pushing his tongue inside. Jesse melted against him, and Dash could feel his desire. They kissed until Dash's head spun, and he couldn't hold back. "I'd rather be on top of you. Inside you. All over you. I love you too, Jesse. And I need you as much as you need me."

Without waiting for a response, Dash took Jesse by the hand and led him to that soft, clean, comfortable bed. He'd never had the luxury of a king-sized bed before; it was almost too much room, so when he lay down with Jesse, he kept him close.

"You love me? You don't have to say it to make me feel good." Jesse's lips moved against his neck.

"You feel damn good no matter what, and don't be ridiculous. You think I'm going to say it if I don't feel it? I've never been in love before, but this is different."

"Yeah?" Jesse propped himself up on his elbow. "How?"

"I don't know.…It's hard to say. I think about you…all the time. I want to be with you and tell you everything." Frustrated, Dash stared into Jesse's eyes. "I guess it's not how many things I can name to show how much you mean to me. Maybe it's that there aren't enough right words…or I can't find enough words to tell you."

His eyes shining, Jesse flung his arms around Dash's neck, lying on top of him. "And you think that isn't exactly what I'd want to hear? That was beautiful."

Dash palmed Jesse's ass and squeezed it. "This is beautiful. You're beautiful, and I want you." He slid his hands underneath to touch Jesse's smooth, hot skin. "Let me make love to you and show you how much I need you." They kissed, his lips moving over Jesse's, coaxing low, throaty moans. "How much I love you."

Jesse's skin burned beneath his fingertips, and he put up no resistance when Dash pulled off his sweats and briefs. "They do say actions speak louder than words." He arched up as Dash nibbled along his collarbone. "So show me."

Six months ago, if anyone had told Dash he'd be in bed with a trust-fund guy who owned an apartment in the Dakota and they'd be exchanging I-love-yous, he'd have thought they were high. But now, with Jesse writhing beneath him, his warm, intoxicating scent rising between them, all Dash could think about was how nothing else mattered but being together.

"I was good at show-and-tell in school." He licked the crown of Jesse's ruddy cock. "I've already told you, so now I'm gonna show you how much you mean to me." Recalling where Jesse kept his condoms and lube from the first time they were together, Dash took them from the drawer and placed them on the bed, then resumed kissing and licking along the length of Jesse's erection.

"I always knew you were a great student," Jesse gritted out before his head fell back and an expression of pure bliss washed over his face. "*Ahhh.*" He sighed and began to flex his hips.

Dash took the entire length of Jesse's cock down his throat, abandoning himself to the absolute joy of having Jesse in his mouth. He licked, tongued, and teased the silky skin, drawing his lips tight as he moved up and down Jesse's shaft.

"Oh…oh," Jesse called out, and Dash, with a final kiss, let go to nuzzle Jesse's muscular thighs, the rough hair tickling his cheeks. He explored Jesse's body with the luxury of time he now knew he had, nipping at the jut of his hip bone and teasing the circle of his belly button. Jesse reached out his hand, and Dash kissed it, then drew each finger into his mouth.

A fierceness he hadn't seen before blazed from Jesse's eyes. "I don't know how I got so lucky, but please, Dash…" His unspoken question hung in the air, but Dash knew.

"I'm the lucky one. You could have anyone, and yet you want me."

Jesse reached up a hand to stroke his cheek, and Dash nuzzled into his warm palm. "You're not anyone. You're the only one. My one. The only one I see."

Some people said actions spoke louder than words, but not so for Dash. Words had power. Words had meaning. And at the end of the day, all people had left were the words spoken between them. Dash would never forget Jesse's words. Jesse saw past his rough clothes and upbringing to who he was inside, and Dash couldn't stop his heart from tumbling over into forever.

"I love you, babe."

The brightness of Jesse's smile lit up the room, and Dash reached for the condom and rolled it on, then slicked himself up. He pushed a slippery finger inside Jesse's snug hole, through that velvety, soft heat, all the while keeping his gaze fastened on Jesse, loving the play of emotions over his face. When Jesse's eyes became unfocused and his breathing erratic, Dash removed his finger and nudged his erection inside, working his way into Jesse. Sinking into him was like sliding into warm butter, and Dash was drawn in deep. His passage clasped him tight, and Dash rested his forehead against Jesse's.

"You okay?"

Jesse kissed his cheek. "So much better than I ever thought I'd be. I thought I'd never get put back together. But I must've been waiting for you to find my pieces."

Dash stroked down the length of Jesse's quivering body. "You feel perfect to me. And whatever skin you're in fits me perfectly." He began to move, slowly at first, and then, at Jesse's urging, with more force, driving in hard. Jesse wrapped his legs around his hips, and Dash thrust deep, their sweaty bodies rocking and sliding together. Jesse grasped his cock, and as Dash continued to pound inside him, came with a harsh cry, spilling warm and wet between them. He shuddered and twitched, his muscles clamping down on Dash's cock, but Dash was caught up in a fervor and pulled Jesse's hips toward him until he'd bent him almost in half.

A golden haze spread before his eyes, and Dash became lost in pleasure as sensation after sensation poured over him. The touch of Jesse's skin against his burned, and Jesse's kisses tasted of fire. Heat suffused him, and with a choked cry, he burst apart and came, letting Jesse's loving arms wrap around him and hold him tight. He came to with his face buried in Jesse's neck and their bodies still warm and plastered together.

"What was that?" Jesse murmured. "I can barely move."

"So don't. I like you right where you are." He kissed and nipped at Jesse's shoulder, loving his taste. God, he could eat the man up; he couldn't get enough. Even now, right after a mind-blowing orgasm that left him breathless, he wanted Jesse again. And again. Dash guessed that was what love was. Never being able to get enough of the person, even when they were right there in your arms.

"I'm not planning on going anywhere." Jesse nuzzled into the spot where his neck and shoulder met. "This spot fits me perfectly."

"We're pretty mushy for two dudes, aren't we?" Dash chuckled a bit and withdrew from Jesse slowly. He knew Jesse had to be sore after the way he'd gone a bit crazy. He pulled off the condom, tied it up, and tossed it in the wastebasket next to the bed, then seeing Jesse watching him, climbed back in and slid under the sheets. "What's the matter?"

"Does it bother you if I say stuff like that to you? I know I'm not one of those tough guys you must be used to being with."

"Do you care that I'm poor, haven't graduated college, and I'm a maintenance worker in your building who picks through garbage?" he countered, watching Jesse's eyes widen with distress.

"Stop saying things like that," Jesse said. "I never cared what you did for a living or any of that other stuff." He slid closer, and reflexively, Dash pulled him into his chest, where Jesse cuddled close, sliding a naked leg over Dash's hip so their bodies molded together. "I only care about you as a person. What's in your heart."

"So we're in agreement, then? You can be as mushy as you want, and I...well, I don't know." Dash grew hot and turned away from Jesse. "I'm still uneducated and a porter."

"Stop putting yourself down. Everything happens for a reason, and you being you is what brought us together. If you were anyone else, I might never have met you, and where would I be? Stuck forever in this apartment, lonely and afraid. Plus, you're going to college and getting your degree, so you need to stop saying you're uneducated." Jesse took his face between his hands and kissed him hard, surprising Dash with his ferocity. "I trust you more than anyone. Which is why it's time."

Warmth flooded through Dash, and he cuddled Jesse closer, running a hand down the smooth length of his back. "Time for what?"

Jesse smiled against his shoulder. "Time for me to fly."

Dash cocked his head, unsure what Jesse meant. "Care to explain?"

"I want to go outside and walk to the park. With you."

Chapter Nineteen

J ESSE HEARD DASH'S quick, indrawn breath.

"I remember you said that before, but I didn't want to push."

"You don't need to push me. I want to do it. Everything that's happened over the last few months has led me to this point. I'm not doing this for you, although I wouldn't—*couldn't*—do it without you. I'm doing it for me. For my life."

His words sounded strong to his ears, but inside, he was melting with fear.

Dash ran a finger down his cheek. "How about we get up, shower, and if you're ready, take that walk? I can't wait to have you by my side."

"Okay." He climbed out of bed, and on shaky legs, made it to the bathroom. Dash followed right behind, and when their eyes met in the mirror, Jesse winced at his pale face.

"It's gonna be fine." Dash placed a hand on his shoulder and gave him a comforting squeeze. "Promise. Now let me take care of you."

At his shrug, Dash left him to turn on the shower taps, and then Jesse allowed himself to be led under the water, where Dash soaped him up and rinsed him off.

"I haven't had anyone wash me since I was a little kid."

Water ran in rivulets down Dash's face, and he brushed them off before answering. "Well, that's gonna have to change. I liked it. I like taking care of you."

He stepped out of the shower and wrapped a large bath sheet around himself. "I'm not a child, Dash. I want to be your lover. Your equal. Not someone you have to protect."

"Is that what you think?" Dash turned off the water and joined him in drying off, his toweling brisk and efficient as he spoke. "You couldn't be more wrong. I want you to lean on me, since that's what I thought friends and lovers did. Lift each other up and help the other through hard times. If I say I want to take care of you, it's because when I think of all you've been through—the death of your father, the mugging—I see red. I want to stand by you. At your side. But being your lover means I like spoiling you too and making sure you're taken care of."

In his prior relationship, he'd been the giver and Sean the taker, so Jesse was at a loss to know how to react. No one had put his needs first in a very long time.

"I guess it'll take some getting used to." He faced Dash. "Stick by me if I make mistakes?"

"Oh, babe." Dash pinned him against the vanity, and Jesse looped his arms around Dash's neck, thrilling to Dash's hot breath against his cheek. "You couldn't get rid of me if you tried."

They dressed quickly, and then Jesse was moving on autopilot, barely noticing that Dash had opened the front door. Dash held on to his arm, and Jesse's heart began to pound. This was it. He was going to do it. Everything was new and happening so fast.

"Are you all right?"

"Uhh...yeah." He swallowed hard but remained determined to carry his plan through. Failure was not acceptable.

"For a second, I thought you were going to bolt." Dash ran his hand up and down Jesse's arm. "Are you sure? We can do it another day if you want."

It would be so easy to say "Fuck it" and lead Dash back into the safety of the apartment, but Jesse couldn't risk it. Not anymore. For five years his mind had made his body a prisoner within these walls of luxury, and while he knew most people would love to switch places with him, he hated it. The spacious rooms closed in and suffocated him. Once his home had spelled safety, and he'd feared what lay outside. But loving Dash had unlocked the iron bars he'd surrounded himself with.

"No," he said with absolute certainty, even though his nerves jangled and his heart pounded. "Let's do this. I want to go to the park." He held Dash's hand tight, hoping his bravado would last once they walked outside.

Riding down in the elevator, Jesse realized with a shock that it was the first time he'd be going outside without Miranda. When he mentioned it to Dash, he found himself enveloped in a hug.

"You see?" Dash whispered. "It's going to be okay.

One step at a time."

Jesse stepped out into the gray twilight of the Dakota courtyard and shivered. He wasn't wearing long sleeves and had forgotten the chill of the outside air on a fall evening.

"Cold?" Dash squeezed his hand, then nudged his shoulder. "I hear body heat can help with that problem. Remind me to show you later."

Jesse snickered. "Don't quit your day job, in case you're planning on becoming a comedian. That's all I gotta say."

"Let's go, wiseass."

Filled with self-confidence, and with Dash at his shoulder, holding his hand, Jesse walked toward the archway leading out of the courtyard. With every step, he shed his old, fragile skin to be reborn into someone strong. Capable.

Fearless.

As they passed by the first security post, Dash dropped his hand, and it was as if the lights turned out in Jesse's mind. He faltered, and Dash stopped walking.

"I'm sorry. Are you going to be okay if we don't hold hands?"

"I wish you could."

"I wish I could too. It's killing me to see you upset like this when you're almost there." With his eyes everywhere but on Jesse, Dash bit his lip, then said, "I shouldn't be hanging out with you, Jess, remember? It's against the co-op rules for workers to fraternize or have social relationships with the residents." He shrugged. "I didn't want the guys at the gate to see."

"That's bullshit," Jesse responded hotly. "They can't tell you who to be friends with."

"Yeah, they kinda can if I want to work here."

Feeling a bit frantic, Jesse clenched his hands into fists and began to shake. "B-but I need you. Please. I'll take responsibility. I'll be okay if you just hold my hand when we walk outside." Maybe he was being irrational, but Dash's touch grounded him. Without it, Jesse wasn't sure he could continue. "You can drop it right before we pass security. If we stand really close they won't even notice." But watching the emotions play over Dash's face, Jesse hated himself for doing this. "You're right. I'm sorry, it's not fair to force you into a position where it's me versus them." Jesse drew in a deep breath and lifted his chin. "I can do it."

"I'm here," Dash said and slid his hand around the nape of Jesse's neck in that possessive hold Jesse loved. Only for a moment, but it helped. "Right by your side. And when we get down the block, I promise to hold your hand."

Shoulder to shoulder, they walked out to the street, Jesse's heart banging with each footstep. At night the noise of the city sounded less harsh, and he gazed up at the dusky sky, watching the clouds. The security guard at the booth glanced at them, and Jesse watched his eyes widen in surprise.

"Evening."

"Have a good one, Spencer," Dash said, and Jesse wondered if they were friends.

After about twenty steps, Jesse needed a moment. "Can we stop?" He had to catch his breath, feeling as though he'd run a marathon. His sweat-soaked T-shirt clung to his back, and his legs shook like limp noodles. He hoped he wouldn't faint.

Anxiously peering into his face, Dash led him over to the side of the building so he could lean against the black metal gate that wrapped around the edge of the facade. "What's wrong?"

"N-nothing. I need a sec." His breath came in short pants, and he blinked rapidly. Things came back into focus, and he gazed at the streetscape.

For the first time in five years, he noticed the sounds he'd missed—the blaring of car horns and the harsh exhaust of a city bus as it stopped to pick up passengers, the noise unfiltered by a window seven stories in the air. The chatter of casual conversation rose around him, and it all became like a din in his head. He heard the children's shrieks of laughter as they played alongside their parents or babysitters. Pigeons cooed and flapped around his feet, and the aromas of the various food carts down the block reached out to tickle his nose. Jesse noticed every detail, from the *click* of a woman's heels on the concrete to the flapping of a businessman's trench coat as it flew around his legs. People still congregated around the front arch of the Dakota, where John Lennon had been shot, taking pictures. Life continued whether he participated or not.

God, he'd missed the city. He didn't know what he'd really lost all these years until now, and tears spilled down his cheeks.

"I'm sorry." He turned his head, ashamed of his response and that Dash had to witness it. "It's a little overwhelming." It was as if he was a tourist in his own city. In his own life.

"I'll bet. But I'm here." Dash slung his arm around Jesse's shoulder and pulled him in close. "You take all the time you need to soak it all in."

From the corner of his eye, he spotted the security guard giving them a hard stare, and though he wanted nothing more than to sink into the strength of Dash's arms, he shook him off and stood tall, his shoulders pulled back.

"I'm okay now, thanks." He pointed down the block. "Can we go to the park? Not inside, of course, but to sit in front. Do you mind?"

"Of course not." This time Dash took his hand, and Jesse, believing they were far enough away that no one working in the front would see, didn't let him go. "Wanna hear something crazy?" Dash's thumb slid up and down his fingers.

"Uh, what? Yeah, sure."

"I don't think I've ever actually been inside Central Park."

At that pronouncement, Jesse stopped short and gaped at Dash. "What? You're kidding."

"Nope. I mean, I live in the Bronx. My father never took me, and my mom didn't take the train. Besides, we have the Bronx Zoo. What's better than that?" Dash tugged at his hand. "Let's go. We have the light." They'd reached the corner of 72nd Street and Central Park West and crossed the street.

A man and his two children rose from a bench and smiled at him. "Kept it warm for you."

Jesse smiled back and dropped down, grateful to be seated. That brief, five-minute walk had taken everything out of him. He stretched his legs, and Dash sat beside him, his muscular thigh pressing close.

"You good? Tell me the truth."

"Ehhh. Okay." He flipped his hand up and down. "I'll live. Which is something I wasn't sure of before I came out."

"I'm so fucking proud of you. Not only did you go out, but you came across the street and to the park." Dash kissed the top of his head. "You're on your way."

Hearing the words should've made him happy, but Jesse was too drained to do anything but give a weak smile in return. It was everything he'd been striving for all these years, but the reality proved almost anticlimactic.

"Yeah. Go me. I crossed the street. Woo-hoo."

Dash sent him a sharp look, but Jesse ignored it, directing his moody gaze down Central Park West. The landscape had changed drastically in the years he'd locked himself away. Glass skyscrapers, their windows alight, stabbed up toward the sky like glittering icicles. He shuddered and turned away.

"What's wrong? And don't try and deny it. Talk to me." Dash swung around halfway to face him. "I know something's bothering you."

"I feel nothing, really. And that's what I'm wondering. I've let this paranoia—or whatever it is—control me for all these years, and now that I'm on the brink of conquering it…" He blinked. "What if that's all I was?"

Dash squinted at him. "I don't get it."

Jesse wasn't sure he understood himself, but he tried to explain. "For five years I was known as Jesse, the agoraphobic. If anyone spoke of me, they'd say, 'Oh, Jesse? He's the guy who never leaves his apartment.' I don't even know who I am anymore outside of my illness. I've let it control every aspect of my life. And if that's the case…what if I'm nothing else?"

Dash's gaze searched his. "I can't understand that. Because I see you as so much more."

"You do?" Jesse propped his chin in his hand. "What? Seriously, I'm not fishing for compliments." He kicked his sneakered foot back and forth. "I just don't know who I am anymore."

Dash took his hands and played with his fingers. "I can tell you who I see. A man who's held himself together after his world fell apart. A man who thinks of others often before himself. A sweet man. A sexy-as-hell man who turns me on like no one else ever has or could. A man who teaches me new things every time I see him." Dash lifted their entwined hands to kiss his fingers. "The man I wish I could stay with every day and night."

"That was nice to hear."

"You sound like you doubt me."

"No." Jesse rubbed his thumb over Dash's. "Never you. Myself."

"I know it's easy for me to say don't, but don't." Dash smiled at him, and Jesse's heart flipped. God, he really loved this man. Dash continued speaking, and Jesse forced himself to listen. "You're looking at it from where you used to be. I'm looking at it from knowing you now. You're fire, baby. You light me up and burn right through me, never stopping."

Could he be that man Dash saw?

"I want to believe you, but—"

"No buts. Sometimes, you have to just go with it. Live your life, grab the happiness you find, and not overthink things. Do you think you can do that?"

"I'm trying. I can't be sure, but I have to try."

Dash's warm, dark eyes kindled with a glow Jesse hadn't seen before.

"Then that's all we can hope for, and I'm holding you to that."

Leaves rustled on the trees behind them, and if Jesse listened hard enough, he could hear the echoes of a little boy's laughter. Memories of days that could never return. Dash remained silent at his side, and Jesse studied his strong profile in the waning light. His dark hair was swept back from his brow, and his cheekbones slashed up straight and strong above curving lips that Jesse knew were soft and giving.

"We should get back."

Dash took his hand, and they walked to the street, where the carriage horses for hire waited patiently, some with their heads buried in their feed buckets. A man lurched toward them, stumbling drunk, hands outstretched and gibbering nonsense. Jesse froze at the man's wild eyes. He smelled the stink of his breath. A buzzing sounded in his head, and his vision grayed.

It's happening again.

"Jesse, *Jess*. It's okay."

Jesse awoke from his trance to allow Dash to pull

him away, and they hurried across the street, where they made it halfway down the block before he pulled at Dash's arm.

"Wait," he gasped. "I need a sec."

Safe. He was safe now. Trembling and weak, Jesse rubbed his eyes. Dash hovered before him, worry puckering his brow. People passed by them, shooting curious looks but not stopping. It took several deep breaths, but Jesse got his thundering heart settled down to where he could speak.

"I'm okay." He paused a moment and gazed at Dash with wonder. A smile broke out across his face, and he repeated, "I'm okay." A moment later Dash crushed him close, and Jesse held on to him. "I'm okay," he whispered, his face pressed into Dash's chest.

"You're better than okay. You're everything."

With his hand held firmly in Dash's, they walked back down the block, the vastness of the sky and the crowds no longer as forbidding and dangerous as Jesse contemplated. Yes, he still shook and his heart still raced with fear when someone came too close to him as they walked. He couldn't imagine doing it alone, but this brief foray outside had shown him that however long he'd hidden away from life, it went on without him. He could either learn that even though his fears were real, he could conquer them, or he could continue to be a spectator of life, watching from his luxury prison, his nose pressed against the window.

"Dash, you working tonight?" The guard, Spencer, greeted them. "How're you doing tonight, Mr. Grace-Martin?"

With a pang, Jesse knew the man addressed him so formally because he didn't know who he really was. Many residents didn't like to be familiar with the staff and have them know their business. Jesse wasn't like that, and he gave the man a friendly smile.

"Please call me Jesse. I'm not that formal."

Spencer nodded, and Jesse saw his eyes flicker to his and Dash's clasped hands. Too late, Jesse remembered what Dash had said earlier and let go. Hopefully nothing would come of it.

"Yeah, I'm working the midnight-to-eight shift now. All the dirty work. Talk to you later."

As they passed the booth, Jesse caught sight of another guard watching them. He gave the man a friendly smile, but all he received in return was a tilt of the head. Anxious to get home, he and Dash crossed the courtyard swiftly, and within minutes, were back in his apartment.

"Go sit." Dash pointed to the living room. "I'll get us something to drink."

"Thanks," he whispered and dragged himself off to collapse on the sofa, feeling as if he'd run a marathon. Uphill. With cement in his shoes. Jesse had never felt so drained, and when Dash handed him a bottle of beer, he drank down half in one noisy, slurping gulp.

"You're not having one?" He wiped his mouth on his sleeve, noticing Dash with a bottle of water.

"I don't think I should show up to work with beer on my breath. They frown on us coming in buzzed," he said with a smile. "But I wouldn't mind a taste."

Jesse held out the bottle, but Dash set it on the

table and grasped him by the neck instead, so their mouths hovered close and he could feel Dash's hot breath on his cheek.

Dash's tongue traced a leisurely path around his lips, and Jesse sighed, sliding his arms around Dash's neck. He flicked his tongue against Dash's and groaned when Dash sucked on it hungrily. His bones turned to mush, and he pressed his lips tightly against Dash's, wishing they could stay like this all night.

Dash buried both hands in his hair, tugging slightly, and Jesse moved closer and straddled him, wrapping his legs around Dash's hips as best he could, given their position on the sofa. Their erections rubbed, and he ground into Dash's lap, his body aflame, hearing nothing but the roaring in his ears and the heavy breaths, grunts, and moans from Dash.

"Oh, fuck. Oh, babe..." Dash stiffened, then let out several heavy sighs. Warmth spread beneath him, and knowing he'd given Dash satisfaction was enough to send Jesse flying over the edge.

"Dash," he sobbed out, holding him tight around the neck. He shuddered to completion, and they lay together for a few minutes before Dash gave his ass a squeeze.

"I haven't come in my pants since I was a kid but damn, that was hot. Good thing I have a change of clothes for tonight. Lemme up, and I'll go take a shower."

Jesse rolled off him to lie on the sofa. Still short of breath, he held his hand out when Dash got up. "Well, I'm coming with you." He gave a grin. "So to speak.

Let's shower together, and then I'll make you a sandwich for dinner."

"Or," Dash said with a sparkle in his eyes, "I can lick you clean, get my protein, then take a quick shower while you make me a sandwich." He sank to his knees and popped the button on Jesse's jeans without waiting for an answer.

"Or that." Jesse sighed, giving himself over to Dash's warm mouth and tongue playing over his skin.

Chapter Twenty

NOT EVEN WORKING the midnight shift could wipe the smile off Dash's face. He strode into the employees' locker room with the taste of Jesse's kiss still warm on his tongue. It was torture to leave him that morning, knowing that he had to go home in the evening because he needed a fresh change of clothes and had to check on his mother.

His good mood soured when he spotted Emilio drinking a cup of coffee, but he forced a smile. The two of them hadn't had much to say to each other since the last time they worked together.

"Hey." Dash figured better to be friendly than short with the man. He had a nasty side. "How'd the night go so far?" He passed by Emilio on his way to the area where the lockers were located, and stood before his, opened the lock, then proceeded to undress to change into his work clothes.

"Quiet here." Emilio finished his coffee and tossed the paper cup in the trash can. He joined Dash by the lockers, leaning his hip against the wall, watching Dash change. "How was *your* night? Do anything fun?"

The slight edge to Emilio's voice sent a warning

flutter through Dash, but he kept an easy smile. "Nah. Nothing big. Just hung out."

"Hung out. Uh-huh. Okay." Emilio pushed off the wall. "I'm outta here."

"No problem." Dash finished buttoning up his uniform. "See ya." Emilio couldn't leave fast enough for Dash. He kept his gaze focused straight ahead, and it wasn't until the door shut behind Emilio that Dash breathed a sigh of relief. Not a minute later, the door bounced open, and Dash tensed, expecting to see Emilio, but it was Hector instead, and his wariness faded. A real smile curved his lips.

"Hey, what's up?" They clasped hands.

"Nothin'. I'm hopin' we have a quiet night."

Dash rolled his eyes. "Yeah. No trash-picking. I had enough of that last night."

Hector snickered. "Better you than me, brother." He folded his arms. "Only this time don't be stupid. Take the fucking tip if someone offers. They can afford it. Ain't no one living here poor."

Thinking of Jesse and feeling a bit defensive, Dash shut his locker and snapped the lock in place. "Well, yeah. I guess. It was pretty stupid of me. She just pissed me off."

"Want a coffee? I'm buying." Hector stood before the urn that held the coffee they had brewing all day for the staff.

Dash chuckled. "Sure, big spender. Milk, no sugar."

"So," Hector said after handing him the cup. "What's the deal with you and that Jesse Grace-

Martin?"

Careful not to react, Dash took a sip before answering. "What're you talking about? Deal?"

Sighing, Hector sat on the long metal table. "Don't screw with me, man. I got eyes and ears. You guys, um…" He paused. "Dating? Hooking up?"

His face hot and the coffee suddenly bitter on his tongue, Dash shrugged. "We're friends."

"Okay. I understand if you're together, not wanting to say nothing. But if that's the case, you need to be careful. 'Cause the talk I'm hearing tonight when I came in was that you two been lookin' all cozy and shit. A lot more than friends, if you know what I mean."

Furious that he'd allowed this to happen, Dash drew in some deep breaths to keep calm and not go off on Hector, who he knew was simply trying to help. "Thanks, man. But we're really just friends." His lips burned, remembering Jesse's tongue in his mouth.

"Okay. I said my piece, and that's it." He slapped his hands on the table. "We'd better get to work."

"Sounds like what we're supposed to be doing, instead of sitting around gabbing about my life." They left the service area to walk through the building.

The night proved uneventful, and Dash worked alongside Hector, moving the day's garbage to the dumpsters, mopping the stairwells, and answering several calls from residents regarding leaky toilets and burned-out lightbulbs in the hallways.

The other evening he'd watched *Rosemary's Baby*, which was filmed at the Dakota in 1968, and he was amazed to see how the outside of the building hadn't changed at all, except for the security booth on the street. The hallways inside, however, looked totally different, and when he asked Eddie about it, the man laughed.

"Yeah, the board told them no way would they let a film crew inside. Even to film a movie. They had to find a different building to film the hallways and stuff. Crazy, right?"

On two separate occasions, one at one a.m. and the other at four a.m., they were each asked to escort residents who'd had too much to drink and needed assistance to find their apartments and open the doors.

"I had to tell the lady that I wasn't able to undress her and put her to bed," Dash said, trying to hold back his laughter. "But she did have enough brain cells working to offer me a tip."

"The question is, did *you* have the brain cells to accept it, or did you act the fool again?"

Dash dug into his pants pocket, pulled out the hundred-dollar bill, and waved it under Hector's bug-eyed stare. "Sure did."

"Damn. You hit it big-time. I only got a twenty." They bumped fists. "Nice work there."

Dash shoved the bill back into his pocket and checked his watch. "Almost that time. I gotta get home. Got stuff to do." He yawned and stretched. "Hope I don't fall asleep on the ride uptown."

They were in the process of changing back into their regular clothes when Paul, the day porter and Emilio's best friend, came in. "Sadiko. Buchanan wants to see you."

Disliking the smirk on Paul's face, Dash wondered what the super wanted to talk to him about. Probably scheduling. He pulled on the leather jacket Jesse had given him and shut the locker door with a bang. "Okay. See you tonight, Hector."

"Daaaaamn. That is one fine-ass jacket."

"Uh, thanks." He mentally kicked himself for wearing it to work.

"They're makin' the fakes you get on Canal Street look as good as the real ones. You're gonna have to hook me up with who you got this from."

"Yeah, sure. I'd better get going. See what Buchanan wants."

"Yup. Have a good one."

Dash left the employees' break room and walked to the end of the hall, to the door marked with faded gold letters that read, Office. He knocked.

"C'min."

Ryan Buchanan sat behind the big metal desk that took up much of the small room. He was a round, teddy-bear type with a white halo of hair surrounding his shiny, freckled scalp. He might have looked like a congenial man, but his light-blue eyes pierced right through most bullshit, and he didn't have to speak loudly to get his point across. He'd been the super of the Dakota for over fifteen years and had the respect of the workers and residents alike.

"Dash, siddown."

Still unsure what this was about, Dash didn't ask questions. He did as he was told.

"How's it goin'? Everything good?"

"Yeah. Fine, thanks."

Buchanan's stubby fingers played with a well-chewed pencil, twirling it before throwing it across the desk. "Shit. I hate this."

Dash's heart fell. He knew what was about to happen but held out hope. Maybe it would be a warning. Maybe…

"Someone came to me. Tole me you were hangin' out with one of the residents. Maybe more than hangin' out."

Dash's face heated and he opened his mouth, but Buchanan kept speaking.

"Look. I don't wanna know your business. What you do on your time is your own. But people have been comin' to me. Tellin' me you been goin' to Jesse Grace-Martin's apartment on your break. They seen you going up after you finish your shift, then come out hours later with the guy, holdin' hands." He put up a palm. "Now before you say something, I don' give a flyin' fuck if you're straight or gay or waddever. But you gotta follow the rules like everyone else."

"I haven't done anything wrong."

"Dash." Buchanan's unexpectedly sympathetic voice gave him no comfort, and Dash braced himself. "You know we got rules about the workers getting close with the residents. It ain't allowed. I gotta let you go. I'm sorry."

"Not even a warning? That's not fair."

"Were you with him yesterday evening? Someone said they saw you holding hands." He dropped his gaze to study something fascinating on the desk. "They said you was kissing him. You gotta understand I can't make exceptions. Last year we fired Pedro, also a great worker, 'cause he was sleeping with one of the residents. It wouldn't be fair that I let you go with a warning and yet I fired him."

Dash knew Buchanan was right, yet it didn't make it easier to swallow.

"If they were wrong, tell me, and I'll believe you. Tell me there ain't nothing between you and him, and I'll tell them they were wrong." Buchanan's gaze locked with his. "Tell me?"

This was the way for him to keep his job. All he had to do was repudiate his relationship with Jesse to Buchanan, even though the man knew he was lying. He and Jesse could keep it on the down-low. If he explained it to Jesse, Dash knew he'd agree. But...no. Jesse needed to walk beside him in the sunlight as well as the shadows, and Dash refused to hide.

"It's okay. I get it. I'll clean out my locker." He stood and stuck out his hand. "No hard feelings. I know you're just doing your job. But I gotta do what's best for me."

"I'm sorry, Dash. It ain't how I wanted this to end."

"Me either." But, Dash thought as he walked out of Buchanan's office, pride was more important than money. And Dash needed to see Jesse and have him say everything was going to be all right.

As he predicted, Jesse was furious when Dash told him. He, Miranda, and Jesse sat around the large island, drinking the coffee Miranda insisted on making when he showed up and said he had to talk.

"This is fucking outrageous and ridiculous," Jesse sputtered. "I'm going to speak to them."

"Who? They're right. I violated their rules. I signed a code of conduct and agreed to be bound by it." As much as Dash was crushed he no longer worked there, he understood. He'd gambled and lost. But watching Jesse storm about the kitchen, his eyes blazing sparks as he continued to rant about the injustice, Dash knew he might've lost the battle but he'd won the war. He had the ultimate prize in Jesse's love.

"But what's going to happen now? Oh, wait. Let's call Harry. I'm sure you can start earlier at the firm. Better for you in the long run."

"I don't want to seem pushy."

"Don't be silly." Jesse pulled his phone to him and hit Speed Dial, while Dash stared into his cup.

He'd used the money from this job to pay his rent, and with the little left over, helped his mother. Now he had nothing. While working at the firm was the solution to paying off his mother's retainer to Harry, Dash still needed to make money to live.

"…Yeah. So they fucking fired him. I know they have those rules, but they're stupid." Jesse's gaze flickered to his. "I'm not sure. I'd better go. I need to talk to him.…I will. Tell my mom I said hi."

Once he'd hung up, Jesse gave him a smile. "Harry said you could start anytime you want. Not to worry."

Not to worry? Easy for Jesse to say. "Uh, that's great and all, but I'm not getting paid for that. I need a paying job. I gotta pay my rent and stuff."

"Oh, that's an easy fix. You'll move in here. Problem solved." Jesse turned to Miranda. "Can you order some extra towels, and Dash, tell her what kind of soap and stuff you like—"

"Whoa, whoa," Dash said, standing up so quickly, the stool screeched across the floor. "Where did you come up with the idea I'm moving in here?"

If he weren't so annoyed with Jesse, Dash would've laughed at how cute he looked with his scrunched-up face.

"What do you mean? It's the perfect solution. You need a place. I have room. End of story. No rent, no harm, no foul."

Tactful as always, Miranda slipped out of the room, but not before Dash saw her shake her head at Jesse. Their time together hadn't changed Jesse's years of conditioning of getting whatever he wanted with no questions asked. He spent money by gazing at a screen, seeing something he wanted and getting it—instant gratification. Dash couldn't wrap his head around that way of life. At all. Not that he wanted the struggle, but what rankled more was Jesse's assumption that he could plan Dash's life without any input from him.

"And what? I live off you? You become my sugar daddy? Are you kidding me?"

The worst thing was how bewildered Jesse looked as Dash spoke to him. Like nothing they'd discussed concerning money had made an impression and he'd been humoring Dash all along.

"Sugar daddy? What the hell? No, of course not. I was just trying to help—"

"By thinking you'll save me with your money? See? This is why I didn't want to accept that jacket from you." He took it off and hung it on the back of the chair. Despite the spaciousness of the room, the walls closed in on him. He needed out. "I gotta go. I…I'll talk to you." Ignoring Jesse's call to come back and talk, Dash couldn't leave fast enough, and after grabbing his backpack, slammed the door behind him. For the first time, he was glad Jesse wouldn't be able to follow him, and he stood, chest heaving, pushing furiously at the elevator button. He left the building and strode through the courtyard and the front gates, not pausing to say anything to the startled guards. Hot tears of humiliation burned his eyes, and he moved as if on automatic, until he found himself inside the train station, waiting for the uptown train. At that moment, Dash wasn't sure he'd ever return to the Dakota again.

Chapter Twenty-One

THEY HADN'T EVEN pretended to work after Dash left. Jesse couldn't believe Dash had walked out instead of talking, and it left him uncertain. For a second he wanted to run after Dash, but then a voice inside him stopped him.

If Dash loved me, he would've stayed. I trusted Dash to always be there, and he left. What if I was outside and Dash walked away from me? Would I be left alone?

He began to shiver, violent shakes sending him to curl up in a ball on the sofa. Love wasn't supposed to hurt.

Was it?

"Why are you putting so much pressure on him?" Miranda set aside her iPad. "His whole life has fallen apart lately."

"I thought I was making it easier. If he moved in with me, he wouldn't have anything to worry about." He gnawed at his bottom lip.

"Oh, Jesse, you know how sensitive he is about your money. You've told me he doesn't like it when you pay for everything all the time or give him gifts. What made you think he'd be okay with this?"

Jesse hugged his legs tight to his chest and rested his cheek on his knees. "I thought he'd want to be with me." And as he spoke, Jesse realized the problem. "But I'm making this about me, aren't I? When it's about him and how he feels."

At Miranda's nod, he ran back to the kitchen to grab his phone and call Dash. As he paced, he called. Nothing. Straight to voice mail. *Dammit.* He hit the button again and again.

"Nothing. No answer." Jesse threw his phone across the sofa. "What the hell."

"Maybe there's no service where he is."

"Or maybe he doesn't want to talk to me."

Miranda left her seat to sit next to him. "Look, Jesse. You hurt his pride. Give him a chance to cool off. He lost his job because of your relationship, and he knew the risk, but he loved you enough to take it. When the dust settles, what risks are you willing to take for him?"

MIRANDA'S WORDS PLAYED through his mind during that day and the next. He knew she was right, but that didn't keep him from calling Dash. It wasn't until later the following evening that Dash finally answered.

"Hi."

"Hi." God, they sounded so formal. Like they hadn't ever said I love you or kissed and held each other all night long. "I'm sorry. I was wrong. I see that now."

"Miranda talked to you?"

Dash sounded odd, and Jesse chose his words carefully. "Well, we talked, yeah. But I realized on my own that I fucked up."

"Oh, yeah?"

"Dash, please." Jesse gripped the phone. "I-I know it was wrong to assume the rest of your life without talking to you. I didn't think about you, only me. I'm sorry."

"I know you are. And so am I. But...I don't know anymore." Jesse strained to hear Dash's voice. "Maybe we're just too different to make this work, 'cause your first thought to solving every problem is to throw money at it to make it go away, and that's not me."

"You make me sound like a terrible person. I was trying to help you, make it easier for you so that you'd have one less thing to worry about while you looked for another job." He swallowed past the tightness in his throat. "I thought that's what you did for the people you loved. I love you, and I thought you loved me too."

"I do love you. That hasn't changed, but it's like you haven't heard anything I said. I can't live off you." He paused. "My mother got the necklaces you sent her and my sister. How expensive were they?"

"Not at all. I swear. I was doing an article on the stones, and Miranda mentioned how pretty they were, and I got one for her too." Jesse's hand curled into a fist. "Please, Dash. Now what? Can't I make it right? I only know who I am because I love you."

"Ahh, babe, that's not true. Maybe I helped along the way, but you did it all on your own. Now you gotta let me do it my own way too."

"I just want to help," Jesse whispered, wondering if the pain in his chest was his heart breaking into pieces. "I don't want to lose you."

He waited, holding his breath, hoping.

"Then let me find myself."

✧　✧　✧　✧

THAT NIGHT, JESSE sat staring out his window into the dark void of the park, only dozing off near twilight. He woke early and watched the clock until Miranda came and handed him his coffee.

"Did you sleep at all?"

"A little," he said, shrugging. "I talked to Dash." He sipped the hot coffee, welcoming the burn through his numb, cold body.

"And?" Miranda took the club chair opposite him and tucked her feet underneath her. "Did you work things out?"

"I don't know. He says he needs time to think about what he wants. That he needs to find himself." The words tasted bitter on his tongue. "I have to talk to Dr. Mingione."

Miranda nodded. "I think that's a good idea. I'll leave you alone and go to the back to check your email."

Absently nodding in her direction, Jesse picked up the phone. Dr. Mingione wouldn't be in her office yet, but he'd leave a message with her service. To his surprise, not even ten minutes passed before she called him back.

"Jesse, what's wrong?"

"I think I messed up the best thing to ever happen to me."

The words tumbled out of him, but to his surprise, he felt immeasurably better after he finished telling his story.

"So that's where we are now. Dash needs to figure himself out, and I feel like if we love each other, I should be part of that process for him."

"Did you say that to him?"

"N-no. I couldn't. I mean, that's not a conversation to have over the phone, but he's not about to come back here right now."

"You're right. Those are words to have face-to-face. So what do you want to do?"

Restlessness welled up inside him, and the urge to be with Dash, to see him and tell him that he didn't care about the money, that he'd give it all up if only he'd come back, grew so strong, he blurted out, "I need to see him. Now. I don't want to wait."

"So," she said, a little softer now and more gently, "what are you going to do?"

His head spun, the years of solitude and agoraphobia battling with the love and desire he felt for Dash. Could he? Was he strong enough to do this? Dash had known the rules and hadn't cared, deliberately breaking them to help him. To be with him. That was love. Feeling resolute, he held the phone tight. "I'm going to let him know how I feel."

"You can do it. I've seen you grow more this year than in the previous four, and I have such faith in you and the bond you created with Dash. And remember, I'm only a phone call away."

"Thanks, I'll be in touch." He exited the call. "Miranda," he yelled.

"What? What's wrong?" She skidded into the room.

"Nothing." Jumpy and incapable of sitting still, he paced the room, his pulse fluttering and heart pounding over what he was about to say. He stood by the window overlooking the park and spotted the bench he and Dash sat on three nights ago. Traffic streamed by, people hurried or strolled leisurely. No one had any idea his whole life had exploded around him. "Will you do something for me?"

"Honey, I'll do anything you want."

"Can you get us a car?" He hugged himself around the waist, sick to his stomach, but never more sure of anything in his life. "I want to go to the Bronx. To Dash."

Miranda's brows shot up and her eyes grew wide as she searched his face. "The Bronx?"

"I need to prove to myself I can do this. For me. When Dash and I sat on the bench outside the park, I saw how much I missed all these past years hiding. If I can do this, it'll show Dash that I'm willing to do anything for us. I don't want to lose myself again to the dark."

"Oh, honey." She hugged him, and he clung to her as the one person in his life who stood by him no matter what. Feeling disloyal, he still couldn't help but wish it were Dash he held on to. "I'm so proud of you."

"I haven't done anything."

"Are you serious?" Miranda let him go to study his face. "You want to travel to the Bronx. That would never have happened last year."

"Let's see how I feel getting into that car," he said grimly, his stomach twisted in a knot of fear.

"Do you have his address?"

"Yeah, and his mother's too from when I sent her the gift. I looked them up."

Miranda had her phone in hand. "You want to do this now? Or take some time to think about it?"

"There's nothing to think about. I need to talk to Dash. Face-to-face. He needs to understand *I* understand his concerns."

Without answering, Miranda pressed a few buttons, then nodded. "Okay. All done. The car will be outside in seven minutes." She gripped his arm. "Ready?"

Cold sweat popped up on his brow, but he forced a thin smile. "As I'll ever be."

Together they walked through the doors, Jesse almost forgetting that last year, or even six months ago, that act alone would've been foreign to him. Now, everything inside him focused on going outside and getting into a car that would take him to Dash. The elevator ride was a blur, and he concentrated on putting one step in front of the other, only dimly realizing he was on the sidewalk when Miranda opened a car door in front of him.

"Okay, honey. Slide in. I'm right next to you."

He gulped air and followed her direction, leaning his head against the window.

"He okay?" the driver asked. "He ain't gonna puke

in my car, is he?"

"I'm fine," Jesse gritted out. "Just drive. Please."

"Okay. Just don't throw up. If you do, I gotta charge you a cleaning fee."

The car lurched forward, and they took off, Jesse's hands digging into the seat as they made their way through midmorning traffic. His breaths came short, and he panted. He tried closing his eyes, but the sway of the car made his nausea worse, so instead he focused on the back of the driver's head. Eventually they drove off the highway and onto city streets, where Jesse could see tall apartment buildings and stores mixed in with modest, single-family homes. The car pulled up in front of a red-brick building, which hadn't managed to escape the scourge of graffiti. Aside from the spray-painted names, the double eagles, which Dash had told him were an Albanian symbol, were featured prominently on several walls, as well as on flags in the neighborhood he'd seen flying in many front yards.

"This is it." The driver glanced over his shoulder. "You gonna need me to wait or somethin'?"

"No," Miranda said and opened the door. "We're fine. Right, Jess?"

He could do this. "Yeah." His voice squeaked, and he cleared his throat. "Yeah. Thanks." He took Miranda's hand, and they stood on the sidewalk and watched the car drive away.

"Ready? Are you sure you want to do this?"

No. I have no idea what I'm doing. I want to be back home. Where it's safe. Where I was safe.

"I have to be. If I'm not, I've got nothing."

Miranda opened her mouth as if she was about to contradict him, then pressed her lips together and gave his hand a hard squeeze. "Then let's go."

The air blew cool, and people passed by them, but for once, Jesse didn't wonder if they were after him. His sole focus was to put one foot in front of the other and get inside Dash's building. They walked up the steps and pushed open the door, coming face-to-face with several rows of names, most foreign to him in spelling and pronunciation. After running his finger down the rows, he came to the label "Dashamir Sadiko" next to Apt. 2J. He pressed the button and waited, still holding on to Miranda.

Nothing. Jesse pressed again, this time in shorter, almost desperate jabs. Dash had to be here. After almost a minute, the box crackled to life.

"Who is it?"

Jesse swallowed. "Dash? It's me."

"Me, who?"

"Jesse. I'm here with Miranda. Can…can we come up?"

"Wait, what? Jesse? You…what the hell?"

Miranda leaned over. "Dash, it's Miranda. Can you let us in? Please?"

"I fucking don't believe this." But the buzzer sounded, and he and Miranda walked inside. The walls were covered with dingy, peeling paint, and a pervasive odor of boiled cabbage and other cooked foods hit Jesse. This was as far from the rarified, lavender-scented air of the Dakota as a person could get. And yet Jesse knew, if presented with the choice, he'd give it all up to have Dash.

Miranda pressed the elevator button. Gears shifted, and then the door slid open. He pressed one and stayed still, hugging his arms around himself, looking at the floor, hoping the elevator wouldn't crash to the ground. When the door opened, Dash stood waiting on the other side.

"It *is* you. I thought I was hearing things."

Jesse gazed at Dash, drinking in the sight of him. Dark circles ringed his eyes, and a rough beard covered his face. "You look tired."

"I haven't been sleeping too well."

Jesse's hands curled into fists at his side. God, he wanted to touch Dash so badly, it was physically painful to stand there and talk as if they were strangers.

"Me either."

A door opened, and an old woman in a housedress and worn slippers shuffled out, holding a plastic bag. She pushed it down a chute in the wall, and after saying something to them in a language Jesse didn't understand, went back into her apartment and slammed the door behind her.

"You'd better come in." Dash led them down the hall to his apartment and hesitated only a moment before opening the door. "Excuse the mess," he mumbled, and Jesse stepped into Dash's world.

The room wasn't more than three hundred square feet. Two small windows with bars flanked the far walls, looking out at the brick wall of the opposite building. A tiny kitchenette was built into a niche to Jesse's right, and a small desk with a laptop faced the double bed, with only a foot or so between them to spare. Dash swept off the seat of the one chair.

"Here, Miranda, please sit." Dash avoided his eyes, and Jesse had the horrible feeling he was embarrassed they saw the cheerless conditions in which he lived.

"Thanks, Dash. It's fine. If you don't mind, I'll just check something while you guys chat." She brought out a pair of earphones, plugged them into her phone, and slipped them on.

"It's no big deal," Jesse said hurriedly. "I made the split-second decision to come see you."

"Uh, yeah, what's this about?" Dash took him by the arm and steered him toward the windows on the other side of the apartment. "I can't believe you're here. Are you okay?" His dark eyes searched Jesse's face.

"I think so. I came because...nothing was right without you. I needed to talk, and what I had to say was too important not to be with you. In person. So here I am." He gave a weak laugh, but Dash didn't smile. He ran his fingers over Jesse's cheek.

"Here you are. It isn't pretty, right?"

Jesse caught Dash's hand and held it against his face.

"I came for you, not to see how big or small your apartment is. You're so caught up in this...stuff." He waved his hand around. "I don't see it. You told me you fell in love with me despite how rich I was. I love you, whether you have money or not. This all means nothing."

"Nothing?" Dash's incredulous laugh rang out harsh. "It's everything. It shapes a person. It can beat them down or make them hungry for more. And I thought that was me...that I wanted more, until I saw maybe that isn't the best way to live either."

"It doesn't have to be either-or. Why are you making life so black-and-white? This isn't about money at all for me." Frustrated, Jesse smacked his thigh. "One thing losing the person I loved most in the world taught me is that money *isn't* everything." He grabbed Dash's hands, hating the doubt in his eyes. "Love is. Rich people, poor people...no one was spared on that day. It's wonderful to have that safety net, but I could go bankrupt tomorrow and I'd still love you and know I'd be happy."

"You say that because you've never been poor. Believe me, money helps."

Tired of beating around the bush, Jesse confronted Dash. "Really? Well, it didn't do a damn bit of good for me these past five years. I was a prisoner in a decorated jail, but make no mistake, I was miserable and unhappy and would've given up everything...*everything* to be like you." He bit his lip. "I'm not here to apologize for having money, Dash. That doesn't make me who I am. I'm more than my bank account, and I thought you of all people saw that. If you can't, I don't know what else to say."

Dash let go of his hands and rubbed his face. "You say it means nothing, but this is it. This is the real me. Now you know. What if this is all we had? Could you be happy living like this?"

"I'd have to make the bed at least." His attempt at humor fell flat, and he changed tactics. "Right. So now

I know. I know how much I missed you not being with me. The halls echoed with nothingness. I know how much I hated that you weren't there to talk to in the evening when I was alone. I know how much I need you, and I'm willing to change. I've learned I can't solve the issues between us with a credit card or by throwing money at them. Please, Dash. Don't leave. Don't you think what we have is worth figuring out?"

With a sigh, Dash leaned against the window. "Can we? I knew from the start loving you would be a risk."

"I risked everything to come here today. Every step I took made me sick. I thought my heart would give out when I got in the car. But you're worth it to me. Life is one big fucking risk every day. We're lucky to wake up. We're lucky to make it through each day. But I know you're worth any risk I could possibly take." He rested his hands on Dash's shoulders. "Please, Dash, I'm not trying to buy you or make you feel like a kept man. Just don't give up on us because of pride."

Dash pulled him close and held him tight. Peace soaked through him, and Jesse rested his cheek against Dash's rough, scratchy beard.

"I guess I could be less touchy about you spending money. But if it affects both of us, I want to be able to give my opinion and ideas and not have you make it a done deal. Lots of things can be accomplished without using money."

"I'm willing." Jesse slid his fingers through Dash's wavy hair. "Are you?" He held his breath, honestly not sure how Dash might answer.

"Now that you're here, I see how stupid I was to

run away. But I have a favor to ask."

Happiness poured through Jesse, and he flung his arms around Dash. "Anything."

"Do you think you can come with me somewhere?" Jesse opened his mouth, but Dash cut him off. "It's to my mom's apartment. Around the corner." He glanced over his shoulder. "Miranda too, of course."

The thought made Jesse sick, but he'd walk through fire to be with Dash. Today had proven he was stronger than he thought.

"Yeah. I'm willing to go anywhere as long as I'm with you."

Chapter Twenty-Two

A N HOUR LATER, Dash sat in his mother's living room in a scenario he'd never dreamed possible. His mother and Miranda flanked Jesse on the sofa while he sat next to his sister and drank the strong coffee served with freshly baked *shendetlie*—a delicious dough sweetened with honey, filled with walnuts, and soaked in a simple syrup mixture. His mother watched Jesse with anxious eyes as he took a bite.

"Oh, my God...this is delicious." Jesse licked his lips and took another bite. "I think I've died and gone to heaven. Thank you so much, Mrs. Sadiko."

"It was nothing. I will send you home with some goodies."

"I could live and die on just this," Jesse said happily.

Miranda sipped her tea and took a piece of *baklava*. "This is better than anything I've ever gotten from any bakery."

"You're making me blush," his mother said, putting her hands to her cheeks. "Dash knows I love having my family around me, and for all you've done for him and me, you are part of ours now."

"Plus"—his sister slipped her arm through his—"it's about time he finally brought home a boyfriend."

"Oh?" His mother's gaze softened. "Is there something you forgot to mention? Last time we discussed it, you told me to stop imagining things. So tell me"—a smile she couldn't contain broke free—"*is* Jesse your boyfriend?"

Jesse remained silent. Waiting. And Dash, who'd never believed he'd reach this point, and could no more deny Jesse and his place in his life than he could his own heart, nodded.

"Yes. He is. I love him."

A beautiful smile bloomed over Jesse's face, and he ducked his head.

"Then I will love him too." His mother gave him a tender smile, her eyes wet and shiny.

"I know you and Drita have always been okay with me being gay, but I've never been in a relationship before. It's different now. When I come to visit, I'm hoping to bring Jesse with me. I won't hide him."

"And why should you?" His mother's mood shifted, her eyes now snapping black fire. Dash couldn't ever recall seeing her so vibrant and alive. "All my life I've been told what I should think or do or feel. But the one thing I've never needed anyone to remind me of is how much I love you and your sister. What I wish for you is what every mother wants for her child. Health. Happiness. Someone to love." She directed her next words to Jesse. "And you, Jesse? What do you have to say?"

"I love Dash. I love him enough to ask him to live

with me, but he said no."

His mother blinked. "What? Move into that beautiful apartment?" Her brow furrowed. "And you said no, Dashamir? Why would you do that?"

"I always knew you were an idiot. This proves it," Drita muttered under her breath.

"Because I don't want to live off Jesse. I need to make it on my own." Even to him, his words sounded weak.

"When you're in love, you're no longer on your own. You'll never be alone again. Love is a partnership. You are gaining something. Togetherness. Jesse." Once again, she addressed Jesse. "Are you willing to move out of your apartment if Dash feels uncomfortable there?"

"You know, having money is a wonderful thing. It gives me the freedom to do what I want. And yet...my money means nothing if I have no one to share my life with. It creates a lifestyle that looks beautiful on the outside but is an empty illusion underneath. I could have almost anything, but nothing satisfied me. Until I met Dash." Jesse turned to him. "You have to believe me," he pleaded, and Dash couldn't look away. "I don't want to own you. I want to be your partner and share my life with you." His eyes twinkled. "And my life happens to come with a multimillion-dollar apartment attached to it." The momentary humor fled, and Dash watched Jesse grow more agitated. "But, um..." He pushed his fingers through his hair, his expression almost haunted, looking everywhere but at Dash. The seconds ticked by, and Dash tensed, gripping the edge of the sofa, waiting for Jesse to battle those inner demons. Their eyes met across the coffee table, and Jesse smiled. "I'm willing to do whatever it takes to be together," he said softly.

"Really?" For Jesse to give up his apartment, his security...the place that held the memories of his father, told Dash more about the bond they shared than anything else could. "Even though it's where you grew up? And your father..." Dash couldn't go on.

"I don't need to live in that apartment to remember my father. He's always with me. I've spent enough of my life living in the past. I think he'd want me to look toward building a future."

"Drita, Miranda." His mother stood and waved her hand, beckoning to the two women, who rose and followed her. "Could you both help me in the kitchen?"

Dash rolled his eyes. "Subtle, Mom."

"Don't be disrespectful to your mother, Dash." Jesse snickered.

"Thank you, Jesse." Dash hadn't seen his mother smile so bright in years. "I'll have some extra *baklava* to send home with you."

"Thank you. You're the best."

Dash glared, but Jesse returned a sunny smile. When it was only the two of them left in the room, Dash joined Jesse on the sofa. "Is that what you really want?"

"*Baklava?* Mmm, yeah, it's delish—*ohhh*."

Dash silenced him with a kiss he meant only to last a moment but tasted like a lifetime on his lips. "Now," he said, breathing heavily against Jesse's cheek, "that's one way to quiet your sassy mouth."

Jesse rested his head against Dash's shoulder. "I can think of others, but I don't want to get you all worked up with them in the kitchen." Dash shivered when Jesse kissed his neck. "Come home with me tonight? We can start looking for a new place together in the morning."

Dash gazed around his mother's apartment. The place he grew up in. He saw the worn carpeting and the stains on the ceiling from the leak caused by the apartment above. He heard the laughter from the kitchen and smelled the scent of honey and vanilla in the air. There might've been poverty and sadness within the walls, but there was also plenty of love. Then he recalled Jesse's beautiful large apartment and the lonely, silent air hanging in every room. There'd been no laughter there for a while. No spilled milk or scents of something delicious cooking in the oven.

"I-I don't want that."

Jesse drew back sharply. "Wh-what? I thought we worked it out. What's wrong now?"

Dash cupped his cheek, grazing Jesse's damp lips with the pad of his thumb. "I'm being selfish. I don't need you to change your life for me to make mine."

"I'm not understanding."

Dash cradled Jesse's face in the palms of his hands. "I'll move in with you. I'd have to be insane not to live in the most beautiful building in New York. I want to make a home with you. Bring love and life back into your apartment. But when I get a job, I want to pay. I know it won't be much, but it'll make me feel as if I'm contributing."

Dash found himself knocked on his back on the sofa with Jesse's arms around his neck. "Don't diminish your contribution. You saved my life. There's no way I can ever repay you. And yes. Yes to it all. Whatever you want. See how agreeable I can be?"

BACK AT THE Dakota, after Dash had collected enough clothing to last him several days, they lay in bed, Dash tracing the ridges of Jesse's abdomen with his tongue before moving lower, teasing him.

"Yes, please," Jesse panted out, wiggling his ass. "See? I'm being agreeable again. Don't I get a reward?"

"I guess I can give you what you need."

Jesse raised himself on an elbow, serious in the late-afternoon sunlight streaming in through the windows. "You. That's all I need. The rest is replaceable."

Dash smiled around the jut of Jesse's hip bone, then licked at the springy hair of his groin before taking Jesse's rigid cock deep. Jesse's taste and scent enveloped him, filled him up until their very essence mixed and mingled. He could feel himself sinking into Jesse's blood and bones, imprinting himself on Jesse's heart. Forever. Together.

Dash licked across the slick head of Jesse's cock, his tongue rough and lips pulling hard. Jesse groaned and twisted the bedsheets into knots. He thrashed back and forth on the pillow.

"Dash. Please."

God, he wanted this man and must've been a damn fool to think he could solve their problems by running away. Precome filled his mouth, and his moans joined Jesse's. Beneath the clutch of his fingers, Jesse's thighs trembled as he gasped for air. From his increasingly rapid hip pumping, Dash guessed Jesse wasn't far off from coming.

But he wanted more.

With one final lick, he withdrew off Jesse's cock.

"What the hell...*Dash*," Jesse whined, his frustration obvious, and Dash almost chuckled at the look of outrage on his face.

"Good things come to those who wait." Dash rolled a condom down his own rock-hard dick, and without any niceties, thrust first one, then two lubed fingers inside Jesse's ass. "And this is gonna be good. I promise."

Jesse sighed, a blissful expression settling over his face. "Oh, yeah." He worked himself on Dash's fingers. "It's all good. You're good. I'm good...*uhhh*."

Dash replaced his fingers with the head of his cock and watched as he sank inside Jesse's body. "So much better than good. The best." He flexed his hips, and Jesse held him tight, whispering in his ear.

"I love you. Thank you for taking a chance on me and not giving up."

"I'll never do that." He shifted and drew Jesse's legs over his shoulders. "I'm all in."

"I'll say," Jesse muttered and grabbed his cock, jerking himself off with quick, hard strokes.

Dash chuckled and began to power into Jesse, driving hard, pinning Jesse to the mattress while he bent him almost double. He grunted and pushed in deeper.

"Fuck, Dash." Jesse stiffened and came, spurting hot and sticky across his chest and chin. He lay back, body quivering, his face flushed and full mouth open and gasping for air.

"Damn, you're gorgeous."

Bringing Jesse pleasure was a huge turn-on, and Dash pounded into him harder, his dick clutched tight in the silky heat of Jesse's body. When Jesse reached up and touched his face, Dash leaned in for a kiss, needing even more connection with Jesse than their bodies could give. As their tongues teased and licked, Dash lost control and fell headfirst into the depths of pleasure. Like a giant wave crashing into him, Dash's orgasm knocked him off his feet, leaving him breathless, wet, and shaking.

With his innate sense of Dash's need to touch and be touched, Jesse held him close. They lay together chest to chest, Dash loath to give up the safe haven he found in Jesse's arms.

Jesse bit his earlobe. "If you even want to think about doing this again tonight, you need to get off me before I'm squashed flat."

Chuckling, Dash rolled away, got rid of the condom, and took Jesse back in his arms.

"I plan on doing this with you more than just tonight."

His eyes shining like twin flames, Jesse kissed his cheek. "Like forever?"

"Yeah. And then some."

Epilogue

One month later

"HI, MOM."
"Oh, Jesse." Her eyes filled. "You look so happy."

It had been almost a year since he'd seen his mother in person, and Jesse hadn't realized how much he missed her until that moment. They hugged, and all the old resentment and bitterness faded away.

"I'm so happy you're here."

"You look wonderful."

They laughed, and he held out his hand for Dash. "Mom, this is Dash. Dash—my mom. Finally in the flesh."

For the past month, since Dash moved in, they'd been FaceTiming with his mother and Harry. He'd told her about his walks to the park and how every day he was getting stronger. How his dosage had been lowered further and his nightmares had all but disappeared. And she told him how it snowed, and that she'd had a bad cold but was better. That maybe in the spring, if he was stronger, he could come visit. The prospect of that no longer terrified him.

Finally, she'd decided it was ridiculous to talk only by computer. *"Harry and I are going to come over. I want to see you and meet Dash."*

Nervous and pale, Dash stood beside him. He'd been restless all night, worrying about meeting Jesse's mom, and with Jesse laughing at him from the bed, must've tried on ten different shirts and pants, ultimately deciding on a pale-blue button-down and a pair of dark-washed jeans.

"Hi, Mrs. Grace-Martin. Uh, I'm sorry, I mean Mrs. Spears."

"No worries. I still get confused myself." At her smile, the tension broke, and Jesse blessed her for having that enviable quality of putting everyone at ease around her. "And please, give me a hug and call me Leigh."

Seeing his mother's arms around Dash, the final piece of Jesse's life clicked into place, no longer lost and broken. Against the odds, Dash had found him and brought him back home.

"Dash, good to see you." Harry shook his hand and patted him on the back. "I'm hearing great things from the firm."

"Thank you. I'm giving it my best."

At Jesse's urging, Dash had asked about working full-time at Harry's old firm. He'd hoped that way he'd work off his mother's retainer to Harry as quickly as possible. A week after the paperwork had been delivered to Dash's father, and to everyone's complete surprise, Dash's father had agreed to the divorce and support terms without further threats of court action.

Dash had ended up owing less than a thousand dollars and was now earning a full salary.

"*I'll bet my last dollar that seeing the name of Harry's firm scared the life out of him. He didn't think your mom could have a heavy-hitter behind her.*"

The early afternoon sunlight slanted into the living room. The sky gleamed a brilliant blue, but large white clouds loomed in the distance. Jesse hoped he and Dash could go out for a walk in the park later.

Upon hearing Dash was meeting Jesse's mother for the first time, Dash's mother had insisted on making a special cake and some of the *baklava* Jesse loved, with extra for his mother to take home. They sat down, and his mother spied the *baklava*. "Oh, this looks delicious."

"My mother made it for you," Dash said with pride.

"Oh." She blinked, and Jesse could see she was visibly affected. "That's the nicest thing anyone's ever done for me." She took a bite of the sticky pastry, and Jesse, who'd rarely seen his mother eat, was astonished to see her finish the whole piece and lick the honey from her fingers. "Absolutely delicious. Tell her thank you for me. Or better yet, can you give me her phone number? I'd love to give her a call and talk to her, mother to mother." She gave them both a brilliant smile. "We're basically family now that Dash is living here."

"Is that your underhanded way of asking if we're planning on getting married?" Jesse lazed back on the sofa next to Dash. "Hold off on that for a little while, okay? It's enough that I'm finally able to go outside on a somewhat regular basis."

"I'm so happy with your progress. What does Dr. Mingione think?"

"She's optimistic for a full recovery eventually. I'm taking it step-by-step. Going out to dinner next week will be a big first for me."

"You're gonna do great," Dash said, giving his hand a squeeze. "Every time we go out, you're more confident. I see it in your face and hear it in your voice."

His mother watched them both with a beaming smile. "You've been so wonderful for Jesse, Dash. I couldn't ask for a better partner for him. I'm thrilled you decided to move in." Addressing Jesse, she frowned. "It always worried me that you lived alone."

"We all have to learn to live our lives the best way we can." Tense with what he planned to say, Jesse gave his mother a tight smile. "I need to say a few things, but please know that I love you very much. I've learned a lot in the time Dash and I have been together. But if I push this under the rug, it'll never get settled, and I want it done with."

Wide-eyed, she laced her fingers together in her lap. "You're scaring me. I love you too. You know that, right?"

"Of course," he said but pressed on, Dash's hand resting on his back, giving him the comfort and courage he needed. "And because we love each other, I can tell you this now." He licked his dry lips. "I resented you for leaving me, at first."

She gazed at him, her lips trembling, wide-eyes filling with tears. "I-I'm sorry. You never said..." She wiped at the tears spilling on her cheeks, and Harry slid a protective arm around her. "Don't stop, please. Go on. I need to hear this. I always knew we'd have this talk one day. We'd grown to be loving strangers almost, tiptoeing around all the pain."

He hated making her sad, and faltered, but Dash leaned over to whisper in his ear. "You're okay. She's stronger than you think, and you're going to come out of this better together."

God, he loved him. Dash was his rock. His strength.

"When Dad died you were there for me, but as the years passed, you pulled away and never came back. You were my mother, and I needed you to be there for me, but you weren't. When I got mugged and couldn't leave the house, I thought maybe you'd stay..." He swallowed hard. "Instead you left, moved away to Connecticut, making it impossible for me to see you."

She cried silently now, her head against Harry's shoulder. "I failed you. I know I did. As a mother I should've put your needs before mine, but I ignored the warning signs and cries for help. And there's more. More you don't know." She blew her nose with the tissue Harry gave her.

"Leigh, baby," Harry said, smoothing her hair. "Are you sure you're okay to talk about this?"

"Yes. I owe it to Jesse. He's my son. He has a right to know."

Dash murmured to him, "Any idea what's going

on?"

Never taking his eyes off his mother, Jesse shook his head. "Not a clue."

Pushing her hair off her forehead, she faced him, her eyes red-rimmed and mouth trembling. "I never told you. After you were mugged, I had a breakdown. I left the city and went to Connecticut, not to get away, but because I was hospitalized. I couldn't tell you because you were dealing with your own issues, and I didn't want to burden you with my problems. I couldn't do that to you. What if you got worse because of me? So I hid and begged Harry not to tell you. After six months I was allowed a few phone calls, and that's when I called you."

Stunned, he began to shake. "Mom...why? You should've told me. I would've understood." He left Dash to sit by her side and hugged her slim, shaking body tight.

"Really? I still don't understand myself." She sniffed into his shoulder. "But I'm working on it. With Harry's help, I'm getting better. And being back in your life helps me more than you could ever know."

"I'm sorry, Mom. I love you. I wish you'd told me, even later on, but I understand why you kept it from me. I couldn't help you. I had to get better myself."

"I love you too. Having your father ripped away from us hurt me so much, but I had to stay strong for you. I didn't realize how those years holding myself together left me so weak, I couldn't do it anymore. When you got mugged, I fell apart."

"But you're okay?" They might've lost their way,

but Jesse wouldn't let her go now.

"I'm better. I still have guilt…guilt over not getting to say good-bye to your father, guilt over you." She smiled through her tears, and to Jesse, she'd never looked more beautiful. There was a calm about her now instead of the forced, brittle happiness she'd surrounded herself with these past years. "But I'm going to be okay. I thank Harry every day for standing by me. And I've hoped for you to find your way back. I think you have. With Dash's help?"

His poor mother. Here he'd believed she'd moved on without a second thought to what she'd lost or left behind, when all along she'd lived in her own personal hell, as insidious as his.

"I'm going to be fine. Dash helped, yeah."

"Not true," Dash cut in. "You started before you met me. Don't deny it. We met outside when Jesse was sitting with Miranda. So I came in after he'd already decided to take the first step."

Dash got annoyed when Jesse refused to take credit for his breakthrough. "It's true. But I was terrified that day and had a panic attack. Dash helped me, and that's how we met." He snorted. "A love story for the century—*Finding Love During an Anxiety Attack*."

"Who cares how it happened?" she said with urgency. "Some people never find that one person who gets them. I've been lucky in that I found two men—your father and Harry. You have Dash. Celebrate what you have. I can see how much you care for each other, and in the end, nothing else matters. Not what other people say, not how they act toward you—that's all nonsense in the long run." She held out her hand to Dash, who walked over to join them. She placed his and Dash's hands together and rested her small palm on top. "What matters is how you treat each other. That you always stand by each other and listen when the other has fears or concerns. Most of all, love one another, especially when it gets hard, because it will get hard sometimes. Love is easy when everything goes right, but it's when things go wrong that you'll need each other's love most of all."

"Thanks, Mom. And I hope from now on we won't keep anything from each other?"

"That goes both ways, buddy." She hugged him tight. "If you and Dash get engaged, I'll be the first to know, right?"

He laughed. "I promise."

After they left and he and Dash had put all the food away, they lay on the sofa with his head pillowed in Dash's lap. These were his favorite times—the two of them quietly winding down from the day, Dash's fingers toying with his hair.

"Do you think about it?"

Jesse glanced up to find Dash's gaze on him. "What?"

"Getting married."

He shrugged. "I don't know. Not yet. There's still so much I need to catch up with before we can think about that. I should be able to go outside more than twice a week, don't you think?"

"You'll get there," Dash said staunchly. "That's twice more than you were able to the year before. Look at it that way."

"You're right. I wanted to jump right to *Z* without hitting *A*, *B*, *C* first." Dash's fingers massaged his scalp. "Mmm, that feels good. What about you?"

"One day, sure. When I've passed the CPA exam and feel more settled." Dash wound a curl around his finger. "I registered for it last week."

He dropped that bombshell so casually, it took Jesse a second to pick up on it. He struggled to a sitting position. "You did? Why didn't you say anything? Do you need to register for a review class?"

"Because I didn't want you freaking out like you are now." He sounded amused, and Jesse glared at him.

"You're being silly. It's a huge accomplishment. This is big—God, you're graduating in June. I'm so proud of you. We need to plan something special."

"I haven't done anything yet."

"You keep downplaying your accomplishments. So I'll do it." Jesse ticked off his fingers. "You're graduating college, first in your family to do so. You have a great job, and they already told you they want you after graduation. And," he said with a smirk, "you have a boyfriend who can't get enough of you."

"I'm not downplaying it. I don't wanna jinx it, that's all." Dash gave him a lazy smile. "And I think I might need some convincing on that last one. You know, the can't-get-enough-of-me part?"

"Come on, then." Jesse stood and took his hand. Together they walked across the living room, pausing to stare out the window. The sky, always infinite and mysterious, no longer loomed evil and threatening.

There was beauty now in its transformation from the dusky violet-blue of twilight to the velvet ebony of night.

"What're you thinking?" Dash asked. He put an arm around his shoulders, and Jesse leaned into his solid warmth.

"That I'm the luckiest guy in the world. I have everything I could ever want, the things money can't buy—the support of my family, my slowly returning health, but most of all, the love of a man who stayed with me despite my problems." A star twinkled in the sky, and though Jesse knew it was silly, he liked to think it was his father watching over him.

"Don't ever think you're something less because of what you went through. I love you because of who you are, and that includes your pain. Besides, if it wasn't for your fear of the outside, we might never have met." Dash kissed him slowly, building up the fire that burned between them. "You would've passed me by as being just another guy on the street."

"Impossible," Jesse said, kissing him back. "You were never just another guy. It might've taken me a little bit longer to find you, but what we have is like the rarest of gems. It hides for years and might take a bit of digging to get to, but once exposed, you know you've found the one." He brushed back the mane of black hair hanging in Dash's eyes. "You were waiting for me to find you, and I'm not letting you go. You're my guy, and I love you."

"I love you too, babe. I'm not hiding. I'm here. Forever."

Jesse gave one last glance at the moon shining in through the windows and the bright star in the sky, then with Dash's arm securely around him, they walked to the bedroom.

The End

Want to read a bonus scene with more Jesse and Dash? Subscribe to my newsletter and get an exclusive excerpt!
claims.prolificworks.com/free/PFSO6MDO

Author's Note

Thank you for reading His Uptown Guy! Reviews are like potato chips for authors. We can never have enough! So, if you feel compelled to leave a sentence or two on a retail site, I'd truly appreciate it!

About Felice Stevens

Felice Stevens has always been a romantic at heart. She believes that while life is tough, there is always a happy ending just around the corner. Her characters have to work for it, however. Like life in NYC, nothing comes easy and that includes love. She lives in New York City with her husband and two children. Her day begins with a lot of caffeine and ends with a glass (or two) of red wine. She's retired from practicing law and now daydreams of a time when she can sit by a beach and write beautiful stories of men falling in love. Although there are bound to be a few bumps along the way, a Happily Ever After is always guaranteed.

Join my NEWSLETTER and read exclusive content, see cover reveals and get notified of sales and specials! landing.mailerlite.com/webforms/landing/c3h8p3

You can join my reader group FELICE'S FUN HOUSE to get all the scoop on what I'm up to, along with sneak peeks, giveaways and kisses...lots of kisses. facebook.com/groups/FelicesFunHouse

Follow me on:

BOOKBUB

bookbub.com/profile/felice-stevens

INSTAGRAM

instagram.com/felicestevens

WEBSITE

www.felicestevens.com

FACEBOOK

facebook.com/felice.stevens.1

TWITTER

twitter.com/FeliceStevens1

GOODREADS

goodreads.com/author/show/8432880.Felice_Stevens

Other titles by Felice Stevens

Through Hell and Back Series:

A Walk Through Fire

After the Fire

Embrace the Fire

Memories Series:

Memories of the Heart

One Step Further

The Greatest Gift

Breakfast Club Series:

Beyond the Surface

Betting on Forever

Second to None

What Lies Between Us

A Holiday to Remember: A Second to None Short Story

Hot Date (Memories with the Breakfast Club, A Novella)

Rescued Heart Series:

Rescued

Reunited

Together Series:

Learning to Love

The Way to His Heart

All or Nothing

I do, I do: An All or Nothing Short Story

38347154R00179

Made in the USA
Middletown, DE
07 March 2019